"In this world there are those things which come to be, and which cease to be, and men are of this kind, and beasts. And there are things also which do not come and go, but which remain. Like the weather, the skies, the waters, the land itself. Yet, deeper than these, there may be things which simply Are. What men call the Spirit of Place, or The Dream, or other names, trying to find expression for what is not expressible, but which surely is. These are civilized times. The seas are crowded by ships, the greatest libraries by books ... yet I will use my civilized modern knowledge to put this down, to tell of dark things and enduring things that have touched us, that continue with us, like a long shadow, though the substance is no more."

THE
GORGON
And Other Beastly Tales

by
TANITH LEE

DAW BOOKS, INC.
DONALD A. WOLLHEIM, PUBLISHER

1633 Broadway, New York, NY 10019

ACKNOWLEDGMENTS

The Gorgon: from *Shadows 5*. © 1983 by Tanith Lee.
Meow: from *Shadows 4*. © 1982 by Tanith Lee.
Anna Medea: from *Amazing SF*. © 1982 by TSR, Inc.
Magritte's Secret Agent: from *Twilight Zone*. © 1981 by
TZ Publications, Inc.
Because Our Skins Are Finer: from *Twilight Zone*. © 1981 by
TZ Publications, Inc.
Monkey's Stagger: from *Sorcerer's Apprentice*. © 1979 by Tanith Lee.
Sirriamnis: from *Unsilent Night*. © 1981 by Tanith Lee.
La Reine Blanche. from *Asimov's*. © 1983 by Davis Publications, Inc.

First Printing, February 1985

1 2 3 4 5 6 7 8 9

PRINTED IN U.S.A.

it hit the fangs in the interstices below the terrace. About the smaller island, barely a ruffle showed. It seemed to glide up from the sea, smooth as a mirror. The little island was verdant, also. Unlike Daphaeu's limited stands of stone-pine, cypress and cedar, the smaller sister was clouded by a still, lambent haze of foliage, that looked to be woods. Visions of groves, springs, a ruined temple, a statue of Pan playing the panpipes forever in some glade—where only yesterday, it might seem, a thin column of aromatic smoke had gone up—these images were enough, fancifully to draw me into inquiries about how the small island might be reached. And when my inquiries met first with a polite bevy of excuses, next with a refusal, lastly with a blank wall of silence, as if whomever I mentioned the little island to had gone temporarily deaf or mad, I became, of course determined to get to it, to find out what odd superstitious thing kept these people away. Naturally, the Daphaeui were not friendly to me at any time, beyond the false friendship one anticipates extended to a man of another nationality and clime, who can be relied on to pay his bills, perhaps allow himself to be overcharged, even made a downright monkey of in order to preserve goodwill. In the normal run of things, I could have had anything I wanted, in exchange for a pack of local lies, a broad local smile, and a broader local price. That I could not get to the little island puzzled me. I tried money, and I tried barter. I even, in a reckless moment, probably knowing I would not succeed, offered Pitos, one of the younger fishermen, the gold and onyx ring he coveted. My sister had made it for me, the faithful copy of an intaglio belonging to the house of Borgia, no less. Generally, Pitos could not pass the time of day with me without mentioning the ring, adding something in the nature of: "If ever you want a great service, any great service, I will do it for that ring." I half believe he would have stolen or murdered for it, certainly shared the bed with me. But he would not, apparently, even for the Borgia ring, take me to the little island.

"You think too much of foolish things," he said to me. "For a big writer, that is not good."

I ignored the humorous aspect of "big," equally inappropriate in the sense of height, girth or fame. Pitos' English was fine, and when he slipped into mild inaccuracies, it was likely to be a decoy.

"You're wrong, Pitos. That island has a story in it somewhere, I'd take a bet on it."

"No fish today," said Pitos. "Why you think that is?"

I refrained from inventing a tale for him that I had seen giant swordfish leaping from the shallows by the smaller island.

I found I was prowling Daphaeu, but only on the one side, the side where I would get a view, or views, of the small island. I would climb down into the welter of coves and smashed emerald water, to look across at the small island. I would climb up and stand, leaning on the sunblasted walls of a crumbling church, and look at the small island. At night, crouched over a bottle of wine, a scatter of manuscript, moths falling like rain in the oil lamp, my stare stayed fixed on the small island, which, as the moon came up, would seem turned to silver, or to some older metal, Nemean metal perhaps, sloughed from the moon herself.

Curiosity accounts for much of this, and contra-suggestiveness. But the influence I presently began to feel, that I cannot account for exactly. Maybe it was only the writer's desire to fantasize rather than to work. But every time I reached for the manuscript I would experience a sort of distraction, a sort of calling, uncanny, poignant, like nostalgia, though for a place I had never visited.

I am very bad at recollecting my dreams, but once or twice, just before sunrise, I had a suspicion I had dreamed of the island. Of walking there, hearing its inner waters, the leaves brushing my hands and face.

Two weeks went by, and precious little had been done in the line of work. And I had come to Daphaeu with the sole intention of working. The year before, I had accomplished so much in a month of similar islands—or had they been similar?—that I had looked for results of some magnitude. In all of fourteen days I must have squeezed out two thousand words, and most of those dreary enough that the only covers they would ever get between, would be those of the trash can. And yet, it was not that I could not produce work, it was that I knew, with blind and damnable certainty, that the work I needed to be doing sprang from that spoonful of island.

The first day of the third week I had been swimming in the calm stretch of sea west of the harbour, and had emerged to sun myself and smoke on the parched hot shore. Presently Pitos appeared, having scented cigarettes. Surgical and government health warnings have not yet penetrated to spots like Daphaeu, where filtered tobacco continues to symbolize Hollywood, or some other amorphous, anachronistic surrealism still hankered after and long vanished from the world beyond. Once Pitos had acquired his cigarette, he sprawled down on the dry grass, grinned, indicated the Borgia ring, and mentioned a beautiful cousin of his, whether male or female I cannot be sure. After this had been cleared out of the way, I said to him,

"You know how the currents run. I was thinking

of a slightly more adventurous swim. But I'd like your advice."

Pitos glanced at me warily. I had had the plan as I lazed in the velvet water. Pitos was already starting to guess it.

"Currents are very dangerous. Not to be trusted, except by harbour."

"How about between Daphaeu and the other island? It can't be more than a quarter mile. The sea looks smooth enough, once you break away from the shore-line here."

"No," said Pitos. I waited for him to say there were no fish, or a lot of fish, or that his brother had got a broken thumb, or something of the sort. But Pitos did not resort to this. Troubled and angry, he stabbed my cigarette into the turf half-smoked. "Why do you want to go to the island so much?"

"Why does nobody else want me to go there?"

He looked up then, and into my eyes. His own were very black, sensuous, carnal, earthbound eyes, full of orthodox sins, and extremely young in a sense that had nothing to do with physical age, but with race, I suppose, the youngness of ancient things, like Pan himself, quite possibly.

"Well," I said at last, "are you going to tell me, or not? Because believe me, I intend to swim over there, today or tomorrow."

"No," he said again. And then: "You should not go. On the island there is a—" and he said a word in some tongue neither Greek nor Turkish, not even the corrupt Spanish that sometimes peregrinates from Malta.

"A *what*?"

Pitos shrugged helplessly. He gazed out to sea, safe sea without islands. He seemed to be putting something together in his mind, and I let him do it,

very curious now, pleasantly unnerved by this waft
of the occult I had already suspected to be the root
cause of the ban.

Eventually he turned back to me, treated me once
more to the primordial innocence of his stare, and
announced:

"The cunning one "

"Ah," I said. Both irked and amused, I found
myself smiling. At this, Pitos' face grew savage with
pure rage, an expression I had never witnessed
before—the façade kept for foreigners had well and
truly come down.

"Pitos," I said, "I don't understand."

"*Meda*," he said then, the Greek word, old Greek.

"Wait," I said. I caught at the name, which was
wrong, trying to fit it to a memory. Then the list
came back to me, actually from Graves, the names
which meant "the cunning"—Meda, Medea, Medusa.

"Oh," I said. I hardly wanted to offend him further by bursting into loud mirth. At the same time,
even while I was trying not to laugh, I was aware of
the hair standing up on my scalp and neck. "You're
telling me there is a gorgon on the island."

Pitos grumbled unintelligibly, stabbing the dead
cigarette over and over into the ground.

"I'm sorry, Pitos, but it can't be Medusa. Someone
cut her head off quite a few years ago. A guy called
Perseus."

His face erupted into the awful expression again,
mouth in a rictus, tongue starting to protrude, eyes
flaring at me—quite abruptly I realized he wasn't
raging, but imitating the visual panic-contortions of
a man turning inexorably to stone. Since that is what
the gorgon is credited with, literally petrifying men
by the sheer horror of her countenance, it now seemed
almost pragmatic of Pitos to be demonstrating. It

was, too, a creditable facsimile of the sculpted gorgon's face sometimes used to seal ovens and jars. I wondered where he had seen one to copy it so well.

"All right," I said. "O.K., Pitos, fine." I fished in my shirt, which was lying on the ground, and took out some money to give him, but he recoiled. "I'm sorry," I said, "I don't think it merits the ring. Unless you'd care to row me over there after all."

The boy rose. He looked at me with utter contempt, and without another word, before striding off up the shore. The mashed cigarette protruded from the grass, and I lay and watched it, the tiny strands of tobacco slowly crisping in the heat of the sun, as I plotted my route from Daphaeu.

Dawn seemed an amiable hour. No one in particular about on that side of the island, the water chill but flushing quickly with warmth as the sun reached over it. And the tide in the right place to navigate the rocks. . . .

Yes, dawn would be an excellent time to swim out to the gorgon's island.

The gods were on my side, I concluded, as I eased myself out into the open sea the following morning. Getting clear of the rocks was no problem, their channels only half filled by the returning tide. While just beyond Daphaeu's coast I picked up one of those contrary currents that lace the island's edges and which, tide or no, would funnel me away from shore.

The swim was ideal, the sea limpid and no longer any more than cool. Sunlight filled in the waves and touched Daphaeu's retreating face with gold. Barely altered in a thousand years, either rock or sea or sun. And yet one knew that against all the claims of romantic fiction, this place did not look now as once it had. Some element in the air, or in time itself, changes, things. A young man of the Bronze Age, falling asleep at sunset in his own era, waking at sunrise in mine, looking about him, would not have known where he was. I would swear to that.

Some thoughts I had leisure for in my facile swim across to the the wooded island moored off Daphaeu.

As I had detected, the approach was smooth, virtually inviting. I cruised in as if sliding on butter. A rowboat would have had no more difficulty. The shallows were clear, empty of rocks, and if anything greener than the water off Daphaeu.

I had not looked much at Medusa's Island (I had begun jokingly to call it this), as I crossed, knowing I would have all the space on my arrival. So I found myself wading in on a seamless beach of rare glycerine sand, and looking up, saw the mass of trees spilling from the sky.

The effect was incredibly lush, so much heavy green, and seemingly quite impenetrable, although the sun struck in glistening shafts, lodging like arrows in the foliage, which reminded me very intensely of huge clusters of grapes on a vine. Anything might lie behind such a barricade.

It was already beginning to be hot. Dry, I put on the loose cotton shirt, and ate breakfast packed in the same waterproof wrapper, standing on the beach impatient to get on.

As I moved forward, a bird shrilled somewhere in its cage of boughs, sounding an alarm of invasion. But surely the birds, too, would be stone, on Medusa's Island, if the legends were correct? And when I stumbled across the remarkable stone carving of a man in the forest, I would pause in shocked amazement at its verisimilitude to the life. . . .

Five minutes into the thickets of the wood, I did

indeed stumble on a carving, but it was of a moss-grown little faun. My pleasure in the discovery was considerably lessened, however, when investigation told me it was scarcely classical in origin. Circa 1920 would be nearer the mark.

A further minute and I had put the faun from my mind. The riot of waterfalling plants through which I had been picking my way broke open suddenly on an inner vista much wider than I had anticipated, while the focal point of the vista threw me completely. I cannot say what I had really been expecting. The grey-white stalks of pillars, some temple shrine, the spring with its votary of greenish rotted bronze, none of these would have surprised me. On the other hand, to find a house before me took me completely by surprise. I stood and looked at it in abject dismay, cursing its wretched normalcy, until I gradually began to see the house was not normal, in the accepted sense.

It had been erected probably at the turn of the century, when such things were done. An eccentric two-storeyed building, intransigently European, that is, the Europe of the north, with its dark walls and arched roofing. Long windows, smothered by the proximity of the wood, received and refracted no light. The one unique and startling feature—startling because of its beauty—was the parade of columns that ran along the terrace, in form and choreography for all the world like the columns of Knossos, differing only in colour. For these stems of the gloomy house were of a luminous sea-green marble, and shone as the windows did not.

Before the house was a stretch of rough-cut lawn, tamarisk, and one lost dying olive tree. As I was staring, an apparition seemed to manifest out of the centre of the tree. For a second we peered at each other, before he came from the bushes with a clashing of gnarled brown forearms. He might have been an elderly satyr; I, patently, was only a swimmer, with my pale foreigner's tan, my bathing trunks, the loose shirt. It occurred to me at last that I was conceivably trespassing. I wished my Greek were better.

He planted himself before me and shouted intolerantly, and anyone's Greek was good enough to get his drift. "Go! Go!" He was ranting, and he began to wave a knife with which, presumably, he had been pruning or mutilating something. "Go, you *go!*"

I said I had been unaware anybody lived on the island. He took no notice. He went on waving the knife, and his attitude provoked me. I told him sternly to put the knife down, that I would leave when I was ready, that I had seen no notice to the effect that the island was private property. Generally I would never take a chance like this with someone so obviously qualified to be a lunatic, but my position was so vulnerable, so ludicrous, so entirely indefensible, that I felt bound to act firmly. Besides which, having reached the magic grotto and found it was not as I had visualized, I was still very reluctant to abscond with only a memory of dark windows and sea-green columns to brood upon.

The maniac was by now quite literally foaming, due most likely to a shortage of teeth, but the effect was alarming, not to mention unaesthetic. As I was deciding which fresh course to take and if there might be one, a woman's figure came out on to the terrace. I had the impression of a white frock, before an odd, muffled voice called out a rapid—too rapid for my translation—stream of peculiarly accented Greek. The old man swung around, gazed at the figure, raised his arms, and bawled another foaming torrent to the effect that I was a bandit, or some other kind of malcontent. While he did so, agitated as I was becoming, I nevertheless took in what I could of the woman standing between the columns. She was mostly in shadow, just the faded white dress, with a white scarf at the neck, marking her position. And then there was an abrupt flash of warmer pallor that was her hair. A blonde Greek, or maybe just a peroxided Greek. At any rate, no snakes.

The drama went on, from his side, from hers. I finally got tired of it, went by him and walked toward the terrace, pondering, rather too late, if I might not be awarded the knife in my back. But almost as soon as I started to move, she leaned forward a little, and she called another phrase to him, which this time I made out, telling him to let me come on.

When I reached the foot of the terrace steps, I halted, really involuntarily, struck by something strange about her. Just as the strangeness of the house had begun to strike me, not its evident strangeness, the ill-marriage to location, the green pillars, but a strangeness of atmosphere, items the unconscious eye notices, where the physical eye is blind, and will not explain. And so with her. What was it? Still in shadow, I had the impression she might be in her early thirties, from her figure, her movements, but she had turned away as I approached, adjusting some papers on a wicker table.

"Excuse me," I said. I stopped, and spoke in English. For some reason I guessed she would be familiar with the language, perhaps only since it was current on Daphaeu. "Excuse me. I had no idea the island was private. No one gave me the slightest hint—"

"You are English," she broke in, in the vernacular, proving the guess to be correct.

"Near enough. I find it easier to handle than Greek, I confess."

"Your Greek is very good," she said, with the indifferent patronage of one who is multi-lingual. I stood there under the steps, already fascinated. Her voice was the weirdest I had ever heard, muffled, almost unattractive, and with the most incredible accent, not Greek at all. The nearest approximation I could come up with was Russian, but I could not be sure.

"Well," I said. I glanced over my shoulder and registered that the frothy satyr had retired into his shrubbery; the knife glinted as it slashed tamarisk in lieu of me. "Well, I suppose I should retreat to Daphaeu. Or am I permitted to stay?"

"Go, stay," she said. "I do not care at all."

She turned then, abruptly, and my heart slammed into the base of my throat. A childish silly reaction, yet I was quite unnerved, for now I saw what it was that had seemed vaguely peculiar from a distance. The lady on Medusa's island was masked.

She remained totally still, and let me have my reaction, neither helping nor hindering me.

It was an unusual mask, or usual—I am unfamiliar with the norm of such things. It was made of some matte light substance that toned well with the skin of her arms and hands, possibly not so well with that of her neck, where the scarf provided camouflage. Besides which, the chin of the mask, this certainly an extra to any mask I had ever seen, continued under her own. The mask's physiognomy was bland, nondescriptly pretty in a way that was somehow grossly insulting to her. Before confronting the mask, if I had tried to judge the sort of face she would have, I would have suspected a coarse, rather heavy beauty, probably redeemed by one chisled feature, a small slender nose, perhaps. The mask, however, was vacuous. It did not suit her, was not true to her. Even after three minutes I could tell as much, or thought I could, which amounts to the same thing.

The blonde hair, seeming natural as the mask was not, cascaded down, lush as the foliage of the island. A blonde Greek, then, like the golden Greeks of Homer's time, when gods walked the earth in disguise.

In the end, without any help or hindrance from her, as I have said, I pulled myself together. As she had mentioned no aspect of her state, neither did I. I simply repeated what I had said before: "Am I permitted to stay?"

The mask went on looking at me. The astonishing voice said:

"You wish to stay so much; what do you mean to do here?"

Talk to you, oblique lady, and wonder what lies behind the painted veil.

"Look at the island, if you'll let me. I found the statue of a faun near the beach," elaboration implied I should lie: "Someone told me there was an old shrine here."

"Ah!" She barked. It was apparently a laugh. "No one," she said, "*told* you anything about this place."

I was at a loss. Did she know what she said? "Frankly then, I romantically hoped there might be."

"Unromantically, there is not. No shrine. No temple. My father bought the faun in a shop, in Athens. A tourist shop. He had vulgar tastes, but he knew it, and that has a certain charm, does it not?"

"Yes, I suppose it does. Your father—"

She cut me short again.

"The woods cover all the island. Except for an area behind the house. We grow things there, and we keep goats and chickens. We are very domesticated.

Very sufficient for ourselves. There is a spring of
fresh water, but no votary. No *genius loci*. I am *so*
sorry to dash your dreams to pieces."

It suggested itself to me, from her tone of amusement, from little inflections in her shoulders, that
she might be enjoying this, enjoying, if you like,
putting me down as an idiot. Presumably visitors
were rare. Perhaps it was even fun for her to talk to
a man, youngish and unknown, though admittedly
never likely to qualify for anyone's centrefold.

"But you have no objections to my being here," I
pursued. "And your father?"

"My parents are dead," she informed me. "When I
employed the plural, I referred to him," she gestured,
a broad sweep of her hand, to the monster on the
lawn, "and a woman who attends to the house. My
servants, my unpaid servants. I have no money
anymore. Do you see this dress? It is my mother's
dress. How lucky I am the same fitting as my mother,
do you not think?"

"Yes. . . ."

I was put in mind, suddenly, of myself as an am-
bassador at the court of some notorious female
potentate, Cleopatra, say, or Catherine de Medici.

"You are very polite," she said, as if telepathically
privy to my fantasies.

"I have every reason to be."

"What reason?"

"I'm trespassing. You treat me like a guest."

"And how," she said, vainglorious all at once, "do
you rate my English?"

"It's wonderful."

"I speak eleven languages fluently," she said, with
off-handed boastfulness. "Three more I can read
very well."

I liked her. This display, touching and magnificent at once, her angular theatrical gesturings, which now came more and more often, her hair, her flat-waisted figure in its 1940's dress, her large, well-made hands, and her challenging me with the mask, saying nothing to explain it, all this hypnotised me.

I said something to express admiration, and she barked again, throwing back her blonde head and irresistibly, though only for a moment, conjuring Garbo's Queen Christina.

Then she walked down the steps, straight to me, demonstrating something else I had deduced, that she was only about an inch shorter than I.

"I," she said, "will show you the island. Come."

She showed me the island. Unsurprisingly, it was small. To go directly round it would maybe have taken less than thirty minutes. But we lingered, over a particular tree, a view, and once we sat down on the ground near the gushing milk-white spring. The basin under the spring, she informed me, had been added in 1910. A little bronze nymph presided over the spot, dating from the same year, which you could tell in any case from the way her classical costume and her filetted hair had been adapted to the fashions of hobble skirt and Edwardian coiffeur. Each age imposes its own overlay on the past.

Behind the house was a scatter of the meagre white dwellings that make up such places as the village on Daphaeu, now plainly unoccupied and put to other uses. Sheltered from the sun by a colossal cypress, six goats played about in the grass. Chickens, and an assortment of other fowl, strutted up and down, while a pig, or pigs, grunted somewhere out of sight. Things grew in strips and patches, and fruit trees and vines ended the miniature plantation before the woods resumed. Self-sufficiency of a tolerable kind, I suppose. But there seemed, from what she said, no contact maintained with any other area, as if the world did not exist. Postulate that a blight, or harsh weather, intervened, what then? And the old satyr, how long would he last to tend the plots? He looked two hundred now, which on the islands probably meant sixty. I did not ask her what contingency plans she had for these emergencies and inevitabilities. What good, after all, are most plans? We could be invaded from Andromeda tomorrow, and what help for us all then? Either it is in your nature to survive, somehow, anyhow, or it is not.

She had well and truly hooked me, of course. If I had met her in Athens, some sun-baked afternoon, I would have felt decidedly out of my depth, taken her for cocktails, and foundered before we had even reached the dinner hour. But here, in this pulsing green bubble of light and leaves straight out of one's most irrational visions of the glades of Arcadia, conversation, however erratic, communication, however eccentric, was happening. The most inexplicable thing of all was that the mask had ceased, almost immediately, to bother me. I cannot, as I look back, properly account for this, for to spend a morning, a noon, an afternoon, allowing yourself to become fundamentally engaged by a woman whose face you have not seen, whose face you are actively being prevented from seeing, seems now incongruous, to the point of perversity. But there it is. We discussed Ibsen, Dickens, Euripides and Jung. I remembered trawling anecdotes of a grandfather, mentioned my sister's jewellery store in St. Louis, listened to an astonishing description of wild birds flying in across a desert from a sea. I assisted her over rocky turf, flirted with her, felt excited by and familiar with her, all this with her masked face before me. As if the mask, rather than being a part of her, meant no more than the frock she had elected to wear, or the narrow-heeled vanilla shoes she had chosen to put on. As if I knew her face totally and had no need to be shown it, the face of her movements and her ridiculous voice.

But in fact, I could not even make out her eyes, only the shine in them when they caught the light, flecks of luminescence but not colour, for the eye-holes of the mask were long-lidded and rather small. I must have noticed, too, that there was no aperture in the lips, and this may have informed me that the mask must be removed for purposes of eating or drinking. I really do not know. I can neither excuse nor quite understand myself, seen in the distance there, with her, on her island. Hartley tells us that the past is another country. Perhaps we also were other people, strangers, yesterday. But when I think of this, I remember, too, the sense of drawing I had had, of being magnetised to that shore, those trees, the nostalgia for a place I had never been to. For she, it may be true to say, was a figment of that nostalgia, as if I had known her and come back to her. Some enchantment, then. Not Medusa's island, but Circe's.

The afternoon, even through the dapple *L'Apres Midi d'Un Faun* effect of the leaves, was a viridian furnace, when we regained the house. I sat in one of the wicker chairs on the terrace, and woke with a start of embarrassment to hear her laughing at me.

"You are tired and hungry. I must go into the house for a while. I will send Kleia to you with some wine and food."

It made a bleary sense, and when I woke again it was to find an old fat woman in the ubiquitous Grecian island black—demonstrably Kleia—setting down a tray of pale red wine, amber cheese and dark bread.

"Where is—" I realized I did not know the enchantress's name.

In any event, the woman only shook her head. saying brusquely in Greek: "No English. No English."

And when I attempted to ask again in Greek where my hostess had got to, Kleia waddled away leaving me unanswered. So I ate the food, which was passable, and drank the wine, which was very good, imagining her faun-buying father putting down an enormous patrician cellar, then fell alseep again, sprawled in the chair.

When I wakened, the sun was setting and the clearing was swimming in red light and rusty violet shadows. The columns burned as if they were internally on fire, holding the core of the sunset, it appeared, some while after the sky had cooled and the stars became visible, a trick of architectural positioning that won my awe and envy. I was making a mental note to ask her who had been responsible for the columns, and jumped when she spoke to me, softly and hoarsely, almost seductively, from just behind my chair—thereby promptly making me forget to ask any such thing.

"Come into the house, now. We will dine soon."

I got up, saying something lame about imposing on her, though we were far beyond that stage.

"Always," she said to me, "you apologise. There is no imposition. You will be gone tomorrow."

How do you know? I nearly inquired, but prevented myself. What guarantee? Even if the magic food did not change me into a swine, perhaps my poisoned dead body would be carried from the feast and cast into the sea, gone, well and truly, to Poseidon's fishes. You see, I did not trust her, even though I was somewhat in love with her. The element of her danger—for she *was* dangerous in some obscure way—may well have contributed to her attraction.

We went into the house, which in itself alerted me. I had forgotten a great curiosity I had had to look inside it. There was a shadowy unlit entrance hall, a sort of Roman atrium of a thing. Then we passed, she leading, into a small salon that took my breath away. It was lined, all over, floor, ceiling, walls, with the sea-green marble the columns were made of. Whether in good taste or bad I am not qualified to say, but the effect, instantaneous and utter, was of being beneath the sea. Smoky oil lamps of a very beautiful Art Nouveau design, hung from the profundity of the green ceiling, lighting the dreamlike swirls and oceanic variations of the marble, so they seemed to breathe, definitely to move, like nothing else but waves. Shoes on that floor would have squeaked or clattered unbearably, but I was barefoot, and now so was she.

A mahogany table, with a modest placing for eight, stood centrally. Only one place was laid.

I looked at it, and she said,

"I do not dine, but that will not prevent you."

An order. I considered vampires, idly, but mainly I was subject to an infantile annoyance. I had looked for the subtraction of the mask when she ate, without quite realizing it, and now this made me very conscious of the mask for the first time since I had originally seen it.

We seated ourselves, she two places away from me. And I began to feel nervous. To eat this meal while she watched me did not appeal. And now the idea of the mask, unconsidered all morning, all afternoon, stole over me like an incoming tide.

Inevitably, I had not dressed for dinner, having no means, but she had changed her clothes, and was now wearing a high-collared long grey gown, her mother's again, no doubt. It had the fragile look of age, but was very feminine and appealing for all that. Above it, the mask now reared, stuck out like the proverbial sore thumb.

The mask. What on earth was I going to do, leered at by the myopic soulless face which had suddenly assumed such disastrous importance.

Kleia waddled in with the dishes. I cannot recall the meal, save that it was spicey, and mostly vegetable. The wine came too, and I drank it. As I drank the wine, I began to consider seriously, for the first time (which seems very curious indeed to me now), the reason for the mask. What did it hide? A scar, a birthmark? I drank her wine, and I saw myself snatch off the mask, take in the disfigurement, unquelled, and behold the painful gratitude in her eyes as she watched me. I would inform her of the genius of surgeons. She would repeat, she had no money. I would promise to pay for the operation.

Suddenly she startled me by saying: "Do you believe that we have lived before?"

I looked in my glass, that fount of wisdom and possibility, and said, "It seems as sensible a proposition as any of the others I've ever heard."

I fancied she smiled to herself, and do not know why I thought that; I know now I was wrong.

Her accent had thickened and distorted further when she said,

"I rather hope that I have lived before. I could wish to think I may live again."

"To compensate for this life?" I said brutishly. I had not needed to be so obvious when already I had been given the implication on a salver.

"Yes. To compensate for this."

I downed all the wisdom and possibility left in my glass, swallowed an extra couple of times, and said, "Are you going to tell me why you wear a mask?"

As soon as I had said it, I grasped that I was drunk. Nor was it a pleasant drunkeness. I did not like the demanding tone I had taken with her, but I was angry at having allowed the game to go on for so long. I had no knowledge of the rules, or pretended I had not. And I could not stop myself. When she did not reply, I added on a note of ghastly banter, "Or shall I guess?"

She was still, seeming very composed. Had this scene been enacted before? Finally she said, "I would suppose you do guess it is to conceal something that I wear it."

"Something you imagine worth concealing, which, perhaps, isn't."

That was the stilted fanfare of bravado. I had braced myself, flushed with such stupid confidence.

"Why not," I said, and I grow cold when I remember how I spoke to her, "take the damn thing off. Take off the mask, and drink a glass of wine with me."

A pause. Then, "No," she said.

Her voice was level and calm. There was neither eagerness nor fear in it.

"Go on," I said, the drunk not getting his way, aware, (oh God), he could get it by the power of his intention alone, "please. You're an astounding woman. You're like this island. A fascinating mystery. But I've seen the island. Let me see you."

"No," she said.

I started to feel, even through the wine, that I had made an indecent suggestion to her, and this, along with the awful clichés I was bringing out increased my anger and my discomfort.

"For Heaven's sake," I said. "Do you know what they call you on Daphaeu?"

"Yes."

"This is absurd. You're frightened—"

"No. I am not afraid."

"Afraid. Afraid to let me see. But maybe I can help you."

"No. You cannot help me."

"How can you be sure?"

She turned in her chair, and all the way to face me with the mask. Behind her, everywhere about her, the green marble dazzled.

"If you know," she said, "what I am called on Daphaeu, are you not uneasy as to what you may see?"

"Jesus. Mythology and superstition and ignorance. I assure you, I won't turn to stone."

"It is I," she said quietly, "who have done that."

Something about the phrase, the way in which she said it, chilled me. I put down my glass, and in that instant, her hands went to the sides of the mask and her fingers worked at some complicated strap arrangement which her hair had covered.

"Good," I said, "good. I'm glad—"

But I faltered over it. The cold night sea seemed to fill my veins where the warm red wine had been. I had been heroic and sure and bold, the stuff of celluloid. But now I had my way, with hardly any preliminary, what *would* I see? And then she drew the plastic away and I saw.

I sat there, and then I stood up. The reflex was violent, and the chair scraped over the marble with an unbearable noise. There are occasions, though rare, when the human mind grows blank of all thought. I had no thought as I looked at her. Even now, I can evoke those long, long empty seconds, that lapse of time. I recollect only the briefest confusion, when I believe she still played some kind of hideous game, that what I witnessed was a product of her decision and her will, a gesture—

After all, Pitos had done this very thing to illustrate and endorse his argument, produced this very expression, the eyes bursting from the head, the jaw rigidly outthrust, the tendons in the neck straining, the mouth in the grimace of a frozen, agonised scream, the teeth visible, the tongue slightly protruding. The gorgon's face on the jar or the oven. The face so ugly, so demented, so terrible, it could petrify.

The awful mouth writhed.

"You have seen," she said. Somehow the stretched and distorted lips brought out these words. There was even that nuance of humour I had heard before, the smile, although physically, a smile would have been out of the question. "You have seen."

She picked up the mask again, gently, and put it on, easing the underpart of the plastic beneath her chin, to hide the convulsed tendons in her throat. I stood there, motionless. Childishly I informed myself that now I comprehended the reason for her peculiar accent, which was caused, not by some exotic foreign extraction, but by the atrocious malformation of jaw, tongue and lips, which somehow must be fought against for every sound she made.

I went on standing there, and now the mask was back in place.

"When I was very young," she said, "I suffered, without warning, from a form of fit, or stroke. Various nerve centres were paralysed. My father took me to the very best of surgeons, you may comfort yourself with that. Unfortunately, any effort to correct the damage entailed a penetration of my brain so uncompromisingly delicate that it was reckoned impossible, for it would surely render me an idiot. Since my senses, faculties and intelligence were otherwise unaffected, it was decided not to risk this dire surgery, and my doctors resorted instead to alternative therapies, which, patently, were unsuccessful. As the months passed, my body adjusted to the unnatural physical tensions resulting from my facial paralysis. The pain of the rictus faded, or grew acceptable. I learned both how to eat, and how to converse, although the former activity is not attractive, and I attend to it in private. The mask was made for me in Athens. I am quite fond of it. The man who designed it had worked a great many years in the theatre, and could have made me a face of enormous beauty or character, but this seemed pointless, even wasteful."

There was a silence, and I realized her explanation was finished.

Not once had she stumbled. There was neither hurt nor madness in her inflexion. There *was* something . . . at the time, I missed it, though it came to me after. Then I knew only that she was far beyond my pity or my anguish, far away indeed from my terror.

"And now," she said, rising gracefully, "I will leave you to eat your meal in peace. Good night."

I wanted, or rather I felt impelled, to stay her with actions or sentences, but I was incapable of either. She walked out of the green marble room, and left me there. It is a fact that for a considerable space of time, I did not move.

*   *   *

I did not engage the swim back to Daphaeu that night, I judged myself too drunk, and slept on the beach at the edge of the trees, where at sunrise the tidal water woke me with a strange low hissing. Green sea, green sunlight through leaves. I swam away and found my course through the warming ocean and fetched up, exhausted and swearing, bruising myself on Daphaeu's fangs that had not harmed me when I left her. I did not see Pitos anywhere about, and that evening I caught the boat which would take me to the mainland.

There is a curious thing which can happen with human beings. It is the ability to perform for days or weeks like balanced and cheerful automata, when some substrata, something upon which our codes or our hopes had firmly rested has given way. Men who lose their wives or their God are quite capable of behaving in this manner, for an indefinite season. After which the collapse is brilliant and total. Something of this sort had happened to me. Yet, to fathom what I had lost, what she had deprived me of, is hard to say. I found its symptoms, but not the sickness which it was.

Medusa (I must call her that, she has no other name I know), struck by the extraordinary arrow of her misfortune, condemned to her relentless, uncanny, horrible isolation, her tragedy most deeply rooted in the fact that she was not a myth, not a fabulous and glamorous monster . . . For it came to me one night in a bar in Corinth, to consider if the first Medusa might have been also such a victim, felled by some awsome fit, not petrifying but petrified, so appalling to the eyes, and, more significantly, to the brooding aesthetic spirit that lives in man, that she too was shunned and hated, and slain by a murderer who would observe her only in a polished surface.

I spent some while in bars that summer. And later, much later, when the cold climate of the year's end closed the prospect of travel and adventure, I became afraid for myself, that dreadful writer's fear which has to do with the death of the idea, with the inertia of hand and heart and mind. Like one of the broken leaves, the summer's withered plants, I had dried. My block was sheer. I had expected a multitude of pages from the island, but instead I saw those unborn pages die on the horizon, where the beach met the sea.

And this, merely a record of marble, water, a plastic shell strapped across a woman's face, this is the last thing, it seems, which I shall commit to paper. Why? Perhaps only because she was to me such a lesson in the futility of things, the waiting fist of chance, the random despair we name the World.

And yet, now and then, I hear that voice of hers, I hear the way she spoke to me. I know now what I heard in her voice, which had neither pain nor shame in it, nor pleading, nor whining, nor even a hint of the tragedy, the Greek tragedy, of her life. And what I heard was not dignity, either, or acceptance, or nobleness. It was *contempt*. She despised me. She despised all of us who live without her odds, who struggle with our small struggles, incomparable to hers. "Your Greek is very good," she said to me, with the patronage of one who is multi-lingual. And in that same disdain she says, over and over to me: "that you live is very good." Compared to her life, her existence, her multi-lingual endurance, what are my life, or my ambitions worth? Or anything.

It did not occur immediately, but still it occurred.

In its way, the myth is perfectly accurate. I see it in myself, scent it, taste it, like the onset of inescapable disease. What they say about the gorgon is true. She has turned me to stone.

ANNA MEDEA

"She will have to go."

Claude Irving swam slowly upward until vision created the surface of *The Times*. His wife very seldom spoke in this chill, clear little voice. He could, offhand, recall only one other occasion on which she had used it. That had been on the morning she had, standing beside him at the altar, declared, in that exact tone of an icy razor, "I do." It meant duty and utter determination. Conceivably, if thwarted, danger.

"Who, my love, will have to go?" inquired Claude Irving.

"The governess," said Chloe Irving. Her voice had not altered. "And the sooner the better."

"But, my love. The children have accepted her. Let me stress that word *accept*. You know how difficult they can be. Fourteen governesses have galloped through this house in the past year—"

"Fifteen," corrected Chloe impassively.

"Well then. This one has lasted a whole month and shows no symptom of impending flight. The others were usually hysterical inside a day."

"I don't care," said Chloe. "She will have to go."

Claude Irving sighed, and laid down *The Times*,

gently, like an old friend who has fainted. "May I ask why?"

Chloe lowered her eyes. Now her voice did alter.

"I'm not quite sure. But—I don't care for her. It's something—like a smell."

"A smell? She seemed most fastidious."

"No, no, I don't mean that she smells. But I have a reaction to her, as one does to a particular odour one simply can't stand—like white spirit, or geraniums."

"I like the odour of geraniums."

Chloe was her normal self now. She had flushed. She appealed to her husband with soft, vague gestures.

"I told you, I can't explain. Perhaps it's instinct. She might—harm the children."

"Do you really think so?" Claude Irving asked with some eagerness.

That, of course, ended the discussion.

Later, on the train up to town, he found himself reviewing the conversation and presently those glimpses he had had of the governess.

She was young; and, though not at all pretty, she did have most definitely a curious sort of style. Indeed, to a man, there was something insidiously attractive in her slender, partly-slinking dark grace, the neatly pinned abundance of black tresses augmented by neat black clothing. She had small feet, come to think of it, and strange black eyes. Did they slant a fraction at the outer corners? Something oriental there, though her skin was flawlessly pale. No hint of a cosmetic. Nor, so far as he could remember, a hair or a sentiment out of place.

And yet, with all this quietude, she had kept the children in order. The awful episodes that had marked the coming and going of the other governesses had been absent from the term of Anna Medea. Yes, that was her name. Most odd.

Roger and Sibelle were really dreadful offspring. Claude sometimes wondered if they were the curse some arcane god had finally decided to vent on a placid well-ordered life. Precocious, canny and cunning, the beastly duet had squalled through infancy into an evil childhood. The servants were terrified of them, and visitors arriving for dinner would tend to glance about anxiously and say: "Children in bed, old man?" Not that the hour of bedtime actually guaranteed safety. Worms had been known to sprawl from a decanter, and treacle and dead mice to have been poured into umbrellas, even so late as midnight. The governesses themselves had suffered in like and most ghastly manner. One, a strict and elderly sadist, of whom Claude had had some hopes, waking to find her hair striped green and, for good measure, on fire, had run from the house screaming in her nightwear, never to be seen again. Although the packing up of her belongings for charity months after had provided some curious surprises, these were only temporary solace.

When Anne Medea arrived, in the driving dusk of an autumn evening, Claude had not thought she would fare any better than the rest.

But the first week went by, and then the second, and so the third; and peace persisted: the dreaded Ragnarok did not transpire. Claude began to relax. Even when he learned that in fact, Anna Medea had not come precisely in answer to the advertisement, but rather on hearsay acquired in the village, and that possibly her references were a touch more weightless than they had at first seemed, he did not balk; and neither did he inform Chloe. His wife had a strange attitude towards the children. She liked them.

He could only conclude they had in some way lied and misled her into this condition, or else that she had mesmerized herself into believing them lovable. Claude, however, had often day-dreamed of such stories as the *Babes in the Wood*, or *Hansel and Gretel*, suitably personalised and with tragic endings. Between himself and Roger and Sibelle there existed a rather flawed, armed truce. He was, for the duration, master of the house. They knew better than to practice directly upon him. But he had wondered now and then how long they would brook this state of affairs when once they were older.

With the advent of the new governess, all such macabre musings had begun to drift away. Recently, he had even dared predict life might settle to the placid pond of the first year of marriage.

And now Chloe had taken against the governess.

Could it be jealousy?

He decided to consider this idea on the train down in the evening. He reminded himself that Anna Medea was, after all, exquisitely young. He realized that she had, besides, cast some spell on the children; and maybe their mother was envious of that.

Claude Irving resolved mildly to interrogate the governess that night before dinner.

The planned interview, as it turned out, was the second of the evening. He had scarcely been back in the house half an hour, and was standing at the drawing room windows with a glass of tolerable Amontillado, admiring the last light and the last economical auburn traces on the autumn trees, when the gamekeeper appeared in the window and shook before his eyes a very dead and bloody piece of fur. Claude opened the window.

"What is it?"

"I should think you can see what un is, sir."

"A rabbit with its throat torn out."

"Found it this morning, at the edge of the woods."

Claude visualised the gamekeeper plodding about all day with the mutilated rabbit, waiting for this moment of confrontation. The gamekeeper, a relic of Claude's father's interest in killing things, did not get on with the present regime, which allowed the Irvings' sportsman friends to spill across the coverts with blazing guns at very irregular intervals, Claude lagging guiltily to the rear, white-handed.

The rabbit was shaken again.

"I didn't do it," said Claude, taking refuge in facetiousness, which was useless.

"Fox didn't do it neither," said the gamekeeper. "Look at these here marks." Claude obliged and became aware he might not want his dinner. "Something big got this un. Slaughtered it, drunk some of the blood, and left the meat. Not hungry, d'you see. If you was to ask me," said the gamekeeper, "a dog did this."

"Oh, dear," said Claude.

"It's happened before," said the gamekeeper resentfully, "and I've told you before. Three or four times now, in the last month. And Bilkers"—Bilkers was the assistant—"he said he seen something a few nights ago, loping through your woods. Big black thing, like a great dog."

"He didn't shoot at it, I hope."

"No, sir, no more he did. But we'd be in our rights."

Claude sent the man off as soon as possible, and tried to relax with a second and then a third sherry. Things like this happened on country estates. Then some fool took a pot-shot, and you ended up with the corpse of your least amenable neighbour's favourite setter.

In the irritation of it, Claude forgot he had requested the presence of Anna Medea at seven o'clock, and when the light firm knock came on the door, he told her to enter, falling into a mood of vexation he had not intended.

"How are you getting on with Roger and Sibelle?" he snapped.

But the governess remained impervious. She stood before him, discreet and still, her pale hands folded meekly, her black eyes—they did indeed slant upwards—unblinking.

"Excellently, thank you."

"You don't find them," he barked, "difficult?"

"In my profession difficulties are not unheard of. They are there to be conquered."

"In fact their very difficulty may have enticed you here, since you sought this position *after* hearing a description of them." The governess stayed mute. "But are they learning anything?"

"Everything that is proper."

"I shall have to see," he said. "No one else has been able to teach them a single thing."

"Your children are most unusual, Mr. Irving," said Anna Medea. "But I am sanguine."

Claude Irving seemed to fall to Earth with a thud. He suddenly saw he was defensive and the governess was not. There she stood, lissome and frankly alluring in a foreign, almost an antique way—like something on a Greek vase—while he ranted.

"I don't think you know," he said rather apologetically now, "my wife may not have stressed it. The other governesses ran away. Most of them quite literally."

"It is necessary," said Anna Medea, "when treating

with children, to understand they are not merely mutable but savages."

Claude was quite shocked. At the same time, he found himself in complete agreement. He could select no retort.

Anna Medea said, "Left in my care, they will acquire only the correct form of knowledge. Nor will they ever be a burden to you, or a source of distress. If that is all, and you are satisfied, I trust you will excuse me."

It was said with impeccable courtesy. Only when she had gone did it occur to him that he had been dismissed. Even then he did not brood on it. Instead he brooded on another, irrelevant, detail. It was growing dark in the room, and the gas was not yet lit. As she turned towards the door, Anna Medea's black, slanting eyes had seemed to give off a peculiar flash, like those of some wild beast caught by a lamp in a thicket.

That night, Claude Irving dreamed there was a wolf in his woods. It came out of the undergrowth, black and sleek and with eyes of fire, carrying little Sibelle neatly in its jaws. Although he was sure little Sibelle deserved it, Claude awoke in a dew of cold sweat.

The village clock was chiming three in the morning across the fields, and the air was crisp and brittle with frost. Something, however, impelled Claude to get up. Padding to the window, he gazed out. There were no lights in the house, not even at the windows of his wife's room, which often bloomed yellow with insomnia. There was, nevertheless, a full moon rising over the woods. In the light of this he presently saw a dark shape slipping from among the trees.

Despite himself, Claude experienced a wave of

horror. He had an insane impulse to cover his eyes and not look. This infantile and primitive urge he furiously quelled. So he was able to watch the governess gliding over the lawn and around to the back of the house, presumably to let herself in at the servants' entrance.

Claude was not reassured by this spectacle.

In the morning he rose late, having stayed restless until dawn. Chloe herself appeared tired and wan. They squinted at each other hauntedly, each it seemed on the verge of mentioning a particular matter, and neither quite able to do so.

Since he was not going to town, Claude had, by midday, forced himself out for a stroll on the estate. The weather was cool rather than cold, the frost dissipated, and at the end of the north lawn, there was a sudden sighting of Anna Medea and the children, stalking beside the pond, perhaps on some form of impromptu nature walk. Shielded by a large beech tree, Claude paused to spy.

Fallen leaves lay thick on the water, which Roger poked with a long twig. Sibelle, holding the governess by the hand, chattered. They looked astonishingly normal, his atrocious children. They were not pulling faces, or the wings off small insects, not whispering evilly, not doing anything overtly nasty or even dubious. Of course, he was not close enough to hear what was being said. But the scene looked acceptable.

What bizarre occultism had Anna Medea bound them with? Was it terror of her person, or the promised revelation of some obscene science or philosophy dredged from the murks of time and all the sinks of Man's primeval past—Claude caught himself with a jolt. What on earth was he thinking? He must be going mad.

He stamped off briskly through the leaf-flecked grass, and before he exactly knew it had arrived at the outskirts of the woods.

The woods, whose trees, unlike those about the house, still retained most of their flamey foliage, occupied almost two miles of ground. At its edges the growth was wide-spaced and slim, but there were parts further in which were dense and old, remnants, it was said, of a more ancient forest dating from before the Norman Conquest.

Claude was quite familiar with the woods. To ramble through them at all seasons was an entirely ordinary pleasure, never laced with overtones of sinister romance. Until today. Today, he found himself wary, trailing through the periphery, peering down the aisles to the red and ebony sequesterings of elder oaks and conifers. Images of popular fiction, druidic sacrifice and such like, did not spring to mind, but he sensed something repellent about the dreaming age within the woods, all the worse because it had always been there, unnoted. The ominous words of Bilkers floated on these thoughts. Was it *there* the assistant keeper had witnessed the 'big black thing' loping between the trees: Or *here* . . .

"G'morning, sir."

As soon as Claude returned to his skin, he reciprocated in kind. It struck him as ironic that Bilkers himself had stolen upon him exactly now.

"Seen any more of your wolf, Bilkers?"

Of course Bilkers had never claimed to see anything of the sort. Perhaps the remark would be taken as friendly sarcasm. Bilkers seemed inclined to take it as truth.

"Yes, like a wolf it were, sir. If I'd spotted un anywhere but here, I'd've had no doubts."

"Maybe some local zoo has lost one of its boarders. Lord Verbrace has a menagerie, I believe." When Bilkers received this information stonily, Claude felt pushed to ask, "Where in fact did you come across the thing?"

"Near the old pines. Had a toothache and couldn't sleep that night, so I went out to check the fences. About midnight it were, but the moon was up, nearly full. Suddenly, out slopes this devil. I don't mind saying, the look of it scared me for a minute. But it took no notice of me. There's a fox been through there recently. I don't think the beast could scent me through all that fox stink, or it might have come at me. I'd've had to shoot un then."

"It's probably harmless. A dog," said Claude feebly. He no longer believed this. Bilkers seemed not to believe it either.

They parted uneasily, like men going out upon a secret mission the world must never learn.

Claude could not deny that when Bilkers had mentioned the pines—certainly one of the most antiquated portions of the woods—the hair had crinkled on his neck.

To feel compelled to march in that direction therefore disconcerted him.

A dank, abyssmal shadow overlay the stand of pines. Even at noon it was gloomy. Aromas of rot and moss drifted. Birds did not nest in the vicinity, and seldom sang.

It was with a despondent unsurprise that Claude, having entered the enclosure, swiftly stumbled on a stone with a kind of gluey mess all over it. This looked only herbal, if uncivilised. There were also odd runnels cut in the damp earth. He did not like to tread on these or walk across them. Ashes and a charred stick gave evidence of burning.

Even to the layman, it was fairly obvious that witchcraft had been practiced in the area.

After luncheon, which he could not eat, Claude retired to the library. His father had been one of those who bought their books by the yard. But it seemed to Claude he had once come on a small collection of volumes dealing with the supernatural. It was an hour before he unearthed them.

Until the sky began to alter colour with the dusk, then, he sat reading. When he emerged he did so clad in a knowledge that was not cheering.

All through dinner, his mind was occupied with the predilections of sorcerers and shape-changers, their rites for summoning familiars, their practices upon babies, their more than platonic involvement with the full moon. Worst of all, perhaps, was the vile assurance that such monsters might pass as mortal, even live under one's roof for considerable periods, the bestial inclination quiescent, or, when active, so disguised with human daylight aspects as to go undetected. Werewolves had been known to live out long and respectable lives among their fellow men, only death by senile decay, or a stray shot finally revealing the Unthinkable to appalled relatives and lovers.

It had been all very well to wish the children some comfortable ill—immolation by a runnaway carriage or a collapsing chandelier—but did even they deserve such a fate as this? For Claude had no doubt Anna Medea was winning their confidence as a prelude to devouring them alive. The tomes of the library had been crammed by such instances.

After dinner, Chloe began to play some skittish

pieces of Greig on the piano. She seemed abstracted. Although she had not referred to her distrust of the governess again, it was obviously preying upon her mind.

Uppermost in his own awareness, however, was not a need for silver bullets or holy water. Claude, even now he believed, remained the Modern Man. He had determined on his course, which was to be that of sweet reason.

After all, the books had informed him that, once slain, the were-beast would revert to its human shape. A momentary vision of himself digging a furtive grave for Anna Medea under the wailing pines did not appeal.

He knew at least she was not of the kind constrained to undergo metamorphosis immediately at sunset, but could effect the change at her own will. He had spoken to her after twilight. Only the flash of her eyes had given her away as someone gifted by dark magic.

Before seeking her, however, Claude tiptoed to gaze upon his son and daughter, something he had not been prompted to do in years. They lay asleep, snuffling faintly, innocuous; and Claude permitted himself a second's sentimentality. After all, they were his. Leaning nearer, astonished by emotion, he saw the night light flicker at each of their throats on a thin metal chain.

In another instant, uproar ensued.

His afternoon's reading had been most comprehensive.

Not until his children were shaken alert and with shrieks of malevolent outrage despoiled of the presents their governess had placed on their throats, not until Anna Medea was pursued to her private parlour and had the two herbal-scented pendants thrust under her small straight nose, did Claude feel justified in broaching the originally intended topic. Nor was he any longer prepared to be reasonable, let alone sweet.

"You are to be given notice," he announced, standing firmly at bay. "The terms are these. You will leave tomorrow morning. Any monetary recompense you think due, and which I consider sensible, will be sent to your next address."

Such a bribe had seemed wise. Actually, he was simply terrified. The need to get her out of the house with a show of strength was paramount. Not to incur too much malice was also important. She was, after all, high in the Satanic social order.

After the ultimatum there followed silence. Anna Medea poised before him, utterly composed, her cameo face a mask of ice.

"And this," she eventually said, "is because you object to the amulets I awarded your children."

"Unhygienic," said Claude. He did not say he knew they were forms of thaumaturgic thrall meant to bind the victims as surely as chains. He had not admitted at any time that he had fathomed her game. "Altogether, we don't find you suitable."

"Indeed."

"Your gypsyish mode of arrival. Your strange methods of tuition—"

"I must warn you," Anna Medea interrupted softly, "that these actions will bear you headlong into disaster."

Claude paled.

"Is that a threat?"

"If you wish. Send me away, and I cannot answer for the consequences."

Claude swallowed and squared his shoulders.

"Then I must warn you in turn. I am armed against you."

Anna Medea gave him a prolonged and terrible look, deeper and blacker than the vaults of time. Claude quailed, but would not budge. He held his position before the fire which still crackled from the pendants he had thrown in there.

Suddenly the woman shrugged.

"You are a fool, Mr. Irving," said Anna Medea.

Downstairs, he took a large brandy. His hands trembled so some was spilled on the rug.

That night his dreams, or the woods, were fraught with howling.

In the morning she was gone.

The succeeding days were not precisely halcyon. After the swiftest interval, free now of restraint, Roger and Sibelle again commenced the overthrow of the household. Dead shrews and abrupt encounters with live and energetic frogs became once more the norm. Close upon a local shopping expedition which the children accompanied, three emporiums sent word they would no longer be able to accomodate the Irvings. The children's mother laughed this off. But then, she was the only adult on the premises who seemed in good spirits. With the vanishment of the eldritch governess, Chloe had blossomed. Though Claude was glad of it, he himself had reservations. Something seemed to tell him the dramatics in Anna Medea's parlour had not comprised the final scene of the act. For one thing, she had since claimed no wages. As she was hardly a timid creature, one was led to assume therefore she did not reckon cash a proper sop to her annoyance. And what would be? The children, one felt, could no longer suffice. Her vengeance would be turned against her employers.

At first, Claude maintained a serene front. But as time crept on and the nights of the full moon started to close in again, his nerves suffered. To wake in a white sweat was a commonplace. To lie sleepless more common still. The journeys to and from town became nightmarish in a literal sense. More than once, having dropped into an exhausted stupor, he had woken himself—and the rest of the railway compartment—with wild cries. There was even an embarrassing incident with a fellow traveller in a wolfskin coat, which was best forgotten.

During this period, he was driven to visit a blacksmith half a day's drive beyond the village. The explanation for his requirements, which were two silver bullets, was so blandly eccentric that the man accepted it without a flicker of concern. On the other hand, werewolves might be more prevalent in Hampshire than one had supposed.

Three evenings later, Chloe said, "It's really too exasperating. I think one of the servants has stolen that little silver paper knife from the morning room."

Claude, who had been staring through the darkened window towards the east, blushed. Next moment he entered one of those small oases of logic, wherein he asked himself if he might not be taking a lot of nonsense too seriously.

"Perhaps," he therefore lightly said, "Anna Medea took the knife to spite us."

Chloe laughed. She came across the room and pressed his hand.

"How understanding you were of my silly prejudice. I almost feel guilty now that you made her go. And yet, I was rather frightened of her."

They stood at the window and presently the full moon rose. The oasis of logic faded in its frigid gleam so many centuries old.

Claude shuddered.

"And really," Chloe murmured, "I do believe the children have been much better behaved since she left."

Claude passed the night in a succession of scares, waking and sleeping, that anyone who had not experienced them would be hard put to envisage. Wolves leaped from the pelmets and off the ottoman, or crawled down the chimney to emerge from the dead fire with burning eyes. Claude ran through forests and tumbled over precipices with fangs in his ankles. Anna Medea stood in the air, black and white as an etching, and said to him: "You are a fool, Mr. Irving."

In the morning, slumped wanly at the breakfast table, a message was brought him. An hour later he stood with Bilkers at the edge of the woods, regarding a collection of little bloody corpses and trying not to be sick. It seemed the shape-changer had returned and left her calling card.

"This un's no dog," said Bilkers. "I heard un last night. No dog ever made a noise like that. The hair near started out of my scalp. It's something not natural if you ask me. And it's got that bold, it's laughing at us."

Claude was on the verge of appealing for aid, but honour stopped him. He had not confided in Chloe. Bilkers was only an employee. Claude made some further comments on Lord Verbrace's menagerie of pumas and jackals, and hurried off to the library.

Here he spent most of the day, re-reading his instructions, wiping sweat from his brow, shivering, and loading and re-loading a newly-cleaned pistol with two bright lozenges.

*   *   *

The house was entirely black that night when he left it, blacker than the moonlit lawns beyond.

At the last, a desperate courage came upon him. Hearing no sound from the woods, he grew to think the monster awaited him. He strode forth, a knight to meet a dragon.

Not only was the darkness silent, nothing moved.

Reaching the brink of the trees, he hesitated, then plunged forward. It was, with the utmost loathing, for the aged pines that he headed. On the way, his own crashing might have obliterated many a stealthier noise, though once a bullet was almost wasted on an incautious owl.

Arriving at the stand of pines, a black clot where even the moon was lost, Claude was shaky but determined. A few minutes more, and he felt like a jilted duellist. The beast was nowhere to be found. A long anguished frozen wait then commenced, which took him through to one in the morning, as he heard it eerily tolled from the village.

Could it be the demon was not even abroad tonight, taunting him? Or was it somewhere nearby, watching, amused. At this notion Claude scrambled forward on numbed feet and pitched full length.

It was as he was lurching up again that a grisly howl split the air.

Claude's knees turned to suet, but he grasped the pistol and staggered in the direction from which the awesome noise had come. Fantasies about knights had vanished with the brandy which inspired them. This horror was from the primal beginning.

A quarter of a mile from the pines, he exploded into a clearing filmed by young beeches, beyond which he could see the pond and the north lawn of the house.

And there, between himself and home, was a low

black shape, with two glitterings for eyes like two silver bullets.

Claude did not falter. The pistol was primed, the catch came off like butter; and, straightening his arm, he fired point blank: once, twice, into the hellish apparition before him.

It spun away and dropped prone. Nor did it move thereafter.

It was some little while before Claude could bring himself to examine his trophy. When he did go near he caught his breath, although he had anticipated nothing else, at the pale body of a woman flung where the wolf had gone down.

It was not until he knelt beside it, and the moonlight crossed into the beeches, that he began to think there had been some kind of practical joke, and then some sort of dire mistake. For the corpse in the grass was that of the wrong woman.

The court, as it turned out, failed to look with sympathy or understanding on the plaintiff's statement. That the husband of Chloe Irving had shot her under the misapprehension she was a wolf did not suggest grounds for leniency.

In the time that was left to him, Claude puzzled over the affair, maniacally desperate to make sense of it. Despite all he had read, it did not seem possible he could have been so permanently deceived. The only real clues he had ever had, he declared to his jailors, were his wife's insomniac nights. Of course, he had shrugged off the other clue, the gamekeeper's complaints of murdered mammals, until they had coincided with the mysterious governess and her doings, and with Bilkers's sighting in the woods.

Bilkers himself was now saying nothing. His face, at the back of the courtroom, was melancholy but unencouraging. He knew when he was beaten. Claude knew it too. His only last-ditch effort was attempting to place, from the condemned cell, an advertisement requesting the appearance of an itinerant female excorcist of foreign extraction, possessed of hypnotic eyes, and answering to the name of Anna Medea. But either Anna Medea never succumbed to newspaper, or else her proud unbending soul took its vengeance for ignorant dismissal, after all, in silence.

So Claude Irving ended on the gallows, as Chloe Irving ended on receipt of her silver paper knife in somewhat remodelled form.

The notorious Wolf Murder was then gradually forgotten, which was a pity. Ten years later, without benefit of either parental or sorcerous check, and reverting to the maternal strain, Sibelle and Roger Irving began to terrorize the countryside. The carnage was subsequently blamed on Lord Verbrace's innocent jackals.

MEOW

I was young, last year. I was twenty-six. That was the year I met Cathy.

I was writing a novel that year, too. Maybe you never read it. Midnight and four a.m., five or six nights a week, I used to do my magician act at the King of Cups, on Aster. It paid some bills, and it was fun, that act. Even more fun when you suddenly look out over the room, and there's a girl with hair like white wine, and the flexible fluid shape of a ballet dancer, looking back at you, hanging on every breath you take.

Later, around four-thirty, when we were sitting in a corner together, I saw there was a little gold cat pendant in the hollow of her throat. Later still, when we'd walked back, all across the murmuring frosty pre-dawn city, with the candy-wrapper leaves blowing and crackling underfoot, I brushed the cat aside so I could kiss her neck.

I didn't realize then, I was going to have trouble with cats.

I might have thought the trouble could have been over money. You know the sort of thing—well-off girl meets male parasite. Somehow we worked it out.

53

keeping our distance where we had to, not keeping it where we didn't. We were still finding the way, and she was shy enough, it was kind of nice to go slowly.

But, she did own this graystone house, which her parents had left her when they went blazing off in a great big car and killed themselves. She's been six- teen then. She'd just made it into adulthood before they ditched life and her. Somehow, I'd always re- sented them. They'd done a pretty good job of tying her up in their own hang-ups, before they split and gave her another one.

The house was still their house, too. It was jammed full of their trendy knick-knacks and put-ons, and their innovative furniture you couldn't sit on or eat off. And it was also full of five cats.

Cathy had acquired the cats, one by one, after her parents died. Or the cats had acquired her. After that, the house was also theirs. They personally en- graved the woodwork, and put expert fringes on the drapes. And on anything else handy, like me. You're right. I had a slight phobia. Maybe something about the fanged snake effect of a cat's head, if you forget the ears. Cathy was always telling me how beautiful the cats were, and I was always trying to duck the issue. And the cats. They knew, of course, about my unadmiration, I'd have sworn that right from the start. They'd leap out on me and biff me with their handfulls of nails. They'd jump on the couch behind my shoulders and bite. When Cathy and I made love, I'd shut the bedroom door, and the cats would crouch outside, ripping the rug. I'd never dared make it with her where they could see and get at me.

I'd spot their eyes in the early morning darkness when I brought her home, ten disembodied dots of creme de menthe neon spilled over the air. Demons would manifest like that. Ever seen a cat with a mouse or a bird? I used to have a dumb dove in my act, called Bernie, and one day Bernie got out on the sidewalk. He was such a klutz, he thought everyone was his damn friend, even the cat that came up and put its teeth through his back. No. I didn't like cats much.

One night it was Cathy's birthday, and we had to be in at the house. Cathy was rather strange about her birthdays, as if the ghosts of Mom and Pop walked that night, and maybe they did. I'd tried to get her to come out, but she wouldn't, so we sat in the white-and-sepia sitting room, under the abstract that looked like three melting strawberries, and ate tuna fish and drank wine. I'd managed to get the cash and buy her a jade bracelet that had sat in a store window the past five weeks, crying to encircle her wrist. When I'd given it to her, she too cried for half a second. It was often harder to get closer to her when she was emotional, than at any other time. By now the jade was warm as her own smooth skin, and the wine not much cooler. The cats sat round us in a ring, except when Cathy went out to the kitchen; then they followed her with weird screechings. The cats always responded to activity in the kitchen in the same way, even to something so small as the dim, far-off clink of a plate. When the house was empty of humans, I could imagine every pan and pot holding its breath for fear of attracting attention.

Finally, Cathy stopped playing with her tuna, and gave it to the cats.

"Oh, look, Stil," she said, gazing at them Madonna-like as they fell in the dish. "Just look."

"I'm looking."

"No you're not," she said. "You're glaring."

I lifted the guitar from the couch and started to

play some music for us, and the cats sucked and chewed louder, to show me what they thought of it.

We sang Happy Birthday to the tune of an old Stones number, and some other stuff. Then we went up to the bedroom and I shut the door. She cried again, afterwards, but she held on to me as if afraid of being swept away out to sea. I was the first human thing she'd really come across since her parents left her. That night at the King had been going to be her experiment in failure. She thought she'd fail at communicating, at being gregarious, and she'd meant to fail, I guess. That would give her the excuse for never trying again. But somehow she'd found me. I didn't really think about the responsibility on my side of all this. It was all too dreamy, too easy.

A couple of the cats noisily puked back the tuna on the Picasso rug outside.

"Why don't you," I said, "leave this godawful house. Let's take an apartment together."

"You have an apartment."

"I have a room. I mean space."

"You can't afford it."

"I might."

"You want to live off me." she said. The first time she ever said it.

"Oh look," I said, "if that's what you think."

"I didn't mean it."

"Sure you did. Just don't mean it again. Next year M.G.M.'ll be making a movie of my book."

"It isn't even published yet."

"So, it will be."

"I'd better go and clean up after the cats," she said.

"Why don't you train them to clean up after themselves?"

We lay awhile, and pictured the cats manipulating

mop, pail and disinfectant. But somewhere in me, I was saying to them: If there are any parasites round here, I know just who. Make the most of it, you gigolos. Your days are numbered.

I really did have it all worked out. Cathy was going to sell the house and I was going to sell the book. We were going to take an apartment, and I was going to keep us in a style to which I was unaccustomed. Cats aren't so hot ten floors up in the air. And five of them, in those conditions, are just not on. Of course, I knew she wouldn't leave them without a roof, and I'd already become a used cat salesman. But suddenly it seemed everyone I knew had one cat, two cats or three. Except Genevieve, who had a singularly xenophobic dog. Everybody, even Genevieve, told me cats are bee-ootiful, and I should let Cathy educate me over my phobia.

Then someone got interested in the book. Things seemed to be coming along, so I sat up from five in the morning until eleven the next night a few times, and finished the beast with heavy hatchet blows from the typer.

I got ready to broach the apartment idea again to Cathy. I began to dream crazy schemes. Like renting out Cathy's parents' house, and whoever took it on got the cats as a bonus, while we had the cats to visit us twice a week. Or buying the cats a ranch in Texas. Or slipping them cyanide in their Tiger-Cookies.

I was fantasizing because I basically understood Cathy wouldn't agree. And she didn't agree.

"No, Stil, I can't," she said. "Can't and won't. You're not making me leave my cats."

"I need you," I said, striking a pose like Errol Flynn. It wasn't only the pose that wasn't one hundred percent true. I was wondering how exactly I did analyse my feelings for her, the first time I'd had to do that, when, brittle and hard as dry cement, she said: "You just need my money."

"Oh Jesus."

"You want to use me."

"Yeah, yeah. Of course I do."

I stood and wondered now if I was only demanding we live together because I wanted her to choose between me and the zoo. Did I really want to be with her that much, this white-faced maniac with green electric eyes?

"You bastard," she whispered. "Dad always told me I'd meet men like you."

And she pulled off the jade bracelet and flung it at me, the way girls fling their engagement rings in old B movies. Like a dope, I neatly caught it. Then she turned and ran.

I stood and looked at the sidewalk where the coloured lights of the King of Cups were going like a migraine attack. I now had the third wonder, wondering what I felt. But I felt too numb to feel anything. Then I went into the club and perpetrated the worst goddam magician act I hope never to live through again.

Two weeks laters Carthage Press bought my book, with an option on two more. I got a standing ovation at the King, got drunk, slept with a girl I can't remember. Three weeks later, Genevieve, who reads Tarot at the King, came over and stood looking at me as I was feeding the dental-floss-white rabbit I'd just accumulated to put in the act as a cliché.

"You know, Stil," said Genevieve, gazing up at me from her clever, paintable, lookable-at face, and all of her five foot one inch, "you are going all to hell."

"I'd better pack a bag, then."

"I mean it, Stil," said Genevieve, helping me post the rabbit full of lettuce. "The act is lousy."

"Gee thanks, Genevieve," I gushed.

"It's technically perfect, and it's getting better, and it's about dead as Julius Caesar."

"Gosh, is he *dead*? How'd it happen, hit and run?"

"No, I'm not laughing," said Genevieve, not laughing. "I want to know where that girl is, the blonde girl." She waited a while, and when I didn't say anything, Genevieve said: "Let's get this straight. I'm worried about *her*. She was on a knife-edge, and you were easing her off it. Now I guess she's back on the knife-edge. You're not usually so obtuse."

"Not that it's any of your business, but we had nothing left to say to each other."

"To coin a phrase. That's why the act stinks. That's why the next novel will stink."

"Genevieve, I honestly don't know if I want to see her again or I don't."

"I know," said Genevieve. She smiled, riffled the cards, and picked the Lovers straight out of the pack. "Just," said Genevieve, "go knock on her door, and see what happens to you when she opens it."

I went out, to the pay-phone in the Piper Building down the block. I didn't realise till I came to put in the dime I still had a leaf of lettuce in my hand.

I didn't think anyone would answer. Or maybe one of the cats would take the call, and spit. Then there was her voice.

"Hi, Cathy," I said.

I heard her drag in a deep breath, and then she said, "I'm glad you called. It doesn't make any difference, but I want to apologise for what I said to you."

"It does make a difference," I said.

"Thank you for mailing me back the bracelet," she said. "I'm going to hang up now."

"Carthage are doing my book," I said.

"I'm so glad. You'd never read me any. I'll be sure and buy it. I'm going to hang up right now."

"O.K. I'll be with you in twenty minutes."

"No—"

"Yes. Give the cats a dust."

It was a quarter to five when I reached the house, and a premature white snow was coming down like blossom on the lawns along the street.

Here goes, Genevieve, I thought, as I pressed the doorbell. Now let's see what *does* happen to me when Cathy opens the door.

What happened was a strange, strange thing, because I looked at Cathy, and I just didn't know her. For one thing, I'd never properly seen how beautiful she was, because she'd looked somehow familiar from the first time I saw her. But now, she was brand new, unidentifiable. And looking in her artificial face, I wondered (always wondering), if I was ready to break the cellophane wrapper.

"There's snow in your hair," she said quietly, and with awe. And I comprehended she, too, was seeing something new and uncannily special in me. "Are you sure you want to come in?"

"You're damn right I do. I'm getting cold out here."

"If you come in," she said, "please don't try and make me agree to anything I don't want. Please, Stil."

"Cross my heart."

She let me in then, solemnly. We went into the living room. The once-conversation-piece electric fire, which didn't look like a fire at all but some sort of space-rocket about to take off and blast its way through the ceiling of Venus, exuded a rich red glow. It enveloped five squatting forms, and their fur was limned as if in blood.

"Hi, cats," I said. I knew by now I was probably going to have to concede, perhaps even share my life with them. Maybe I could get to love them. I reached down slowly, and a fistful of scythes sloughed off some topskin. So. I could tie their paws up in dinky little velvet bags, I could cover the floors with washable polythene, I could always carry a gun. Cats don't live so long as humans. Unless they get you first.

We sat by the fire, the seven of us. Cathy and I drank China tea. The cats drank single cream from five dishes.

There were some enormous fresh claw-marks along the fire's wood surround, bigger and higher than any of their previous original etchings. Cathy must have gone out at some point and missed one of their ten or eleven mealtimes, and they'd got fed up waiting. I surreptitiously licked my bleeding hand.

"Genevieve told me," I said, "About a ground-floor apartment just off Aster. There's a back yard with lilac trees. They'd enjoy scratching those."

"You still want me to sell this house," said Cathy. "My parents' house, they wanted me to have."

"Not sell. You could rent it."

She looked at the fire, which also limned her now, her bone-china profile, the strands of her hair, with blood.

"I thought I'd never see you again," she said.

"The Invisible Man. It's O.K. I took the antidote."

"I thought I'd just go back to where I was, the years before I met you. That I'd always be alone. Me, and the cats. I thought that was how it would be."

I took her hand. It was cold and stiff, and her nails were long and ragged. Down below, the cats were poised over their empty plates, staring up at her, their eyes like blank glass buttons.

"So I said to myself," she said, "I don't need anyone. I've got the cats. I don't need anyone human at all."

She pulled her hand out of mine, and got up.

"I'm not," she said, "leaving this house."

"All right. Good. Sit down."

"In a minute," she said. "I have to feed the cats."

"Oh, sure. The cream was an apéritif. Which is the starter: Salmon or caviar?"

She considered me, her eyes just like theirs. She wasn't laughing, either. She went out to the kitchen, and the cats trotted after her. They didn't screech this time, but I could imagine all that cream slopping loudly about in their multiplicity of guts.

Alone, I sat and contemplated the Venus rocket, and the huge new claw-marks up the wood. It looked, on reflection, really too high for the cats to have reached, even balanced on tip-claw. Maybe one had teetered on another one's head.

After a while, none of the cats, or Cathy, had come back.

The tea was stone cold, and I could hear the snow tapping on the windows, the house was so quiet, as if no one else but me was in it. Finally I got up, and walked softly, the way you tread in a museum, along to the kitchen door. There was no light anywhere, not in the passage, not in the dining area, or the kitchen itself. And scarcely a sound. Then I heard a sound, a regular crunching, mumbling sound. It was the cats eating, there in the dark. I must have heard it a thousand times, but suddenly it had a unique syncopation all its own. It was the noise of the jungle, and I was right in the midst of it. And the hair crawled over my scalp.

I hit the light switch on a reflex, and then I saw.

There on the floor, in a row, were the five cats. And Cathy.

The cats were leaning forward over their paws, chomping steadily. Cathy lay on her stomach, the soles of her feet pressed hard against the freezer, supporting her upper torso on her elbows. Her hair had been draped back over one shoulder so it wouldn't get in the way as she licked up the single cream from the saucer.

She continued this about a couple of seconds after the light came on, long enough for me to be sure I wasn't hallucinating. Then she raised her head like a snake, and licked her lips, and watched me with her glass-button eyes.

I backed out the kitchen. I went on backing until I was half along the passage. Then I turned like a zombie and walked into the living room.

Nothing was altered. Not even the big new runnels in the wood surround of the fire.

I was sweating a dank cold sweat and breathing as fast as if I'd just got out from a lion's cage, which I hadn't, yet. It was some kind of primitive reaction, because what I'd seen was really very funny, a joke. But I don't think I could have been more shaken if she'd come at me with a steak knife.

I pondered my alternatives. I could make it out the door, and run. I needn't come back. She'd know why not. Or I could stay and try to figure her out, try to persuade her to tell me what the game was and why she was playing it, and how I could help stop her going insane.

I was deliberating, when she came into the room.

She looked straight at me, and she said, "I'm sorry you saw that."

"Are you? Somehow I had the feeling I was meant to see. What's the idea?"

"No idea. I like it. I like scratching the wood, too. Over the fire. See? You look nervous."

"Must be because I am."

She glided across the room, and slid her arms round my ribs.

"You're nervous of me."

"I'm terrified of you."

She kissed my jaw, and each time she kissed, I felt the edges of her teeth. I could imagine what she'd be like if I made love to her now. Not that I wanted to make love to her.

I wanted to leave her and run. That was all I wanted, but concern gets to be a habit, and I guess we all know about habits. Besides, you find a girl sitting with a bottle of pills and a razor blade, and you go out and shut the door? And then, in any case, I realised, she was trembling. I'd thought it was just me.

"Get your coat and your boots," I said.

"It's snowing."

"Excuses, excuses. Get your coat."

"All right."

Ten minutes later, we were on the street. The cold silvery air seemed to blow through my head, and I started to ask myself where I was taking her. But Cathy didn't speak, just walked beside me, like a good little girl doing what the adults tell her though she doesn't understand.

We rode the subway, and came back up out of the ground and walked to my place, to which I never take anyone unless I must, not even a rabbit. The King of Cups is where I live; 23 Mason is where I

occasionally eat, and less occasionally sleep, thrash a
typewriter, and worry. And that's the way it looks.
It's a couple of flights up, or chiropractical jerks if
you use the elevator. In the snow-light, it was grey
and chill and scattered with reams of paper, maga-
zines and dust. My world and no one else's, and I
didn't want her here, and this was where I'd brought
her. Why? Because part of me had subconsciously
worked it out that this place had been built from my
own individual ectoplasm, and I was going to use it
to bawl her out and back to sanity, louder than any
shout I could make with my throat.

We got inside the door, and she glanced drearily
around. We hadn't offered a word to each other
since leaving the house.

"Every luxury fitment," I now said. "Most of them
not working."

Cathy crossed to the window, and stood there in
her coat with the snow dissolving on its shoulders.
She looked at the yard two floors down, and the
trash-cans and broken bottles in their own cake-
frosting of snow. When she turned round, her face
was gleaming, waves of tears running over it. She
sprang to me suddenly and held on to me. I knew
the grip. I knew I'd gotten her back. If I wanted her.
Her hair seemed the only thing in the room which
had colour, and which shone.

"I'm sorry," she muttered, "sorry, sorry."

I felt tired and it all seemed faintly absurd. I
stroked her hair, and knew in the morning I was
going to call Genevieve, and ask her what the hell to
do next.

In the morning, about seven, I slunk out of bed, put
some clothes on, and went out, leaving Cathy asleep.
The pay-phone in the entry, as usual, was bust, so I

walked down to the booth on the corner of Mason and Quale. The snow lay thin and moistly crisp as water-ice, and the sky was painting itself in blue as high summer. It was an optimistic morning, full of promises of something. I got through to Genevieve, who hardly ever sleeps, and told her all of it, feeling a fool.

"Oh boy," said Genevieve. And then: "Bring her over here to breakfast, why don't you. Maybe the dog'll chase her up a tree."

"You think I'm on something and I imagined it."

"No."

"You think I should laugh it off, it doesn't matter."

"It matters."

"Well?"

"Well. I think you're going as bats as she is. I don't know what I can do except feed you pancakes—little children like those, don't they? But I know a guy might help."

Genevieve genuinely knows a remarkable number of guys who can help. Help you get to sing with the opera, help you find out who you were six hundred years ago in Mediaeval Europe, or help you find a cop who cares somebody mugged you and stole the fillings in your teeth.

"A shrink."

"Sort of. Wait and see."

"It has to be gentle, Genevieve, Very, very gentle."

"It will be. Bring her. I'll expect you by eight."

Once you've passed the buck, you feel better. I felt better. I walked back through the snow, identifying the footprints in it like a kid: human, bird, dog. I knew I could leave all the delicate manoeuvring to Genevieve, who is one of the best social surgeons there are. Sometime later, I'd have to decide where

I wanted to be in all of this, but I didn't have to do it right now.

I got up to the second floor, and let myself in the apartment, and Cathy was gone.

The bed was empty, the bathroom, even the closet. I was working myself into a panicky rage when I saw her purse lying under the window. The window was just open, and the dust-drape of snow on the fire-escape had neat dark cuts in it the shape of shoe-soles. I climbed through onto it, and looked down and saw Cathy standing in the yard, with her back to me.

I didn't react properly. I was just so relieved to find her. I leaned on the rail and shouted.

"Hey Cathy. We're going to Genevieve's for breakfast."

She turned round, then, and her eyes came up to mine, but without a trace of recognition. And then I saw what it was she had in her mouth. It was a bleeding, fluttering, almost-but-not-quite-dead pigeon.

Cathy had found her breakfast already.

THE HUNTING OF DEATH: THE UNICORN

One: The Hunting

In the first life, Lasephun was a young man.

He was reasonably tall, of slender active build, and auburn-haired. His skin, which was to be a feature of all this group of lives, was extremely pale, and lent him an air of great intensity. By nature, the being of Lasephun was obsessive. Charged with fleshly shape, the obsessiveness took several forms, each loosely linked. The first life, the young man who was called Lauro, became obsessed with those things which were unobtainable, and hungered for them with a mysterious, gnawing hunger.

Firstly then, the motive force, which was creative and sought an outlet, drove him from place to place. In one, he would find a forest, and in the forest a shaft of light like golden rain, and the sight of this would expand in him like anguish. In a city, he would see a high wall, and over the wall the tops of crenellated towers and beyond the towers the sky with thunderclouds, and somewhere a bell would slowly ring and a woman would go by picking up the whispering debris from the gutter. These images and these sounds would stay with him. He did not know what to do with them. Sometimes, like some intangible unnamed scent, there would be only a feeling within him that seemed to have no cause, a deep swirling, disturbing and possessing him, which could neither be dismissed nor conjured into anything real.

At length, he learned how to make music on the twenty-two strings of a lutelin, and how to fashion songs, and he sang these in markets, inns, and on the steps of cathedrals for cash, or alone on the billowing roads and the sky-dashed face of the land for nothing—or for himself. But his songs and his music filled him with blunted anger. And as he grew, by mere habit, more polished, his anger also grew. For what he could make never matched the essence of what he had felt. The creation was like a mockery of the stirring and the dream within him. He almost hated himself, he almost hated the gift of music.

To others, he was a cause of some fascination. To still others he was attractive, phantasmal, like a moving light. They would come to him, and sometimes even follow him a short distance, before they perceived he no longer saw them. He never stayed long in any one place. As if he felt the movement of the earth under him, he travelled, trying to keep pace with it.

Proceeding in this way, it occurred to him one night that he himself did not move at all, but simply paced on one spot, while the landscape slid towards him and away behind him, bringing him now a dark wood, and now a pool dippered by stars, and now a town on a high rock where wild trees poured down like hanging gardens.

It was well past midnight. The morning, disguised as the night, was already evident on the faces of any clocks the town might hold. Lauro leaned on a tree in the vale below the town, not far from the pool which glittered, and the dark wood which had gathered all the darkness to itself as if to be cool.

Was a world so beautiful, so unfathomable, also a disappointment to its Creator? Had the world failed to match the vision of the God who devised it? On His seventh day, not resting but lamenting, had He gone away and left His work unfinished, and somewhere else did some other world exist, like but unlike, in which had been captured the creative impulse entire and perfectly?

Lauro touched the lutelin and the strings spoke as softly as the falling of a leaf—

And in that moment a white leaf blew out of the dark wood and flickered to the edge of the pool.

Lauro stared. He saw a shape, which was not like the shape of a horse, but more like that of a huge greyhound, and all of one unvariegated paleness so absolute it seemed to glow. He saw a long head, also more like that of some enormous dog, a head chiseled and lean, with folded glimmering eyes. And from the forehead, like the rising of a comet (frozen), the tapering crystaline finger of the fearful horn. And the horn lowered and lowered to meet the horn of another in the pool. Where the two horns met each other, a ring of silver opened and fled away. Then the mouth cupped the water and the creature drank.

As the unicorn was drinking, Lauro only watched it. To him it would have seemed, if he had considered it at all, that the unicorn was not drinking, but only carrying out some ethereal custom special to its kind. For the unicorn was unearthly and therefore did not need to accomplish earthly things. The unicorn had strayed into this world, which was God's disappointment, out of that other world, the second creation God had made, when the form had finally matched the vision.

So Lauro watched and did not move, probably did not even blink, his back against the tree's trunk, his hands spread on the strings of the lutelin. But then the unicorn raised its head from the pool, and turned a little, and began to come towards him.

All creative beings are capable of seeing in symbols, and each will seek analogy and omen, even while denying the fact. Embryonic though Lauro's creative gift might be, his beautiful voice unfined and his song-making erratic, uneven and a source of rage to him, still, presented with this unique symbol, he recognised it. The sorcerous quality of the unicorn was inevitably to be felt. No one, however dull, could have mistaken that, and Lauro was not dull at all, but if anything too aware and too sensitised. The sight of the unicorn touched him and he resonated to the touch as the strings of the lutelin had resonated. It was not a voice which spoke to him, and there were no words uttered either in the darkness or within his own heart or brain, yet it was as if something said plainly to him: *Here it is, here it approaches you, that which you require, that which for ever and ever you have pursued, not knowing it. The wellspring within yourself you cannot tap, the jewel in your mind you cannot uncover.* And in that moment the miracle of the unicorn seemed to be that if he could only lay his skin against the skin of it, even so small an area of skin as a finger's tip, everything that burned and smoked within him would be, at last, his to use. He, too, laying hands on this creature of the second perfect world, would gain the power of perfect creation. But maybe also there was a part of him which recognised the unicorn in another way, as that thing which must always *be* pursued and *never* taken, the inconsolable hunger, the mirage which runs before and can never be come up with, since the consolation of hunger is satiety, and the end of the chase is stillness and death.

And so, for one reason or another, as the unicorn moved towards him, Lauro broke from his trance and moved forward one step in answer.

At which the unicorn, perhaps seeing him for the first time, stopped.

At which Lauro took another step.

At which the unicorn became a single blink of a white lid on the night, and was gone.

Nothing natural could have moved so very fast. It had not even seemed to turn, but just to wink out like a flame. Nevertheless, Lauro knew it had gone back into the wood, which must be its habitation. A vague succession of stories came to him which explained how a unicorn's wood might be beset by perils, by phantoms, by disasters. These did not stop him. He ran at the wood and straight into it.

It was like falling off the edge of the night into a black pit. The pit was barred over by raucous branches which slashed his face and slammed across his body, full of earth which gave way under his feet and the tall columns of the trees which met his body with their own. He fell many times, and once he was almost blinded when an antler of branches stabbed into his face. But presently he glimpsed a white gleam ahead of him, and knew it for the unicorn, and he shouted with fury and joy. And then he fell a long way down, as it seemed into the black soul of the wood, and lying there on the black soul's floor, where there were decayed leaves like old parchment, and some tiny flowers that shone in the darkness, he dazedly saw the white light coming back to him. This time for sure the unicorn might savage him. He thought of this with awe but not terror. The touch that would unlock the genuis within him could not kill. Whatever wound there was, he would be healed of it. The fall had stunned him, and he was conscious that the neck of the lutelin was snapped off from the body.

Then the unicorn came between the trees, and it was only the moon.

Lauro knew despair then, and a sort of anger he had never felt before. He lay watching the moon, its light making his face into a bone in the black cavity of the wood.

When the day came, he was able to climb out of the cavity, which had not seemed possible before, although conceivably it had been possible. He put the broken lutelin into his pack, and walked out of the trees. By day, the wood had a different appearance. It was very green, but the green of undisturbed deep water. On all sides the trees, though struck by sunlight, seemed impenetrable.

It was silent. No birds, no winds moved in the unicorn wood.

A while before noon, Lauro entered the town on the rock.

It was like many other towns, and he scarcely looked about him. Others looked at him, and he felt their eyes on him. This was because he was a stranger, but also because he was himself and there was that quality to him of the fire, or the moving light, a quality in fact curiously like that he had noted in the unicorn.

And today, beside his obsessive intensity was very great. It was like a wave banked up behind his eyes. And when he sat on the steps of the stone church,

under the high doors and their carvings of martyrs
and demons, his face was like these stones faces, with
the reddish autumnal hair falling leadenly round it.
His hands were stiffly clasped, without even the lutelin
now to lend them life.

After a while, a woman came to him and offered
him bread from a basket, and he would not take it,
and later another offered him fish and he refused
this too. Then a priest came out, and offered him
holy comfort, and Lauro laughed, high, and pitched
as if he sang. There were others, all eager, in their
timid solicitous ways, to aid him, for they sensed his
pain, and they came to him and the cold fire of his
pain, like moths to the candle. He refused them all.
They could not help him. They knew it and they
went away. Even the child who tugged on his sleeve,
looking up into his eyes and their black centres, even
the child—at whom he briefly smiled—ran away.

The day gathered in the town until it was the
colour of strawberries, and the rays of the sunset fell
through the church windows from within and out
upon the steps, and upon the face of Lauro. He
could not play or sing what he had known, could
only speak it, and had not been able to.

He had been there seven hours when the Lord of
the town came riding to Mass in the church, a thing
he did not generally do. The strawberry sky was
behind him and behind the eight dark horses and
the dark forms of the men who rode on them. The
horses were not remotely like the unicorn. Even if
they had been given crystaline horns that flamed in
the sunset, they would not have been like. Someone
had told the Lord of the stranger with the lank red
hair and the frozen face and hands. They had re-
ported him as a seer or poet—one who has witnessed
some portentous thing: and so he had.

The Lord reined in his horse at the foot of the stair.

He looked at the stranger with his Lord's proud and self-blind eyes, and suddenly the stranger looked back at him with eyes that had seen far too much.

"You," the Lord said. "Why are you sitting there? What do you want?"

Lauro said, "There is a unicorn in your wood."

"A unicorn," said the Lord. "Who reckons so?"

"I do."

"You may be mistaken. You may be drunk or mad. Or a liar. *You.* What are you?"

"I forget," said Lauro. "I forget who I am. I forgot in the moment I saw the unicorn."

The Lord smiled. He glanced about. His men smiled to demonstrate they were of one mind with him. The townspeople smiled, or else lowered their eyes.

"Perhaps," said the Lord, "I do not believe in unicorns. A fable for children. Describe what you saw. Probably it was a wild horse."

Lauro got to his feet, slowly, His eyes were now wise and looked quite devilish—this was because he did not know any more what to do. He turned and walked, without another word, up the steps and in at the church doors.

The Lord of the town was unused to men with devil's eyes who turned and walked wordlessly away from him. The Lord gestured two of his men from their mounts.

"Go after him. Tell him to come back."

"If he will not obey, my lord?"

The Lord frowned, visualising a scuffle in the precincts of the church, damaging to his reputation. He dismounted suddenly. The Lord himself, with his two men at his back, strode up the steps into the church after the stranger.

Lauro was standing at the church's remotest end, in shadow before the darkened window. His hands hung at his sides and his head was bowed. The Lord gripped him by the shoulder, and Lauro wheeled round with a vicious oath. Lauro had been in the other, second world, aeons away, where the unicorn was. His eyes flared up and dazzled, luminous as a cat's, and the Lord hastily gave ground.

"Swear to me, on God's altar," said the Lord.

"Swear to what?"

"The unicorn."

"An hallucination," said Lauro. "I am a liar. Or drunk. Or mad."

"Swear to me," said the Lord.

Lauro grinned, with his long mouth closed, a narrow sickle.

"What will you do if you believe me?"

"There were stories before," said the Lord, "when I was a boy. Years ago. I dreamed then I should hunt such a beast, and capture it. And possess it."

Lauro put back his head and laughed. When he laughed, he looked like a wolf. Laughing, the wolf went to the altar and placed his hand on it.

"I swear by God and the angels of God and the Will and Works of God, that there is a unicorn in your wood. And God knows, too, you will never take, capture or possess a unicorn."

The Lord said: "Come to my stone house with me. Eat and drink. Tomorrow you shall ride with us and see."

So Lauro lay that night in the Lord's stone house with its three dog-toothed towers. Sometimes before he had lain in the houses of lords. His envy and his ambition were not exacerbated by anything of theirs.

Preparations for the hunting of the unicorn had

begun almost at once. It occurred to Lauro that the Lord wished to credit the unicorn's existence, that on some very personal level the reality of the legend was highly important to him. But Lauro cared nothing for the desires and dreams of the Lord. The hunt was less convincing to Lauro than the memory of the unicorn itself—which had now become ghostly. He believed in the unicorn rather less than the Lord believed, and yet he knew he had beheld it, knew that it waited for him in the wood. If it was possible to come at the unicorn by means of dogs and horses and snares, then he would accompany the hunt. But he did not believe in this, either, as he had said. It had come to be that what he believed credible was useless to him, and that what he did not believe could happen at all yet he believed *would* happen; since it had already happned once, and because it was essential to him. Actually, the hunt was as his song-making had been, a needful but flawed expression, inadequate but unavoidable. So he lay in the house, but did not sleep.

In the morning, the Lord's underlings brought Lauro down again into the hall. People hastened about there with a lot of noises, and food was piled high on platters and wine stood by, just as on the night before. The dogs were out in the yard, a sea of brown and white that came and went in tides past the open door.

Presently a girl was conducted in at the door. She was fair-skinned, and had been dressed in a long green gown. Her hair and her eyes were both dark as the wood, and Lauro, looking at her as she curtseyed for the Lord, knew her purpose. She knew it too. She was very solemn, and her eyes were strangely impenetrable, as if the lids were invisibly closed not over, but *behind* them.

The Lord came to Lauro eventually.

"I have only to give the word, now. Are you ready?"

"Are you?" asked Lauro.

"You show me no respect," said the Lord peevishly. "I do not trust you."

"Did I say you should trust me?"

"You have nervous hands," said the Lord. "I would think you were a musician, but you have no instrument with you. Walk with the grooms, in front of me. I want you in sight."

Lauro shrugged, unaware.

They went out into the courtyard, and the dogs began to bark. Overhead the sky was clear, and all around the air was sweet. The girl in green was put up on a horse, which she rode with both her legs on one side, in the manner of a lady. Because it was the custom of the legends and stories, she had been set at the head of the hunt, and the dogs, which were leashed, tumbled after the tasselled hooves of her horse. Lauro walked with the grooms, behind the dogs and before the horses. The hunt-master, and the Lord and his men, each with their swords and knives, came clanking on. There were three bowmen, and two boys to sound the horns. The hunt-master himself carried a long blade in an ornate scabbard, but he was frowning, angry and unnerved.

The townspeople stood watching in the streets, and they scarcely made a sound, though some of them indicated Lauro to others who had not seen him previously.

As the hunt left the town and began to pick a way down the rock, with the dogs whining impatiently and the green-clad virgin riding side-saddle before them all, everything became, for Lauro, measured as a planned and stately dance. The falling verdure of the trees that flooded round the track as they descended, meshed with the sun and confused his eyes, so he partly closed them, and the noises of the dogs and the metal noises of the men made his ears sing, so he ceased mostly to listen.

Apart from the girl, it was like any other hunt, for meat or sport. He knew, when they reached the wood—day-green and opaque—they would not find the unicorn. The wood was like a curtain or a tapestry. It was possible to thrust through to its other side, but not to discover any substance in it.

They entered the vale under the town. They rode through the vale, between the solitary trees with their caps of sunlight, and over the long rivers of their shadows. The pool appeared, a shallow rent in the fabric of the land, with the sky apparently beneath and showing through it. At this sky-pool, the unicorn had drunk, or performed its ritual of drinking. Behind lay the wood like a low cloud balanced against the earth and the horizon. He remembered the wood and the pool as if he had lived in this spot since childhood, he who had always been wandering. But then, these also had become figments of the second perfect world which, in some esoteric way, he had indeed always known.

The girl cast one glance behind her before she rode among the trees. As she lowered her eyes, they met Lauro's; then she turned away again.

The hunt trotted into the wood about twenty paces, and then stopped still, while the hunt-master ordered his men ahead to search for droppings and other indications of the presence of a large beast. Lauro moved aside and leaned on a tree, and smiled coldly at the ground. A unicorn could not be taken in such a fashion. His mind seemed to drift out into the wood, searching and searching itself for some permissible, ethereal trace, like an echo, of the unicorn, but the greenness was a labyrinth where his mind soon lost itself. He sensed the girl had moved ahead alone. He closed his eyes, and all of them were gone.

Then—he did not see or sense it, he *knew* it—then the unicorn came, as if from nothingness, and stepped across the turf, ignoring the hunt, the dogs, the girl, looking at him. And Lauro felt the shadow of the unicorn wash over him, like a faint breeze.

Lauro opened his eyes. There was nothing there, where he was gazing. But something was happening to the Lord's men, a susurration not of noise but of silence. There was a great heat in the wood.

The girl had indeed moved forward alone, and she had dismounted or been lifted down. She stood between two trees, and the unicorn stood beyond her. It was like a statue, immobile. It did not look real.

There was nothing to be done. The creature did not move. If the men should have, the unicorn would run. So much was obvious. But the hunt-master, used to his craft, to the unsupernatural deer and starting panic-swift hares, signalled to one of the boys who carried a hunting horn, and the boy, his eyes bursting, blew the horn—since he had always done so—and the men by the hounds slipped their leashes, again from habit.

The pack flung itself forward and the surge of it hit the girl as she stood there before the unicorn. She was tossed sideways, and would have gone down, but one of the grooms snatched her up and away out of the foam of dogs.

Everyone seemed taken by surprise at his own actions. The unicorn, for an instant, seemed surprised, too. But Lauro laughed again, as he had in the church. He was furiously glad the hunt had come to defile the unicorn's sanctity and purity and solitude. Glad for the yelping and shouting, and the blundering of hoofs. Yet he did not suppose any true defilement was likely.

But the unicorn ran, and the dogs belled and swirled after it. Men and horses rushed by.

There was a long aisle between the trees, tenuously barricaded at intervals by screens and sheer sloping walls of blinding sunlight. Down this aisle the unicorn ran. And suddenly Lauro realized he could see the unicorn running, that it was perceptible to him. Before, the speed and articulation of the unicorn had been quite invisible.

As he noticed this, with a kind of slow and searing shock, one of the bowmen let fly an arrow.

The unicorn was so white, so luminescent even by day—it seemed the shaft was drawn after it by magic, magnetised to the shining skin—

Lauro saw, or thought he saw, the arrow penetrate the right flank of the unicorn. It seemed to stumble. It was like a star clumsily reeling in its smooth and faultless flight. Lauro could not now believe what he saw. The unicorn had become a deer, a white stag, nothing more. Lauro was running, with the rest. So he beheld the foremost handful of dogs catch up to and leap on their prey.

The unicorn fell. It was very sudden, and the dogs gushed over it. He saw teeth meeting in the sorcerous skin. And then, something more terrible. The unicorn, like almost anything at bay and pulled down, began to fight. First one dog was spitted, screaming and lathering on the slender tower of the impossible horn, and then another. Each, as it was impaled, was thrown away, its entrails loose as ribbons. And the fabulous horn was red.

A man raced forward shouting, laughing or ap-

pearing to laugh. He thrust the tip of his short knife
into the unicorn's side. Another was driving a blade
into the arching throat. The blood of the unicorn,
just like that of the dogs, was only red.

Lauro dropped to his knees, and the hunt went by
him and covered the sight of the fallen unicorn
which was only a white stag. It had not made a single
sound.

Someone, dashing by, kicked Lauro. He felt the
blow from a distance of many miles. No blow, no
pain, no warmth could come at the cold thing inside
him.

The horns were winded, and the hunt-master swore
in a businesslike way. They had hunted the unicorn,
wounded it, bound it. It was taken. The whole event
had been very quick.

Lauro continued to kneel, as if he prayed, on the
trampled turf.

At some juncture, he was offered payment. This was
after he had followed the hunt back into the town.
He had walked a quarter of a mile behind them,
then a mile, two miles. He had not seen what had
happened as they entered the town, but when he
came there the streets were empty. It had begun to
rain, gently at first, but with increasing violence. If
blood had trickled into the streets from the unicorn's
wounds, it had been washed away. The people, too.

If any had watched the hunt's return, they would
have seen an animal, slung between staves, obscurely
roped, its head hanging down. It had looked dead,
dead and bloody and of a surpassing, horrid ordi-
nariness.

But the slung carcass of the unicorn was not dead.
Lauro followed them all, and come in the end to

the three-towered house, and at the door men were waiting and took him in.

The Lord sat in a carved chair and drank wine. He was rain-wet, and his clothing steamed. The hall was full of such steam, and the yard full of the steaming, snarling hounds, who had tasted blood and been given no portion of the slain beast to devour.

The Lord stared at Lauro. The Lord was gross and ruddy.

"Well. You will wish to be paid. I have gained a rare animal. I may henceforward collect such oddities. It might amuse me to do so. What price do you ask for your information?" And when Lauro said nothing, staring back with his cold inhuman eyes, the Lord said: "It was worth something, and you know it. I had heard rumours, from my boyhood. Many heard such tales. But it took you, stranger and vagabond, to suss the creature out for me."

"For you," Lauro said.

"For me. What price, then?"

Lauro said, "Where do you mean to keep it?"

"Penned. On grass, under trees, A pavilion. Something pretty. The ladies shall tame it. In three months it will eat from my hand, like a lap dog."

Lauro looked right through the Lord and his hall, and saw a pavilion of grass, and the unicorn gamboling. It occurred to him, with an uncanny frightening certainty, that since the unicorn had only been a legend before, he himself, by his desire and his desperation, had somehow conjured it. Conjured, witnessed, and betrayed.

"By the Christ," said the Lord, growing furious all at once, "name your price, you insolent devil."

The thoughts and the words combined. Lauro smiled.

"Thirty," he said, "pieces of silver."

With a curse or two, and a clinking of coins like curses, they paid him. Afterwards, he went outside, and around the wall of the Lord's house, from sight. He sat down by the wall, in the rain. He could think of nothing, yet the image of the unicorn remained. After a time, deep within himself, he felt the mysterious formless shining which tortured him, as always, unable to find its expression. He understood that this occasion was no different. But he was not like a dumb man in enormous pain who could not cry out.

At some point he slept under the blanket of the rain.

When he woke, there were warm and fluttering lights in certain high windows of the house. He wondered where the unicorn was, in some stable or outhouse, perhaps, and he wondered if it would die, but it did not seem to him it had lived. He slept again, and on the second awakening the lights in the house were out. He got to his feet and rain fell from him like water from a bucket. He began to move around the wall, searching for something, at first not comprehending his search. Eventually, he became conscious that he was seeking a secretive way back in, a way to reach the unicorn. But he did not know why he did so, or what use it might be. He did not even know where the unicorn had been imprisoned.

He came to a part of the wall which seemed, even in the wet darkness, to be different. He could not tell what it was. But then the notion began to grow that it was different in some mode of the spirit, because it was connected to his purpose. Almost immediately he found a thin wooden door. He rapped on the door, and received no answer. There were rotted timbers in the door, that sagged when his knuckles met them.

For maybe an hour he worked at the rotten wood,

and when some of it gave way, he worked on the rusty bar within. Ivy clung to the bar and insects skittered away from his probing, wrenching hands. The joints of his shoulders jarred in their sockets and sweat ran down his back and across his breast, turning icy cold when it touched the heavy rain in his clothes.

When the door opened he no longer thought it would, and had been working on it from mere momentum, as if hypnotised.

Inside the door was an obscure stone-arched walk. Lauro went into it, and through it, and came out in an old yard framed by the tall blank walls of the house. Another door, this one unbarred, led into a little garden. Beyond the garden, still inside the precinct of the house, was a patch of muddy ground. Distantly a tower loomed up; before the tower several cumulose trees rose in a bank of shadow. A lamp burned, showing two men asleep under an awning, an empty wine-skin between them. These things were like messages inscribed on the stones, the earth, the dark. In the very centre of the dark, far beyond the scope of the lamp, against the trees, was a dim low smoulder, like a dying fire, except it was white. It was the unicorn.

A fading ember, a candle guttering. The flame of the unicorn dying down, put out by rain and blood.

Lauro went forward, past the drunken sleepers, out of the light. He padded across the grass, and came under the rustling, dripping trees. The rain eased as he did so, and then stopped. He saw the unicorn clearly.

It was seated, with its forelegs tucked under it, like a lamb or a foal. The fringe of its mane was sombre with water. Its head was lowered, the horn pointing directly before it. And the horn was dull. It looked

unburnished, ugly, *natural*, like a huge nail-paring.
He could not see its eyes. Though they were open,
they were glazed; they had paled to match the darkening of its flesh until the two things were one.

There was no protection for the unicorn from the
elements, but then, it had lived in the wild wood.
What held it penned was a fence of gilded posts, no
more. They were not even high enough that it could
not have jumped over them. What truly held it was
the collar of iron at its neck, and the chain that ran
from the collar to an iron stake in the ground.

Something glittered in the mud, more brilliantly
than the unicorn now glittered. As Lauro came nearer,
he saw there were small gems and coins lying all
about the unicorn. A ruby winked like a drop of
wine. Some man had thrown a jewelled dagger, some
woman a wristlet of pearls.

Bemused, Lauro stood about five paces from the
gilded fence. There had been no emotion in him he
could identify, until now. But now an emotion came.
It was disgust, mingled with hatred.

He approached two more paces, and hated the
unicorn.

He hated it because it had failed him. It had proved
attainable, and vulnerable. It had let itself be dirtied.
It was inadequate, as he was.

Its wounds, of course, marred it. There would
always be scars, now, from the teeth of the dogs, the
arrow, the knives. But its fading was not due to these
alone.

He had reached the fence. He waited, in an appalled foreknowing, for the beast to turn to him, to
plead with him by means of its lustreless eyes. If it
did so, he might kill it. For he knew, at last, it too
was mortal, and could die. It had never existed in a
second world of perfection at all. His mistake.

It lay like a sick dog and did not look at him, while the night murmured with the aftermath of the rain. Some minutes elapsed before Lauro leaned in across the gilded posts and stretched down to take the rich man's dagger from the mud.

An hour later, when his limbs were numb from standing rigidly in one place so long, and his spine ached and his head and his very brain ached, and the moon appeared over the trees and the unicorn had not looked at him, Lauro threw the dagger at the unicorn.

As he did so a cry burst from him. There were no words in it. Then the dagger struck the unicorn in the neck, or rather, it struck against the area where the chain had been locked to the collar.

Something happened. Something snapped inside the case of the lock. The lock mouthed open, and the chain snaked away and lay coiled on the mud among the scattered jewels. The collar spun from the neck of the unicorn as if propelled.

Lauro took a step backward. Then many more steps.

What had freed the unicorn seemed to be an act of magic, perpetrated through him, and through what had been intended as an act of malicious harm. A theory that the force and angle of the blow might simply have sprung the crude mechanism of the lock did not temper Lauro's reaction. As he stepped back, he examined the fence of posts, expecting it to dissolve or collapse. This did not happen.

Not did the unicorn respond to its freedom for some moments. It seemed almost to consider, to debate within itself. Then, when the response came, it was complete. It sprang up, deftly, and the night seemed to slough from its body like a skin.

Set loose from this skin, as from the chain, the

unicorn began to glow. It altered. Its eyes filled as if from a ewer and were charged again with depth and nameless colour. The wounds glared, also charged, also like peculiar eyes, shot with incandescence—its new skin, or the skin beneath, was white again.

Lightly, and with no preliminary, it leapt the posts of the pen. And then, once more, it halted.

Lauro was closer now to the unicorn, or the fantasy which was the unicorn, than he had ever been. He was not afraid, and no longer was he consumed with hatred or disgust or disapointment in it. These also had been sloughed. The unicorn was renascent, beautifully and totally. The wet mane was like silver. The horn of its head was translucent and the night showed through it faintly, and there seemed to be stars trapped within the horn.

Lauro waited, like a lover who is willing to permit an old love to resume its mislaid power upon him. He waited for his belief in the miracle of the unicorn to come back. And slowly and irresistibly it did come back, flowing in, touching him as before, so he felt the certainty of it in his bones, sounding them like a chord.

The unicorn began to move again. Its head was slightly tilted sideways. It looked at Lauro with one eye which had grown denser than the night.

He had believed in it, betrayed it, freed it. This time, he knew, the unicorn must acknowledge him. Lauro's awareness was unarguable. It was a fact for him. Perhaps it was his sureness itself which would cause the unicorn to do so.

The unicorn hesitated yet again. Lauro gripped the air and the darkness in each of his hands. He tried to memorise the image of the unicorn. Soon, it would be gone. Only the unlocking it would give to him, only this would remain. Twinned, bonded, they would have freed each other of their separate chains. That must last a lifetime. It would.

Then the unicorn moved. It raced towards the little garden and the walk beyond, unerringly seeking the environs outside the house. And, for a frantic instant, he thought it would avoid him. But as it passed Lauro, it turned its head once more. The silken, star-containing spike of the horn drove forward and to one side, laying Lauro's breast open, cloth and flesh and tissue peeled away, the beating heart itself revealed, and ceasing to beat.

As the ultimate inaudible leaf-sounds of the unicorn's feet died in his ears, Lauro, lying on a bed of blood and hair and mud and rain, understood at last the rhythms and the means of his expression. The feeling like pain, like a death wound, swelled inside him, carrying him upward, and he was able, finally, to give it utterance. His lips parted to speak the glowing exactitude of the words which came. His lips stayed open, and when the rain began again, it fell into his mouth.

Two: Of Death

But in the second life, Lasephun was a young girl.

She was small in stature and slim. The pale skin was now, in her, almost white. Her hair was long and very dark, falling to her waist in black, shining streamers. The character of the being Lasephun's obsessiveness, in this, the second life, was muted and quiescent, although still in evidence in particular ways. But this life, a girl of sixteen who was called Sephaina, had been cared for in a unique manner, grown almost like a cherished plant. She had not yet had occasion to seek within herself, and so to be astonished, or to become dissatisfied.

Where Sephaina had been born she did not know, neither her parentage. These things did not matter to her. They had no relevance. Sephaina's awareness had begun in a slate-blue house, moated by brown water. Lillaceous willows let down their nets into the moat, and birds flew by the narrow windows with which the walls were pierced. Such pictures were set like stained glass into each of her days. The calm of the house, certain architectures, certain lights and shades incorporated in its geography, these were the balm in which the years of Sephaina floated. Her companions were several, and choice. The women who firstly cared for and then waited on her, were kind and elegant. The girl children who played with her grew up into beautiful maidens. Nothing ugly came in her way, and nothing more distressful than the death of a bird or a small animal from the meadows beyond the high walls of the house.

Within, the house was a puzzle of rooms bound by winding stairs and carven doors. From its tallest turrets, the meadows, pale golden with summer and blue pale with flowers, might be seen stretching away to a sort of interesting nothingness, which was the edge of vision. Sephaina had seldom entered the meadows, then only to picnic beneath a tree, her girl companions spread about her, birdsong and the notes of mandolettes mingling. For Sephaina, the world was no more than these things. She had never been sick, or truly sad. The only melancholy she had known had been slight, and bittersweet. She was surrounded by love and devotion, and it was in the nature of this life to accept these gifts, and dulcetly reflect them. To be valued was as integral to her days as her curious adopted state. For she understood that others did not live as she did, while never questioning how she lived. From her first awareness, a sense of her own purpose, though unexplained, had been communicated to her.

Not however until the day preceding her sixteenth birthday was her destiny announced, and placed before her like a newly opened flower.

Shortly after noon, as Sephaina sat quietly with two of her women, a priest entered the room, and a group of men with him. Sephaina had, of course, seen and conversed with men, but never with so many at once. She was not shy with them, but she guessed instantly, and faultlessly, that something of great import was about to happen.

The priest addressed her without preamble.

"Tomorrow you will be sixteen years of age, and on that day your fate, which has always been with you, governing your existence—although unknown—will be fulfilled."

Then he extended his holy ring to her, and Sephaina kissed it.

The men nodded. None of them spoke.

The priest said to her: "Follow then, and learn what your fate is."

So she rose, and the priest went from the room, up a winding stair and into one of the turrets. Sephaina followed him, with her women, and the men walked after, the heavy brocade of their garments making a syrupy sweeping noise on the steps.

If Sephaina had entered this turret before, she was uncertain. If she had ever come there, then the turret had since been much changed. There was a long and exotic tapestry, worked in a multitude of colours, which covered every wall. A candle-branch burned in the middle of the floor, flickering some-

what, so the figures in the tapestry seemed to quiver
and to breathe.

The subject of the tapestry was a great hunt, which
pursued a white beast with a single horn through the
glades of a wood, until a girl was found in its way,
seated on the grass, and the beast lay down and put
its head in her lap. At which the hunt drew close and
with dogs and bows at first, and thereafter with
knives and spears, appeared to kill the creature. It
bled from many wounds but the blood did not reach
the grass, which was starred instead by rainbow
blossoms.

Sephaina looked at these scenes of cruelty, deceit
and death, and she wept a moment, as at any of the
few deaths she had seen. But her tears ended almost
immediately. She was perturbed, and turned to the
priest for his answer. He gave it.

The creature in the tapestry was a unicorn. A
thing part fabulous and partly earthbound. It was
not necessary that one either believe or disbelieve in
it. There had been an era when the unicorn had
been hunted, had been slain or captured, cut and
roped, demeaned, used to increase some lord's vain-
glory or pride of acquisition, or bloodlust. But the
death of the unicorn was, in fact, largely inconse-
quential. It was conceivable only a single beast had
ever been killed, or that none had been killed. Or
that all the unicorns then extant in the world at that
time had died—only a dream left behind them capable of *seeing* life, or that they had been re-procreated
by mystical means from some eerie quickening between foam and shore, cirrus and mountaintop. Neither did truth or falsehood rate very highly in this
case. The core of the story of the unicorn, its
humiliation, in some ways paralled the history of the
Christ and might be said to represent it. And now, as

the debasement of Christ had been raised to worship, so the unicorn, ghost or truth or simply dream, was propitiated and adored. The clue to existence was the protean ability of man to alter things. To balance the ignominy of the unicorn's death, whether false or actual, the ritual of the hunt had been transformed into a festival of love.

They would advance into the trees of the wood, not with horses, dogs and weapons, but now on foot, unarmed, with flowers and fruit and wine. And to lead the procession there must be a maiden, who would charm by the magic force of her virginity, not in order to betray, but in order that they might do homage. And if it should come to her, laying its long head, horned as if with polished salt, in her lap, then the offerings could be made to it. Or if not, still the beauty of the tradition had been honoured, and the spirit of the unicorn with it.

"And you," the priest said to Sephaina as she stood between him and the circling tapestry, "you have been reared in perfect harmony and happiness to be that maiden who will lead the procession into the wood. Your years have been kept lovely in order that you be wholly lovely for him, the white one, so he will wish to come to you and give his blessing to what we do, and his forgiveness of what has been done. Every sixteen years, this is the custom. You are very special. You were chosen. Do you understand?"

"Yes," she said. The men behind the priest murmured then.

Sephaina lowered her eyes and saw the unicorn imprinted on the floor. It was different from the entity in the tapestry. It glowed, and its horn had a light within it like that of burning phosphorous. In some strange way, she remembered the unicorn. To be told of it was no amazement to her. That it might dwell in the world, that it might come to her indeed, did not seem incredible. For the first time also, something twisted inside her, a feeling very old though new to her: It was fear.

They showed her the gown she was to wear. It was the palest green, sewn with flora of blue thread. They showed her the oils and perfumes they would use for her skin and hair, and these were scented like a forest and the most delicious plants that might be discovered there.

Sephaina walked through the house, gazing at everything in it. She had a feeling of loss, as if she could never come back there. No one had told her if she would. Something had prevented her asking.

As the sun began to set, something odd happened in the meadows beyond the house. There began to be fireflies, dozens of them, scores of them, and then hundreds upon hundreds. They were not, of course, fire-flies, but the flames of torches and of lamps. The meadows, from the far distance to the edge of the moat, were dark with people, and on fire with lights. Bizarre shifting patterns, like those in a weird mosaic, formed and fell apart. Sephaina watched the lights, knowing why people gathered about the house. She had never known her power before, though she had, at some oblique station of her life and mind, accepted her rarity long ago. To see the demonstration of her emblematic worth stunned her.

She brooded on it, pausing for long minutes, transfixed at one after another of high windows. She wondered if they saw her, the ones who waited in the meadows. She imagined that perhaps they did, although not with their eyes.

Eventually her women persuaded her to the bedchamber where she had always slept. They washed and braided her hair with herbs, ready for the morning. When she lay down, they drew the covers over her. One read her a passage from a beautiful book which told of enchanting and lustrous things, towers built upon water, boats sailing the air, lovers who loved and lost and refound each other at the brink of violet seas where birds spoke in human voices. Then, her ladies and her maidens kissed Sephaina, and they went away to the antechamber beyond her door. Here, two of them would sleep each night, in case she should want something and call out. This had not happened since she was a little child.

Sephaina lay in the familiar bed, and watched the bedroom in the mild irradiation of a single low lamp. She remembered nights of her childhood, and how the shadows fell at different seasons, or when the moon was full, and how the room would be when the sun rose again. Her window was sheltered, however, by the ascension of a wall, from the vantage of the meadows, and so from the lights of those who stood about the house. And she wondered all at once if this room, whose window, unlike all the upper windows of the house, was shielded from the meadows, was always given to the chosen maiden for just this reason: To allow her peace on this one night of her life, the even of her sixteenth birthday.

The words of the priest came and went in her head all this time, behind every one of her other thoughts.

She had only seen depictions of woods, she had never seen a real one. The wood in the tapestry had been very dense, very darkly green, with slender tree trunks stitched on it, and with blossoms thick on the grass, and yet there had seemed no way to go through the wood. And the unicorn. How would it be to wait

for it to come to her, how would it be to know she
herself was the magic thing which drew the magic
thing towards her? It was curious. It was as if all this
had happened to her before, yet in some other distorted way—

Sephaina closed her eyes, and was startled that two
tears ran from under her lids.

But she had been trained by serenity to sleep easily and deeply, and already her mind moved forward
from the shore, slipping into the smooth currents of
unconsciousness. A dream rose from the threshold,
and greeted her. She beheld a drinking cup of crystal with a long and fluted stem. The drink in the cup
was very dark. She stared, and saw the wood and the
unicorn inside the drink, inside the cup. Then she
swam by the dream into the depths of sleep.

Sephaina woke to a huge silence that was uncanny.
The silence was an actual presence in the room,
filling and congesting it. It might have been that her
own heart had stopped beating. Or it might have
been the heart of time which had stopped, every clock
in the house, or the world, stilled Yet she breathed,
was capable of movement; her heart sounded. These
things she discovered by cautiously testing them.

At length she sat up, the ultimate test, and so she
saw that a shape crouched in the embrasure of her
sheltered window, between the room and the starry
night.

Fear has many forms. Sephaina's fear burned low
as the low-burning of the lamp, yet, like the lamp,
pervaded the chamber. Fear was also so novel to her
that it seemed quite alien. She could barely control
it. The twisting she had felt within herself when they
had told her of her destiny, the ebbing and swelling
flow of unease and isolation that had mounted as she

watched those hundreds of lights swarm upon the meadows, now gained a quiet and terrible dominion over her.

She could not have cried out, even if she thought to do so, and somehow the sensation of her fear prevented her from thinking of it. She was alone, on the whole earth, with the shape, whatever it should be, which had manifested between light and night.

Then the shape altered, melted upward. It slid from the embrasure, and began to come towards her, gliding, taking no steps. The lamp did not in any way describe it, except that, with no warning, its eyes flashed, catlike. And in the very same second dry summer lightning also flashed. It shattered the window and the room together. By means of this freak illumination, she saw the outline of the invading demon. It had now assumed, or perhaps had consistently possessed, the structure of a man, rather tall, physically agile, and long-haired

It seemed to her he addressed her. In the dreadful silence, she replied.

He said: "Would you see me?"

She replied: "No."

At that, he laughed. She was sure enough of the laugh. He sung it to her, and it was very cruel. Just then the tinderish lightning ignited again through the window, and he seemed to catch flame from it, absorbing, vampire-like, colours and equilibrium. She knew him instantly, the demon. His hair was red as rust, his eyes were bleak, and his face was like a bone. Across his breast a flap of cloth hung loose and ragged. Under this rent was an incoherent darkness that evaded or tricked her gaze.

She knew him. The knowledge was a facet of her fear.

At last she said: "What must I do to be rid of you?"

"Nothing, yet. I shall step from your window, in the same way I stepped up here. You will come with me."

Sephaina visualised the drop from the window to the moat below.

"You mean to kill me?"

"No. Why not put your trust in me? You are willing to trust all others—your servants, your friends, the priest. The unicorn."

Sephaina stared. She began to pray, and fell quiet.

The demon only said, "Give me your hand."

At which Sephaina, without knowing why, gave him her hand.

Immediately she was weightless. The covers of the bed drifted away from her. Linked to the demon she, too, now drifted across the room, her feet half the distance of her own body from the ground. Seeing which, she would have let go of him, but her hand would not leave go.

"Why fear this?" he inquired of her, almost with irritation. "There are other things you should fear."

And even as he spoke, he passed through the window and out on to the broad cool highway of the night sky, and she was taken with him.

The roofs of the house lay below, uncertainly gleaming, like tarnished pearl. The moat had become a circle of mist. The meadows were a great fire which had burned down to embers, for only here and there were the lamps still lit, and these looked very small to one who moved through the air, as if they no longer had any significance for her.

How was it possible to travel in this way? It occurred to Sephaina that maybe she had left her body behind. Yet her form was opaque, though weightless as a feather. The demon, too, appeared physical rather than astral, and as they clove the dark air, sometimes strands of his hair would blow across her face, stinging her cheeks: Both things had substance and were real.

The arc of the sky, like a glorious cathedral ceiling, benighted, swung and dipped above them.

The land below sheared away, amalgamated and no longer discernible. Sephaina, who all her days, as he said, had been able to trust—and so was in the habit of trusting—commenced trusting her devilish guide. She was not afraid of being suspended in space. In her limited experience so many things were miraculous. Anything different was a wonder. A wonder, therefore, eventually seemed merely different. And besides, she knew him. (Of course, one life ago she had *been* him, or she had been what he appeared to be.) She became relaxed, and it made her impatient that she could not tell what the landscape was that unfolded below them. She wanted to see it; she had seen so little, save in books.

Then the flowing abstract knit together. Sephaina saw they hovered like two birds above an ebony cloud, which, as they sank lower, grew gilded veins and smoky fissures. A waterfall of leaves brushed her face. They had come to a wood.

Inside the upper levels of the trees they moved with a darting precision, like that of fish. There was an opening, a glade like a bubble, and the demon drew her into it. They rested on invisible nothingness.

"Look down," he said to her. "Look about. What do you see, now?"

Sephaina looked into the slightly luminous black heart of the glade. Enormous sallow flowers dimly shone back into her eyes.

At last he said, "Did you never see bones before?"

"Yes—the bones of a bird—once."

"These are the bones of other things," he said.

They dipped again, and the grass-heads met their feet. She stood a few inches above the carpet of the glade, and he recalled irresistibly the tapestry of the unicorn, where the ground was strewn with blossoms. Here, bones lay thick as snow.

He led her. They spun over the glade. She was glad she need not walk on the bones. So she looked into the sockets of skulls and of pelvises. The demon drew a thigh bone from the grass. He examined it and threw it aside with the contempt of some great inner pain. The form of this long bone, as it fell, reminded Sephaina of the spike on the unicorn's forehead.

They came into a second glade, adjacent to the first. Here too there were bones, but fewer of them. In a third glade, the bones were scarce and mostly concealed among the tree roots, or in the tangle of the undergrowth. Some of the bones were smudged with moss.

"And who do you suppose left their skeletons here?"

"Are these—" she whispered, "—are these the bones of unicorns?"

"These are the bones of countless young girls that unicorns have killed."

Although she did not want to, Sephaina raised her head and looked into his eyes. His eyes were unkind and clever, and exceedingly honest.

She did not question him. Presently he said, "In reparation for the ancient hunting, for capture and for death. A sacrifice. The maiden is perfect and her life is also without blemish. No disease. No sorrow. They have told, you will wait, and the unicorn will come to lay his head in your lap. That is true enough."

He continued to speak to her, and after a moment Sephaina screamed.

He was a demon. He told her lies. Yet behind her lay the snow of glistening bones. The bones of the young girls who had been pegged out, naked and spreadeagled, awaiting the supernatural beast from the wood. Which, scenting them, did indeed come, and did indeed lay its head in the lap of each— breaching her virginity and impaling her womb upon the blade of its monstrous horn.

The chosen sacrifice, brought to death by those she loved. Judas' kiss. The crucificial nailing. A reversal of the image of Christ and of the unicorn. Animal for god, the female for the male. The lore of the wood. Of death.

Her hand was still moulded to the hand of the demon. When she cried out, she felt the cry pass into him.

"You think you do not credit what I say. But what I say is the truth, as the unicorn is also truth."

"No," Sephaina said.

So he made her go back, back through the glades, and he made her see, again and again the bones of dead women. Again and again he murmured to her of how it had been, how it was. Tomorrow she, like the rest, would lie on the floor of the wood, and next year, on her seventeenth birthday, she too would be bones.

At last he drew her away, back up into the night, where the stars hung, brooding on their longevity. She saw the stars, and the world below. They meant nothing to her. This fresh miracle, the miracle of betrayal and horror, she had also accepted, or so it seemed.

"Now you believe," he said to her, "I will tell you

how you may evade your destiny. Would you like to hear?"

"Is there a way?" she asked.

"More than one. I can set you down in the meadows beyond the house. There any able man, ignorant of who you are, can deprive you of your virginity. Without this ceremonial enticement, the unicorn will not seek you out. Or I can carry you to some far-off country where no one will think to search for you."

"But you are a demon," she said. "And this is a dream. Wherever you took me, I should wake in the house."

"Should you? Then do only this: Approach those who come for you tomorrow. Reveal your knowledge and your reluctance. They will not press you, for the sacrifice must go willingly. You will, of course, be cast from the house, and will become an exile. No one, anymore, will care for you, and few will offer you love. But you will avoid the agony and death of the sacrifice."

Sephaina gazed at the stars, which lived forever, or very nearly.

She beheld the land below, so distant it did not seem she need ever return to it.

"I do not know," she said. "Tell me what I must do."

"No," he said. "My part is played out. I will tell you nothing more."

Sephaina shivered. Her hand in his was changing into ice.

"Then let me go. Let me go back and wake."

"This is no dream," he said. He smiled. His mouth was a crescent; his eyes were colder than her hand.

Then the night was emptied away. Winds and stars and darkness and the earth, all emptied at a vast and improbable speed, through her eyes and in through her window.

The last thing she was aware of was the separation of their icy fingers, his dead, hers merely frozen.

She did not sleep after that, but rather she ceased temporarily to exist. When once more she grew to a consciousness of her surroundings, the dream remained vivid and actual, as if it lay in shards about the room. She had only to take up these shards, examine them, bring them together. She did so, trembling. She lived again each minute of the flight and her time in the wood of bones. Very little was missing. And she knew it was not a dream, as in the dream she had known it was not.

When this had been accomplished, Sephaina lay like a stone, and gradually the window, where the stars had framed the demon, began to pale and greyly glow.

Soon the sun would rise, and they would come for her. They would bathe her and anoint her and dress her in the green gown embroidered with blue and heavenly flowers. They would take her among the trees of the wood. They would strip her and chain her and death would come, white as the moon, with starlight caught even by day inside its killing horn.

Sephaina lay, and she considered how the demon had offered her freedom from this death, and how she had not allowed him to help her, and she wondered if he would have helped her.

To lie with a man—she could not have done that. She had been nutured in a certain way, and was quite innocent. Never having thought of the sexual union between man and woman, as if knowing she must die a virgin, such an act was now like a myth, and useless to her. But to be carried to safety in some other place, far from the house, the moat, the meadows. How would she live there? And lastly, if she herself were to deny her fate to her attendants, to the priests—crying out when they came to her that she had learned they meant to give her to death—if she did that, pleaded for her survival, won it. . . . How should she fare on the raw face of the world, untutored, unguided? She who had always been cherished, and trained to find her cherishing natural, therefore necessary?

Yet to live, to evade pain and horror, and what ever abyss or ascent, hellish, supernal, stood beyond mortality. Surely to escape this was worth all exile, despair and loneliness.

Then, she thought in bewilderment of those she loved, and how they had always intended to destroy her. The very shock of it made her, somehow, certain that it was so. Such a thing as this could not have been invented.

But neither had their love been false.

With puzzled wonder, she considered this final absurdity. Love her they did. Simple instinct reaffirmed her belief in their sincerity, just as the same instinct had led her to believe the warning of the demon.

As the warmth of dawn started to powder the greyness, she rose and stood at her window. She watched the birds begin to fly upwards, and the light begin to hang the heads of the willows beyond the wall with thin chains of greenish gold.

When the sun lifted, the sky flushed, blushed with joy. Sephaina felt her own heart lift, despite herself. She felt herself to resemble the sky. She had been cultivated to openness and beauty, and she knew a sudden extraordinary happiness. It dazzled her. She sought for reasons. It had come to her she was an atom of the whole creative, created landscape, of the air, of the sun. Her course, too, had been fixed; to rise and to go down. For this lovely and poignant day she had been bred. Because of her value on this day, she had been loved. She was the sacrifice by means of which earth and heaven might touch. The hands of the clock might not terminate progress. The shadow on the sundial could not hide itself. Some things must be.

With a sigh that was like the loss of blood, and yet also like the loss of poison, Sephaina bowed her head. She would not step aside. She would say nothing. If it must be, she would be hurt and she would die. But not in negation, not from fear of other things, not out of slavish acquiescence and blindness. She saw within herself, as if in a dawn pool, the reflection of all her years. It had been impossible to think of her life drastically changed, continuing elsewhere, not because she was ill-equipped to live it in such a way, but because her whole life had been a building towards this end. Her death, the last stitch in the tapestry. She could not break the thread. Harmony was her familiar. Harmony she recognised, and must yield to.

When the gentle rap came on the door, the early sunshine had overbrimmed the window and lay across Sephaina's body. When her attendants entered, she saw their faces in this silken light. Anguish and pleasure were mixed in each face, and a calm, saddened hope.

She was not afraid of them. She could not hate them. *She* was their hope, and her death was what had saddened them. She would not cry out at them. She touched them as carefully as they touched her.

There was a stillness in her, like death already. Yet is was warm.

*   *   *

So they took her through the meadows where the people kneeled, and along a narrow road, and through a valley, and came to the wood. They entered the wood, entered its hot, green essence where the sunlight dripped down, and the shadows spun like spiders. There were no bones in the grass, nor any flowers.

They brought her a crystal cup with a dark drink in it, but she put the cup aside. She had already begun to cry, but softly, almost unobtrusively. Her maidens kissed her hands, the priests blessed her. The older women took her away, and drew off her garments, concealing her with their bodies. No one explained to her what they did. Sephaina did not question or protest. Her tears fell noiselessly down on to her own skin.

She lay on the ground between the margins of her black hair. The women put the bracelets of the shackles, which were light and delicate and did not chafe her, on her wrists and ankles. With great decorum, circumspectly, they arranged her limbs, until she was a white cross on the grass. Men pegged the ends of the shackles into the ground, some distance from her, their faces averted so they should not shame her by looking at her nakedness.

Then, every one of them left her.

Through the scent of her own tears, Sephaina could smell the fermentations of the wood, like the perfumes with which they had dressed her. She heard the faintest whispering, also, that might have been the wings of insects, or the leaves brushing one another as they grew. Above, the green roof was burnished by the sun. Rays of sun leaned like spears all about her. Like a fence of gilded posts. It was peaceful. These instants seemed timeless, and might go on forever, and while they did so, she was secure. Then she heard something step through the grass towards her, and the sound was scarcely discernible, not remotely human.

The unicorn leaned over her like a tower.

It was dark against the flaring leaves above, its whiteness curbed. It seemed the largest single entity in the world. The horn on its head was like another shaft of sun.

Sephaina clenched her whole body, but she could not shut her eyes, she could not look away from the unicorn. When it touched her, she would die, in terrible agony, and beyond the agony an unknown whirlpool gaped.

There was a pause. She gazed at the mask of death, and felt a stasis, an unconscionable waiting. And then the birdlike soaring sense of rightness, in fact of perfection, came to her again, even in her fear. Her entire body quickened, seemed elevated. She knew pain could not hurt her, and she smiled, in welcome. The unicorn seemed to read her mind. He swung his gigantic head and the blazing spike of the horn ran down.

There was a rending. Feeling nothing at all, she was confused. Then the rending came again, and twice more, and the ropes of grass which had bound her wrists and ankles lay dismembered. The unicorn stepped across her body, laving it with shadow. The curtain of the trees drew back and the unicorn reentered the deep of the wood. There was a flash of whiteness, the curtain fell and the unicorn was gone.

Out of green space, women came and clothed her, and lifted her. A priest came and took her hands. They were ghosts, but the ghostly priest talked to her.

"It is always done in this way," said the priest to

Sephaina, under the sun-broken trees. "There is a warning given. For each, it will be unique; the demon within arises. It may take any form, that of some secret misgiving, perhaps, or some awful memory. It speaks the words of death and nightmare. Many of our daughters cannot endure the thought of what lies before them. They are shown the bones, bedded deep in the wood. The bones, you must understand, do not exist, but seem most real, as you recall. Those young women who cannot bear their fate fly to the meadows or the lands beyond, or else fall to their knees before us begging us to release them. This too is always done, they are sent away, and thereafter without true happiness and without sanctity we must live, until the next sacrifice is due. For almost fifty years, Sephiana, the sacrifice has failed. For she must accept her death, and go consenting, to set the balance right. But to consent is *all*. Then death is not needful. You live, and we are holy, because of you."

Sephaina said, like one waking from a dream, "What now, then?"

And he told her now she would live in honour and luxury in the house, among the women she had always known, who had tended her. And that when the next chosen came to them, a little child, she too would help to care for it and rear it to its purpose, as she had been cared for and as she had been reared.

They carried her back to the slate-blue house, singing, with garlands, wine and laughter. The people in the meadows also sang, and gave her gifts. For today at least, she remained wholly special.

But after today. . . .

Seeing the house she had not expected to see again, the flowers, the lilies on the polished moat, Sephaina knew disillusion in her rescue as she had known a wild elation in her fear. The shining building of her years had collapsed. She had met death, who had turned aside. Her sunset went unrequired, though like the sun her glory faded. She was to be an attendant. She was to wait upon another. She was no longer the chosen one. Another would be that.

After the vision and the vision's ending, how drained and commonplace and far away the world seemed. A collection of plants and stones and random flesh, now only paintings in another book.

It was true, they had not killed her, but she might still die. Of boredom.

Three: The Unicorn

And in the third life, Lasephun was the unicorn.

In the beginning there had been only something white, white and gleaming as the centre of a flame. It moved like marsh gas, a disembodied, cool fire, or a breath of opaline wind. It entranced things to pursue it, may-flies, doves, fawns, but it did not consume them. Nor were they able to pass through it. Sometimes it rested, at others it ran. Its speed seemed dependent upon nothing, not even itself. Its repose was similar. It neither fed nor expelled any waste matter. It was not embryonic. It did not take on the forms of other things. At night, faintly, it emanated a pale, unimaginable glow. It was like the soul of a star, fallen in the wood.

One day, this luminous uncreature drifted from the wood, and skimmed over the surface of a pool. The pool faithfully reflected it for several moments, and then ceased to reflect it. The pool began to show instead another reflection, of something which had once been there, drunk from the pool, and spirited itself away.

This thing in the mirror of the pool touched its long slim horn to the wafting formless whiteness. When the white thing reached the other edge of the pool, it let down slender legs into the grass. A canine beautiful head emerged, an arching body. The starry spike broke from its forehead.

It had no particular memory, the unicorn. It did not know, therefore, if it had been dead and had then existed as a spirit or a fable, or if now it was reborn. The pool had refashioned it in a partially earthly shape, as the eyes of a man would have done. Water, and human eyes, possessed this sorcerous ability.

The unicorn touched the earth with its feet.

The earth knew the feet of a live thing.

The trees, the air, knew it.

The recognition of presences about it solidified the presence of the unicorn. The unicorn was now solid, and externally actual. Inside itself, however, it remained phantasmal and fantastic.

The nature of the unicorn was like a prism, composed of almost countless facets. Each thought was a new dimension. The intensity of Lasephun, the obsessiveness, was demonstrated by the unicorn's adherence to each of these facets as it explored within itself.

Its life became and was self-exploration. It had no other function. It lived *within*, and where the external world brushed it—the scents of the wood, the play of light and shade, day and night, the occasional wish to drink from the pool—it explored these sensations within itself and its reaction to them. It had no gender, no creative or procreative urge. It was timeless, knowing neither birth nor death. It was refined like the purest distillation, and it was totally self-absorbed. So it lived and was happy, learning itself, finding always new aspects of itself and its relation to the objects around it. It was seldom seen, and never disturbed. Possibly, a hundred years went by.

One dawn, the unicorn came from the wood as the sun was coming from the horizon. The world was all one contemplative and idyllic pinkness. Pink seemed in that instant the shade of all things lovely, ethereal and divine. As the unicorn lowered its head towards the spangling water of the pool, it sensed, for the first time it could ever remember, an expression of life nearby.

Startled, the unicorn raised its head, and water-beads glissanded from its brow as if the horn wept tears of fire.

The startlement might have resembled that of a deer disturbed at its drinking, but was not of this order. Never before had it encountered a corresponding life signal from anything about it. It had never known that such a note was capable of being sounded.

After a moment, confused and fascinated, the unicorn moved away from the pool, and glanced around itself.

Above the valley, a ruined town rotted graciously on a rock. Some way off in another direction, a slate-blue house sank in a dry moat: this was not visible from the pool. Beyond the pool another way, lay the wood, while in the valley there were several trees. Beneath one of these a young girl lay asleep. Presently the unicorn came on her and paused.

Her long dark hair ribboned about her, her skin was white as cream, save where the freckling of leaf-shadows patterned it. A pannier lay beside her; she had been gathering roots and plants, perhaps for use in some simple witchcraft.

The unicorn recognised her at some basic inexplicable level, and a fresh facet leapt into being in the prism of its awareness. Decades and decades before, the unicorn had been human and a girl rather like this one. Yet there was more. The girl asleep under the tree was very young, and she was virgin.

The magic of virginity—for magic it was—was quite straightforward. Its sorcerous value was that of energy stored, and was accordingly at its most powerful not in the celibate, but in the celibate who had never yet relinquished celibacy, and better still in one who had not even known himself. This, as it happened, the girl had not. Her life, like the unicorn's had been lived inwardly, had been lived outwardly. Her meditation and her senses turning always outwards, she had not yet found herself, knew herself neither in the spirit, nor in the body. In this manner she was strangely asexual, as the unicorn was. While her extreme youth lent her also, briefly, an air of the ethereal. Her birth was close enough she had overlooked it, her death far enough away she had not considered it. Life and death and sex were, for this time, beyond the periphery of her sphere—yet only that. However, for this short season, the sounding note of her existence had paralled the unicorn's own.

Aside from the sounding note, and despite recognition, the unicorn did not see the girl as what she was, but only as another external object, like a stone or flower.

After it had observed her for some time, the unicorn pawed the turf a little. The gesture was reflexive, a mere exercise. It looked nevertheless ferocious and dangerous, and it wakened the girl, who sat up, staring, her hand to her mouth in fear.

It seemed she had heard old stories of what a unicorn was. She did not appear to be in doubt, only in amazement and fright. Then these emotions visibly faded.

When she spoke aloud, the unicorn, having no longer any knowledge of the human vernacular, did not understand her. Nor did it seek to understand. It sensed exultation in her voice. It sensed itself the cause of this exultation—and not the cause. What in fact she had said amounted to the word: "You are my sign from God. Now I know the one I love will come also to love me." For in fact the very innocence of her meditation had already, through itself, brought itself to an end. She loved.

The unicorn had forgotten almost altogether the aspirations and the inner processes of men and women. It looked, with its shadowy, gleaming eyes, that were like burned yet burning violets. It watched as the girl obeised herself before the unicorn-which-had-become-her-omen-of-love. As she did so, the unicorn felt itself harden once more inside the shell of its physical existence. So all things may be fixed by the regard of others.

But before she could try to touch it—it had some dim memory, perhaps a race memory of its kind, of such touchings—the unicorn drew away and vanished in the wood.

Then from the wood's edge, its eyes piercing through the foliage which was like curious jewelry, the unicorn continued to watch. Rising and picking up her pannier, with a strange half-sweeping sigh, yet smiling, the girl moved away across the valley. She began to climb toward the ruined town.

A village leaned against the walls of the town. The unicorn saw the girl enter the village. It saw her step into a little hovel with a roof of golden thatch. She sat down at a spinning wheel. The wheel spun. The girl whispered dreamily. Magic as well as thread was unfolded from the primitive machine. By now the unicorn felt as much as it saw: It had ceased to view with its eyes alone. Some aspect of itself, still fluid and supernatural, had followed the girl and now hung against a wall. It was reminiscent of a cobweb, pale and luminous; unobserved.

Dusk seemed to enter the room suddenly, like smoke. A moment after, the girl raised her head and her face lost all its faint colour. A shadow fell across the room, the spinning wheel. It was the shadow of a young man. Even in the gathering darkness, the colour of his hair was apparent. It was auburn, as the hair of Lauro had been. The phantasmal cobweb that lay against the wall, the perception of the being which had become a unicorn, clung against itself. It had now recognised, without recognition, the two lives which it had formerly been. The purpose of this representation, its earthly male and female states, filled it with strange longings, a sort of nostalgia for mortality it did not comprehend.

The young man spoke. Then the young girl.

The cobweb essense of the creature which had become a unicorn listened. It began, at last, by some uncanny osmosis of thought—telepathy, perhaps—to distinguish the gist of the conversation.

"I have thought of you all day," the young man said. "I do not know why."

"You are uncivil to say this. Am I not worth recalling?" And the wheel spun, as if it, not she, were excited and unsure.

"I think you are a witch, and put a spell on me," but he laughed. His laugh was Lauro's. In this way the unicorn had laughed, long, long ago.

"So I might. So I meant to."

"And why?"

"To test my skill. Another man would have done as well. You are nothing to me."

"If I am nothing to you, why do you sit and gaze at me in church?"

"Who told you that I did?"

"Your own face, which is red as a rose."

"It is my anger," she said.

But he went close to her and sat beside her, following the wheel with Lauro's eyes, as she followed it with Sephaina's.

The light faded, and at last he said: "Shall I light the lamp for you?"

"You are too kind. Yes, light the lamp, before you go to your own house."

"May I not stay, then, in your house?"

"If you stay," she said above the flying wheel, "the village will remark it. I have neither father nor mother, nor any kin. If you stay, you must wed me, they will all say. And the priest will demand it."

"The priest already knows I am here. I took care that he should."

Then the wheel was left to itself and whirled itself to a standstill.

The cobweb clinging to the wall beheld itself embrace itself, the two it had been as one. But the anguish and the urgency of love it did not pause to examine, for some noiseless clamour drove it abruptly away.

As the lovers twined in the hovel, therefore, the unicorn walked delicately to the pool in the valley. It touched the tip of its unbelievable horn to the reflection there. Its calm eyes were two purple globes, shining, and its whiteness was like summer rain.

A human would have been thinking: Ah, I must consider this. I must *know* this. But the unicorn only considered, only *knew*. It returned to the black wood, wrapping itself in the blackness, fold on fold, until it was utterly invisible, even to itself.

The brief mortal kindling it had witnessed—or possibly imagined that it witnessed—held its awareness as its own life and the manifestations of life had formerly held it, and nourished it. It turned about within itself the images of that perfectly commonplace coupling, the commonplace wishes and desires which had heralded it. It turned them about like rare gems to catch the light of the rising moon.

The unicorn lay down in the blackness of the forest. It drank from its own brain.

Sometimes the blackness of the wood grew green or gold or rose. Sometimes there were faraway voices, or thunder, or the velvet sound of falling snow. Flowers burst out or withered under the body of the unicorn, which was no longer perceptible as anything like a body.

The magic of virginity, which had drawn the symbol of the unicorn on the air, both for the virgin and for itself, a virginity ironically almost instantly given up, drifted like a spring leaf on water. Then down and down through the unicorn's prismatic awareness.

At last this floating leaf, a green mote, struck the floor of the unicorn's intellect. It felt a cry within itself, a terrible cry, aching and raging, and full of inhuman human despair.

What was the meaning of *this*?

The unicorn did not know it, but time was also like the wood. As the wood had grown tall and tangled and old, so time had grown, hedging the unicorn round as if with high reeds, or a fence of gilded posts.

When it ran lightly over the pool, it did not notice it ran across water, as in the beginning.

The trees on the rock had also grown old. The unicorn passed through them, unimpeded, like fluid. The throbbing centre of the pain which had somehow reached the unicorn was to be found on the track that ran through the middle of the village.

Under the broken ancient wall of the town, an elderly woman was crying and lamenting, not loudly, but with a desperate intensity. To the human eye, her trouble was immediately quite plain. Two men had between them a covered figure on a bier. One hand, like a parcel of bones, stuck out, and this the woman held and fondled. Her man was dead and due for burying, and the old woman, probably his wife, overcome at the final undeniable fact of parting, had halted the proceedings with this eruption of passionate grief. All around, others stood, trying to comfort or dissuade.

To the unicorn, only the outcry and the anguish were decipherable. They needed no explanation. And then it saw auburn hair and black, and recognised, or so it seemed, the lovers from the earlier night.

The unicorn moved closer. It stepped across the broken sunlight and the shadows and drew near to the old woman who wept and softly cried out, endeavouring to distinguish the young man and the young woman who were, in their physical forms, its own self from two other ages.

Then came a separation, of persons, of thought. The young man who resembled Lauro was younger than he had been when last the unicorn looked at him, and his hair was blacker than a coal. It was the girl, older than remembered, older than Sephaina, whose hair hung red as rust all down her back as she held the weeping woman, and took her hand from the dead hand on the bier.

"Mother, my mother," said the girl, "my father is

dead and we must let him go to his rest. Has he not earned his rest?" said the girl, gently, calmly, and it was the young man now who began to weep. "Let him be on his way."

The old woman allowed her hand to be removed from the sticklike fingers. She stood in the street, sunken and soulless, staring as the men with the bier moved off from her.

The unicorn sighed.

It had seemed only yesterday, or seven days before, or maybe at most a month, or a season ago, that it had left them, embracing and new and brimmed by life and trust, beyond the spinning wheel. But summers had come and gone, winters, years and decades. Their children had grown. The son had his mother's hair, the girl her father's. And the maiden who had slept under the tree was gnarled and bent like a dehydrated stem, and the young man who had wooed her was an empty sack of flesh, its motive force spilled out.

"No," said the old woman tiredly. "How am I to live, how am I to be, now, alone?"

The unbeautiful incoherent words conveyed her desolation exactly. She was rooted to the track. She saw no need to go on, or to return. Meaningless and stark and horrible, the world leaned all about her, a ruin, shelterless. Her poor face, haggard and puckered, the filmy eyes that had been dark as the pool beside the wood, all of her flaccid as the dead man carried away from her. Her mouth continued to make the shape of crying, but now even the tears would not come. She had reached the ultimate lethargy of wretchedness. And tug at her arm as the red-haired daughter might, or try to steel and support her as the black-haired son did, the old woman who had been young and a virgin, stood on the track and saw her wasted life and the bitter blows of life, and all of its little, little sweetness—now snatched from her forever.

And then something changed behind the dull lenses of her vision. Something seemed to open, some inner eye.

She had seen the unicorn standing out three paces from her.

"Mother—mother, what is it now?" the girl asked anxiously.

"Hush," said the old woman. She was apparently aware her daughter could not see the silver beast with its greyhound's head, its amethystine eyes, its body like a moonburst, its single horn like a cone of stars—that no one could see the unicorn but she. "Hush. Let me listen."

"But what are you hearing?"

"Hush."

So they fell silent in the street. The men and women looked at each other, fearing for the wits of this one of their number. Yet, politely they waited.

The unicorn stood, a few inches from the ground, visible only to one, fixing her first with this lambent eye, then with that. The unicorn, of course, did not speak. It had no speech. But lowering its neck it set the tip of its horn, like a silver pin, to the old woman's forehead.

There is no death. Beyond life, is life. Whatever suffering and whatever disappointment, whatever joy, whatever bewilderment, there is more time than can be measured to learn, and to be comforted. Blindly to demand, meekly to consent, inwardly to know, these are the stages of existence. But beyond all knowledge is another, unknown, knowledge. And beyond that unknown knowledge, another. Progression is endless. And to be alone is the only truth and the only falsehood.

The unicorn vanished on this occasion like a melting of spring snow. The old woman noted it, and she smiled. She walked firmly after the bier, crying still somewhat, from habit. She was to live to a great age. One evening in the future, she would tell her daughter—then rocking her own child in the firelight—"On the day of your father's burying, I saw the Christ. He wore the shape of a white unicorn. He promised life everlasting."

But that was far away, and now the unicorn ran, like a wind, and as it ran it left humanity behind itself forever. It dissolved and was a burning light.

The light asked nothing of itself, it was content to blaze, which also, surely, was another truth.

The being of Lasephun was presently transmuted, passing into some further, extraordinary stage, the name of which creature is unknown, here.

MAGRITTE'S SECRET AGENT

You asked me about it before, didn't you, the picture. And I never told you. But tonight, tonight I think I will. Why not? The wine was very nice, and there's still the other bottle. The autumn dusk is warm, clear and beautiful, and the stars are blazing over the bay. It's so quiet, when the tide starts to come back, we'll hear it. You're absolutely right. I'm obsessive about the sea. And that picture, the Magritte.

Of course, it's a print, nothing more, though that was quite difficult to obtain. I saw it first in a book, when I was eighteen or so. I felt a strangeness about it even then. Naturally, most of Magritte is bizarre. If you respond to him, you get special sensations, special inner stirrings over any or all of what he did, regardless even of whether you care for it or not. But this one—this one. . . . He had a sort of game whereby he'd often call a picture by a name that had no connection—or no apparent connection—with its subject matter. The idea, I believe, was to throw our prior conception. I mean, generally you're told you're looking at a picture called Basket of Apples, and it's apples in a basket. But Magritte calls a painting The Pleasure Principle, and it's a man with a kind of white nova taking place where his head should be.

Except that makes a sort of sense, doesn't it? Think of orgasm, for example, or someone who's crazy over Prokofiev, listening to the third piano concerto. This picture, though. It's called The Secret Agent.

It's one of the strangest pictures in the world to me, partly because it's beautiful and it shocks, but the shock doesn't depend on revulsion or fear. There's another one, a real stinger—a fish lying on a beach, but it has the loins and legs of a girl: a mermaid, but inverted. That has shock value all right, but it's different. This one. . . . The head, neck, breast of a white horse, which is also a chess piece, which is also a girl. A girl's eyes, and hair that's a mane, and yet still hair. And she—it—is lovely. She's in a room, by a window that faces out over heathland under a crescent moon, but she doesn't look at it. There are a few of the inevitable Magritte tricks—for example, the curtain hanging *outside* the window-frame, instead of in, that type of thing. But there's also this other thing. I don't know how I can quite explain it. I think I sensed it from the first, or maybe I only read it into the picture afterwards. Or it's just the idea of white horses and the foam that comes in on a breaker: white horses, or mythological Kelpies that can take the shape of a horse. Somehow, the window ought to show the sea, and it doesn't. It shows the land under the horned moon, not a trace of water anywhere. And her face that's a woman's, even though it's the face of a chess-piece horse. And the title. The Secret Agent, which maybe isn't meant to mean anything. And yet—Sometimes I wonder if Magritte— if he ever—

I was about twenty-three at the time, and it was before I'd got anything settled, my life, my ambitions, anything. I was rooming with a nominative aunt,

about five miles along the coast from here, at Ship
Bay. I'd come out of art school without much hope
of a job, and was using up my time working behind a
lingerie counter in the local chain store, which, if
you're female, is where any sort of diploma frequently gets you. I sorted packets of bras, stopped
little kids putting the frilly knickers on their heads,
and averted my eyes from gargantuan ladies who
were jamming themselves into cubicles, corsets and
complementary heart attack in that order.

Thursday was cinema day at the Bay, when the
movie palace showed its big matinee of the week. I
don't know if there truly is a link between buyers of
body linen and the matinee performance, but from
two to four-thirty on Thursday afternoons, you could
count visitors to our department on two or less fingers.

A slender girl named Jill, ostentatiously braless,
was haughtily pricing B cups for those of us unlucky
enough to require them. I was refolding trays of
black lace slips, thinking about my own black, but
quite laceless, depression, when sounds along the
carpet told me one of our one or two non-film-buff
customers had arrived. There was something a little
odd about the sounds. Since Jill was trapped at the
counter by her pricing activities, I felt safe to turn
and look.

I got the guilty, nervous, flinching-away reaction
one tends to on sight of a wheelchair. An oh-God-I-
mustn't-let-them-think-I'm-staring feelings. Plus, of
course, the unworthy survival-trait which manifests
in the urge to stay uninvolved with anything that
might need help, embarrass, or take time. Actually,
there was someone with the wheelchair, who had
guided it to a stop. An escort normally makes it
worse, since it implies total dependence. I was already looking away before I saw. Let's face it, what

you do see is usually fairly bad. Paralysis, imbecility, encroaching death. I do know I'm most filthily in the wrong, and I thank God there are others who can think differently than I do.

You know how, when you're glancing from one thing to another, a sudden light, or colour, or movement snags the eye somewhere in between—you look away then irresistibly back again. The visual centre has registered something ahead of the brain, and the message got through so many seconds late. This is what happened as I glanced hurriedly aside from the wheelchair. I didn't know what had registered to make me look back, but I did. Then I found out.

In the chair was a young man—a boy—he looked about twenty. He was focusing somewhere ahead, or not focusing, it was a sort of blind look, but somehow there was no doubt he could see, or that he could think. The eyes are frequently the big giveaway when something has gone physically wrong. His eyes were clear, large, utterly contained, *containing,* like two cool cisterns. I didn't even see the colour of them, the construction and the content struck me so forcibly. Rather than an un-seeing look, it was a seeing-through—to something, somewhere, else. He had fair hair, a lot of it, and shining. The skin of his face had the sort of marvellous pale texture most men shave off when they rip the first razor blade through their stubble and the second upper dermis goes with it forever. He was slim, and if he had been standing, would have been tall. He had a rug over his knees like a geriatric. But his legs were long. You see I've described him as analytically as I can, both his appearance and my reply to it. What it comes to is, he was beautiful. I fell in love with him, not in the carnal sense, but aesthetically, artistically. Dramatically. The fact that a woman was wheeling him about, helplessly, into a situation of women's underwear, made him also pathetic in the terms of pathos. He preserved a remote dignity even through this. Or not really; he was simply far away, not here at all.

The woman herself was just a woman. Stoutish, fawnish. I couldn't take her in. She was saying to Jill: "Should have been ready. I don't know why you don't deliver any more like you used to."

And Jill was saying: "I'm sorry, maa-dum, we don't deliver things like this."

It was the sort of utterly futile conversation, redolent of dull sullen frustration on both sides, so common at shop counters everywhere. I wondered if Jill had noticed the young man, but she didn't seem to have done. She usually reacted swiftly to anything youngish and male and platitudinously in trousers, but presumably only when trousers included locomotive limbs inside them.

"Well, I can't stop," said the woman. She had a vague indeterminate Ship Bay accent, flat as the sands. "I really thought it would be ready by now."

"I'm sorry, maa-dum."

"I can't keep coming in. I haven't the time."

Jill stood and looked at her.

I felt blood swarm through my heart and head, which meant I was about to enter the arena, cease my purely observational role.

"Perhaps we could take the lady's name and phone number," I said, walking over to the counter. "We could call her when her purchase arrives."

Jill glowered at me. This offer was a last resort, generally employed to placate only when a customer produced a carving knife.

I found a paper bag and a pen and waited. When the woman didn't speak, I looked up. I was in first gear, unbalanced, and working hard to disguise it.

So I still didn't see her, just a shape where her face was, the shadowy gleam of metal extending away from her hands, the more shattering gleam of his gilded bronze hair. (Did she wash it for him? Maybe he had simply broken his ankle or his knee. Maybe he was no longer there.)

I strove in vain toward the muddy aura of the woman. And she wouldn't meet me.

"If you'd just let me have your name," I said brightly, trying to enunciate like Olivier, which I do at my most desperate.

"There's no phone," she said. She could have been detailing a universal human condition.

"Well . . ." I was offhand ". . . your address. We could probably drop you a card or something." Jill made a noise, but couldn't summon the energy to tell us such a thing was never done. (Yes, he was still there. Perfectly still; perfect, still, a glimpse of long fingers lying on the rug.)

"Besmouth," said the woman, grudging me.

It was a silly name. It sounded like an antacid stomach preparation. What was he called, then: Billy Besmouth? Bonny Billy Besmouth, born broken, bundled babylike, bumped bodily by brassieres—

"I'm sorry?" She'd told me the address and I'd missed it. No I hadn't, I'd written it down.

"19, Sea View Terrace, The Rise."

"Oh yes. Just checking. Thank you."

The woman seemed to guess suddenly it was all a charade. She eased the brake off the chair and wheeled it abruptly away from us.

"What did you do that for?" said Jill. "We don't send cards. What do you think we aar?"

I refrained from telling her. I asked instead what the woman had ordered. Jill showed me the book, it was one of a batlike collection of nylon-fur dressing gowns, in cherry red.

At four-thirty, ten women and a male frillies-freak came in. By five-forty when I left the store, I should have forgotten about Bonny Billy Besmouth, the wheelchair, the vellum skin, the eyes.

That evening I walked along the sands. It was autumn, getting chilly, but the afterglow lingered, and the sky above the town was made of green porcelain. The sea came in, scalloped, darkening, and streaked by the neons off the pier, till whooping untrustworthy voices along the shore drove me back to the promenade. When I was a kid, you could have strolled safely all night by the water. Or does it only seem that way? Once, when I was eight, I walked straight into the sea, and had to be dragged out, screaming at the scald of salt in my sinuses. I never managed to swim. It was as if I expected to know how without ever learning, as a fish does, and when I failed, gave up in despair.

You could see The Rise from the promenade, a humped back flung up from the south side of the bay, with its terraced streets clinging on to it. He was up there somewhere. Not somewhere: 19, Sea View. Banal. I could walk it in half an hour. I went home and ate banal sausages, and watched banal TV.

On Saturday a box of furry bat-gowns came in, and one of them was cherry red.

"Look at this," I said to Jill.

She looked, as if into an open grave.

"Yes. Orrful."

"Don't you remember?"

Jill didn't remember.

Angela, who ran the department, was hungover

from the night before, and was, besides, waiting for her extramarital relationship to call her. I showed her the dressing gown and she winced.

"If she's not on the phone, she's had it."

"I could drop it in to her," I lied ably. "I'm going to meet someone up on The Rise, at the pub. It isn't any trouble to me, and she has a crippled son."

"Poor cow," said Angela. She was touched by pity. Angela always struck me as a kind of Chaucerian character—fun-loving, warm-hearted, raucously glamorous. She was, besides, making almost as much a mess of her life as I was of mine, with a head start on me of about ten years.

She organised everything, and the department did me the great favour of allowing me to become its errand-person. I suppose if the goods had been wild-silk erotica I might not have been allowed to take them from the building at all. But who was going to steal a bat-gown?

"You aar stew-pid," said Jill. "You should never volunteer to do anything like that. They'll have you at it all the time now."

At half past six, for Saturday was the store's late closing, I took the carrier and went out into the night, with my heart beating in slow hard concussions. I didn't know why, or properly what I was doing. The air smelled alcoholically of sea and frost.

I got on the yellow bus that went through The Rise.

I left the bus near the pub, whose broad lights followed me away down the slanting street. I imagined varieties of normal people in it, drinking gins and beers and low-calorie cola. Behind the windows of the houses, I imagined dinners, TV arguments. It had started to rain. What was I doing here? What did I anticipate? (He opened the door, leaning on a crutch, last summer's tennis racket tucked predictably under the other arm. I stood beside his chair, brushing the incense smoke from him, in a long queue at Lourdes.) I thought about his unspeaking far-awayness. Maybe he wasn't crippled, but autistic. I could have been wrong about those strange containing eyes. Anyway, she'd just look at me, grab the bag, shut the door. She had paid for the garment months ago, when she ordered it. I just had to give her the goods, collect her receipt. Afterwards, I'd go home, or at least to the place where I lived. I wouldn't even see him. And then what? Nothing.

Sea View curved right around the bottom of The Rise. Behind its railing, the cliff lurched forward into the night and tumbled on the sea. Number 19. was the farthest house down, the last in the terrace. An odd curly little alley ran off to the side of it, leading along the downslope of the cliff and out of sight, probably to the beach. The sound of the tide, coupled with the rain, was savage, close and immensely wet.

I pushed through the gate and walked up the short path. A dim illumination came from the glass panels of the door. There was no bell, just a knocker. I knocked, and waited like the traveller in the poem. Like him, it didn't seem I was going to get an answer. An even more wretched end to my escapade than I had foreseen. I hadn't considered the possibility of absence. Somehow I'd got the notion Mrs. Besmouth—Antacid seldom went out. It must be difficult, with him the way he was, whichever way that happened to be. So, why did I want to get caught up in it?

A minute more, and I turned with a feeling of letdown and relief. I was halfway along the path when the front door opened.

"Hi you," she said.

At his uninviting salute, I looked back. I didn't recognise her, because I hadn't properly been able to see her on the previous occasion. A fizz of fawn hair, outlined by the inner light, stood round her head like a martyr's crown. She was clad in a fiery apron.

"Mrs. Besmouth." I went towards her, extending the carrier bag like meat offered to a wild dog.

"Besmouth, that's right. What is it?" She didn't know me at all.

I said the name of the store, a password, but she only blinked.

"You came in about your dressing gown, but it hadn't arrived. It came today. I've got it here."

She looked at the bag.

"All right," she said. "What's the delivery charge?"

"No charge. I just thought I'd drop it in to you."

She went on looking at the bag. The rain went on falling.

"You live round here?" she demanded.

"No. The other end of the bay, actually."

"Long way for you to come," she said accusingly.

"Well . . . I had to come up to The Rise tonight. And it seemed a shame, the way you came in and just missed the delivery. Here, do take it, or the rain may get in the bag."

She extended her hand and took the carrier.

"It was kind of you," she said. Her voice was full of dislike because I'd forced her into a show of gratitude. "People don't usually bother nowadays."

"No, I know. But you said you hadn't got time to keep coming back, and I could see that, with—with your son—"

"Son," she interrupted. "So you know he's my son, do you?"

I felt hot with embarrassed fear.

"Well, whoever—"

"Haven't you got an umbrella?" she said.

"Er—no—"

"You're soaked," she said. I smiled foolishly, and her dislike reached its climax. "You'd better come in a minute."

"Oh no, really that isn't—"

She stood aside in the doorway, and I slunk past her into the hall. The door banged to.

I experienced instant claustrophobia and a yearning to run, but it was too late now. The glow was murky, there was a faintly musty smell, not stale exactly, more like the odour of a long closed box.

"This way."

We went by the stairs and a shut door, into a small back room, which in turn opened on a kitchen. There was a smokeless coal fire burning in an old brown fireplace. The curtains were drawn, even at the kitchen windows, which I could see through the doorway. A clock ticked, setting the scene as inexorably as in a radio play. It reminded me of my grandmother's house years before, except that in my grandmother's house you couldn't hear the sea. And then it came to me that I couldn't pick it up here, either. Maybe some freak meander of the cliff blocked off the sound, as it failed to in the street—

I'd been looking for the wheelchair and, not seeing it, had relaxed into an awful scared boredom. Then I registered the high-backed dark red chair, set facing the fire. I couldn't see him, and he was totally silent, yet I knew at once the chair was full of him. A type of electric charge went off under my heart. I felt quite horrible, as if I'd screamed with laughter at a funeral.

"Take your coat off," said Mrs. Besmouth. I protested feebly, trying not to gaze at the red chair. But she was used to managing those who could not help themselves, and she pulled the garment from me. "Sit down by the fire. I'm making a pot of tea."

I wondered why she was doing it, including me, offering her hospitality. She didn't want to, at least, I didn't think she did. Maybe she was lonely. There appeared to be no Mr. Besmouth. Those unmistakable spoors of the suburban male were everywhere absent.

To sit on the settee by the fire, I had to go round the chair. As I did so, he came into view. He was just as I recalled, even his position was unaltered. His hands rested loosely and beautifully on his knees. He watched the fire, or something beyond the fire. He was dressed neatly, as he had been in the shop. I wondered if she dressed him in these universal faded jeans, the dark pullover. Nondescript. The fire streamed down his hair and beaded the ends of his lashes.

"Hallo," I said. I wanted to touch his shoulder quietly, but did not dare.

Immediately I spoke, she called from her kitchen: "It's no good talking to him. Just leave him be, he'll be all right."

Admonished and intimidated, I sat down. The heavy anger was slow in coming. Whatever was wrong with him, this couldn't be the answer. My back to the kitchen, my feet still in their plastic boots which let water, I sat and looked at him.

I hadn't made a mistake. He really was amazing. How could she have mothered anything like this? The looks must have been on the father's side. And where had the illness come from? And what was it? Could I ask her, in front of him?

He was so far away, not here in this room at all. But where was he? He didn't look—oh God what word would do?—*deficient*. Leonardo da Vinci, staring through the face of one of his own half-finished, exquisite, lunar madonnas, staring through at some truth he was still seeking . . . that was the look. Not vacant. Not . . . missing—

She came through with her pot of tea, the cups and sugar and milk.

"This is very kind of you," I said.

She grunted. She poured the tea in a cup and gave it to me. She had put sugar in, without asking me, and I don't take sugar. The tea became a strange, alien, sickly brew, drunk for ritual. She poured tea into a mug, sugared it, and took it to the chair. I watched, breathing through my mouth. What would happen?

She took up his hand briskly, and introduced the mug into it. I saw his long fingers grip the handle. His face did not change. With a remote gliding gesture, he brought the mug to his lips. He drank. We both, she and I, looked up, as if at the first man, drinking.

"That's right," she said.

She fetched her own cup and sat on the settee beside me. I didn't like to be so close to her, and yet, we were now placed together, like an audience, before the profile of the red chair, and the young man.

I wanted to question her, ask a hundred things. His name, his age. If we could get him to speak. If he was receiving any treatment, and for *what*, exactly. *How* I wanted to know that. It burned in me, my heart hammered, I was braised in racing waves of adrenalin.

But I asked her nothing like that.

You could not ask her these things, or I couldn't. And he was there, perhaps understanding, the ultimate constraint.

"It's very cosy here," I said. She grunted. "But I keep wondering why you can't hear the sea. Surely—"

"Yes," she said, "I don't get much time to go into the town centre. What with one thing and another."

That came over as weird. She belonged to the category of person who would do just that—skip an idea that had no interest for her and pass straight on to something that did. And yet, what was it? She'd been a fraction too fast. But I was well out of my depth, and had been from the start.

"Surely," I said, "couldn't the council provide some sort of assistance—a home-help—"

"Don't want anything like that."

"But you'd be entitled—"

"I'm entitled to my peace and quiet."

"Well, yes—"

"Daniel," she said sharply, "drink your tea. Drink it. It'll get cold."

I jumped internally again, and again violently. She'd said his name. Not alliterative after all. Daniel . . . She'd also demonstrated he could hear, and respond to a direct order, for he was raising the mug again, drinking again.

"Now," she said to me, "if you've finished your tea, I'll have to ask you to go. I've his bath to see to, you understand."

I sat petrified, blurting some sort of apology. My brief brush with the bizarre was over and done. I tried not to visualise, irresistibly, his slim, pale, probably flawless male body, naked in water. He would be utterly helpless, passive, and it frightened me.

I got up.

"Thank you," I said.

'No, it was good of you to bring the dressing gown."

I couldn't meet her eyes, and had not been able to do so at any time.

I wanted at least to say his name, before I went away. But I couldn't get it to my lips, my tongue wouldn't form it.

I was out of the room, in my coat, the door was opening. The rain had stopped. There wasn't even an excuse to linger. I stepped on to the path.

"Oh, well. Goodbye, Mrs. Besmouth."

Her face stayed shut, and then she shut the door too.

I walked quickly along Sea View Terrace, walking without having yet caught up to myself, an automaton. This was naturally an act, to convince Mrs. Antacid, and the unseen watchers in their houses, and the huge dark watcher of the night itself, that I knew precisely where I wanted to go now, and had no more time to squander. After about half a minute, self-awareness put me wise, and I stopped dead. Then I did what I really felt compelled to do, still without understanding why. I reversed my direction, walked back along the terrace, and into the curling alley that ran down between Number 19, and the shoulder of the cliff.

I didn't have to go very far to see the truth of the amorphous thing I had somehow deductively fashioned already, in my mind. The back of Number 19, which would normally have looked towards the sea, was enclosed by an enormous brick wall. It was at least fourteen feet high—the topmost windows of the house were barely visible above it. I wondered how the council had been persuaded to permit such a wall. Maybe some consideration of sea-gales had come into it. . . . The next door house, I now noticed for the first time, appeared empty, touched by mild dereliction. A humped black tree that looked like a deformed cypress grew in the garden there, a further barrier against open vistas. No lights were visible in either house, even where the preposterous wall allowed a glimpse of them.

I thought about prisons, while the excluded sea roared ferociously at the bottom of the alley.

I walked along the terrace again, and caught the bus home

Sunday was cold and clear, and I went out with my camera, because there was too much pure-ice wind to sketch. The water was like mercury under colourless sunlight. That evening, Angela had a party to which I had been invited. I drank too much, and a good-looking oaf called Ray mauled me about. I woke on Monday morning with the intense moral shame that results from the knowledge of truly wasted time.

Monday was my free day, or the day on which I performed my personal chores. I was loading the bag ready for the launderette when I remembered—the connection is elusive, but possibly Freudian—that I hadn't got the pre-paid receipt back from Mrs. Besmouth. Not that it would matter too much. Such records tended to be scrappy in Angela's department. I could leave it, and no one would die.

At eleven-thirty, I was standing by the door of Number 19, the knocker knocked and my heart was in my mouth.

I've always been obsessive. It's brought me some success, and quite a lot of disillusion, not to mention definite hurt. But I'm used to the excitement and trauma of it, and even then I was; used to my heart in my mouth, the trembling in my hands, the deep breath I must take before I could speak.

The door opened on this occasion quite quickly. She stood in the pale hard sunlight. I was beginning to learn her face, and its recalcitrant, seldom-varying expression. But she had on a different apron.

"Oh," she said, "it's you."

She'd expected me. She didn't exactly show it, she hadn't guessed what my excuse would be. But she'd known, just as I had, that I would come back.

"Look, I'm sorry to bother you," I said. "I forgot to ask you for the receipt."

"What receipt?"

"When you paid for the garment, they gave you a receipt. That one."

"I threw it away," she said.

"Oh. Oh well, never mind."

"I don't want to get you in trouble."

"No, it's all right. Really." I pulled air down into me like the drag of a cigarette, or a reefer. "How's Daniel today?"

She looked at me, her face unchanging.

"He's all right."

"I hoped I hadn't—well—upset him. By being there," I said.

"He doesn't notice," she said. "He didn't notice you."

There was a tiny flash of spite when she said that. It really was there. Because of it, I knew she had fathomed me, perhaps from the beginning. Now was therefore the moment to retreat in good order.

"I was wondering," I said. "What you told me, that you find it difficult to make the time to get to the town centre."

"I do," she said.

"I have to go shopping there today. If there's anything you need I could get you."

"Oh no," she said swiftly. "There's local shops on The Rise."

"I don't mind," I said.

"I can manage."

"I'd really like to. It's no bother. For one thing," I added, "the local shops are all daylight robbers round here, aren't they?"

She faltered. Part of her wanted to slam the door in my face. The other part was nudging her: Go on, let this stupid girl fetch and carry for you, if she wants to.

"If you want to, there are a few things. I'll make you out a list."

"Yes, do."

"You'd better come in," she said, just like last time.

I followed her, and she left me to close the door, a sign of submission indeed. As we went into the back room, the adrenalin stopped coming, and I knew he wasn't there. There was something else, though. The lights were on, and the curtains were drawn across the windows. She saw me looking, but she said nothing. She began to write on a piece of paper.

I wandered to the red chair, and rested my hands on the back of it.

"Daniel's upstairs," I said.

"That's right."

"But he's—he's well."

"He's all right. I don't get him up until dinner time. He just has to sit anyway, when he's up."

"It must be difficult for you, lifting him."

"I manage. I have to."

"But—"

"It's no use going on about home-helps again," she said. "It's none of their business."

She meant mine, of course. I swallowed, and said: "Was it an accident?" I'm rarely so blunt, and when I am, it somehow comes out rougher from disuse. She reacted obscurely, staring at me across the table.

"No, it wasn't. He's always been that way. He's got

no strength in his lower limbs, he doesn't talk, and he doesn't understand much. His father was at sea, and he went off and left me before Daniel was born. He didn't marry me, either. So now you know everything, don't you?"

I took my hand off the chair.

"But somebody should—"

"No they shouldn't."

"Couldn't he be helped—" I blurted.

"Oh, no," she said. "So if that's what you're after, you can get out now."

I was beginning to be terrified of her. I couldn't work it out if Daniel was officially beyond aid, and that's where her hatred sprang from, or if she had never attempted to have him aided, if she liked or needed or had just reasonlessly decided (God's will, My Cross) to let him rot alive. I didn't ask.

"I think you've got a lot to cope with," I said. "I can give you a hand, if you want it. I'd like to."

She nodded.

"Here's the list."

It was a long list, and after my boast, I'd have to make sure I saved her money on the local shops. She walked into the kitchen and took a box out of a drawer. The kitchen windows were also curtained. She came back with a five-pound note I wasn't sure would be enough.

When I got out of the house, I was coldly sweating. If I had any sense I would now, having stuck myself with it, honourably do her shopping, hand it to her at the door, and get on my way. I wasn't any kind of a crusader, and, as one of life's more accomplished actors, even I could see I had blundered into the wrong play.

* * *

It was one o'clock before I'd finished her shopping. My own excursion to the launderette had been passed over, but her fiver had just lasted. The list was quite commonplace; washing powder, jam, flour, kitchen towels. . . . I went into the pub opposite the store and had a gin and tonic. Nevertheless, I was shaking with nerves by the time I got back to Number 19. This was the last visit. This was it.

Gusts of white sunlight were blowing over the cliff. It was getting up rough in the bay, and the no-swimming notices had gone up.

She was a long while opening the door. When she did, she looked very odd, yellow-pale and tottery. Not as I'd come to anticipate. She was in her fifties, and suddenly childlike, insubstantial.

"Come in," she said, and wandered away down the passage.

There's something unnerving about a big strong persona that abruptly shrinks pale and frail. It duly unnerved me, literally in fact, and my nerves went away. Whatever had happened, I was in command.

I shut the door and followed her into the room. She was on the settee, sitting forward. Daniel still wasn't there. For the first time it occurred to me Daniel might be involved in this collapse, and I said quickly: "Something's wrong. What is it? Is it Daniel? Is he O.K.?"

She gave a feeble contemptuous little laugh.

"Daniel's all right. I just had a bit of an accident. Silly thing, really, but it gave me a bit of a turn for a minute."

She lifted her left hand in which she was clutching a red and white handkerchief. Then I saw the red pattern was drying blood. I put the shopping on the table and approached cautiously.

"What have you done?"

"Just cut myself. Stupid. I was chopping up some veg for our dinner. Haven't done a thing like this since I was a girl."

I winced. Had she slicked her finger off and left it lying among the carrots? No, don't be a fool. Even she wouldn't be so quiescent if she had. Or would she?

"Let me see," I said, putting on my firm and knowledgeable act, which has once or twice kept people from the brink of panic when I was in a worse panic than they were. To my dismay, she let go the handkerchief, and offered me her wound unresistingly.

It wasn't a pretty cut, but a cut was all it was, though deep enough almost to have touched the bone. I could see from her digital movements that nothing vital had been severed, and fingers will bleed profusely if you hit one of the blood vessels at the top.

"It's not too bad," I said. "I can bandage it up for you. Have you got some T.C.P.?"

She told me where the things were in the kitchen, and I went to get them. The lights were still on, the curtains were still drawn. Through the thin plastic of the kitchen drapes I could detect only flat darkness. Maybe the prison wall around the garden kept daylight at bay.

I did a good amateur job on her finger. The bleeding had slackened off.

"I should get a doctor to have a look at it, if you're worried."

"I never use doctors," she predictably said.

"Well, a chemist then."

"It'll be all right. You've done it nicely. Just a bit of a shock." Her colour was coming back, what she had of it.

"Shall I make you a cup of tea?"

"That'd be nice."

I returned to the kitchen and put on the kettle. The tea apparatus sat all together on a tray, as if waiting. I looked at her fawn fizzy head over the settee back, and the soft coal-fire glows disturbing the room. It was always nighttime here, and always nineteen-thirty.

The psychological aspect of her accident hadn't been lost on me. I supposed, always looking after someone, always independently alone, she'd abruptly given way to the subconscious urge to be in her turn looked after. She'd given me control. It frightened me.

The kettle started to boil, and I arranged the pot. I knew how she'd want her tea, nigrescently stewed and violently sweet. Her head elevated. She was on her feet.

"I'll just go and check Daniel."

"I can do that, if you like," I said before I could hold my tongue.

"That's all right," she said. She went out and I heard her go slowly up the stairs. Big and strong, how did she, even so, carry him down them?

I made the tea. I could hear nothing from upstairs. The vegetables lay scattered where she had left them, though the dangerous knife had been put from sight. On an impulse, I pulled aside a handful of kitchen curtain.

I wasn't surprised at what I saw. Somehow I must have worked it out, though not been aware I had. I let the curtain coil again into place, then carried the tea tray into the room. I set it down, and went to the room's back window, and methodically inspected that, too. It was identical to the windows of the kitchen. Both had been boarded over outside with planks of wood behind the glass. Not a chink of light showed. It must have been one terrific gale that smashed these windows and necessitated such a barricade. Strange the boarding was still there, after she'd had the glass replaced.

I heard her coming down again, but she had given me control, however briefly. I'd caught the unmistakable scent of something that wants to lean, to confess. I was curious, or maybe it was the double gin catching up on me. Curiosity was going to master fear. I stayed looking at the boarding, and let her discover me at it when she came in.

I turned when she didn't say anything. She simply looked blankly at me, and went to sit on the settee.

"Daniel's fine," she said. "He's got some of his books. Picture books. He can see the pictures, though he can't read the stories. You can go up and look at him, if you like."

That was a bribe. I went to the tea and started to pour it, spooning a mountain of sugar in her cup.

"You must be expecting a lot of bad weather, Mrs. Besmouth."

"Oh yes?"

"Yes. The windows."

I didn't think she was going to say anything. Then she said: "They're boarded over upstairs too, on the one side."

"The side facing out to sea."

"That's right."

"Did you build the wall up, too?"

She said, without a trace of humour: "Oh no. I got a man in to do that."

I gave her the tea, and she took it, and drank it straight down, and held the cup out to me.

"I could fancy another."

I repeated the actions with the tea. She took the

second cup, but looked at it, not drinking. The clock ticked somnolently. The room felt hot and heavy and peculiarly still, out of place and time and light of sun or moon.

"You don't like the sea, do you?" I said. I sat on the arm of the red chair, and watched her.

"Not much. Never did. This was my dad's house. When he died, I kept on here. Nowhere else to go." She raised her elastoplasted hand and stared at it. She looked very tired, very flaccid, as if she'd given up. "You know," she said, "I'd like a drop of something in this. Open that cupboard, will you? There's a bottle just inside."

I wondered if she were the proverbial secret drinker, but the bottle was alone, and three quarters full, quite a good whiskey.

She drank some of the tea and held the cup so I could ruin the whisky by pouring it in. I poured, to the cup's brim.

"You have one," she said. She drank, and smacked her lips softly. "You've earned it. You've been a good little girl."

I poured the whisky neat into the other tealess cup and drank some, imagining it smiting the gin below with a clash of swords.

"I'll get merry," she said desolately. "I didn't have my dinner. The pie'll be spoiled. I turned the oven out."

"Shall I get you a sandwich?"

"No. But you can make one for Daniel, if you like."

"Yes," I said.

I got up and went into the kitchen. It was a relief to move away from her. Something was happening to Daniel's mother, something insidious and profound.

She was accepting me, drawing me in. I could feel myself sinking in the quagmire.

As I made the sandwich from ingredients I came on more or less at random, she started to talk to me. It was a ramble of things, brought on by the relaxation of spilled blood and liquor, and the fact that there has seldom been anyone to talk *to*. As I buttered bread, sliced cheese and green cucumber, I learned how she had waited on and borne with a cantankerous father, nursed him, finally seen him off through the door in a box. I learned how she weighed meat behind the butcher's counter and did home-sewing, and how she had been courted by a plain stodgy young man, a plumber's assistant, and all she could come by in era when it was essential to come by something. And how eventually he jilted her.

The whisky lay in a little warm pool across the floor of my mind. I began irresistibly to withdraw inside myself, comparing her hopeless life with mine, the deadly job leading nowhere, the loneliness. And all at once I saw a horrid thing, the horrid thing I had brought upon myself. Her position was not hereditary, and might be bestowed. By speaking freely, she was making the first moves. She was offering me, slyly, her mantle. The role of protectress, nurse and mother, to Daniel—

I arranged the sandwich slowly on a plate. There was still time to run away. Lots of time.

"Just walking," I heard her say. "You didn't think about it then. Not like now. The sea was right out, and it was dark. I never saw him properly. They'd make a fuss about it now, all right. Rape. You didn't, then. I was that innocent, I didn't really know what he was doing. And then he let go and left me. He crawled off. I think he must have run along the edge of the sea, because I heard a splashing. And when the tide started to come in again, I got up and tidied myself, and I walked home."

I stood quite still in the kitchen, the sandwich on its plate in my hands, wide-eyed, listening.

"I didn't know I was pregnant, thought I'd eaten something. The doctor put me right. He told me what he thought of me, too. Not in words, exactly, just his manner. Rotten old bugger. I went away to have the baby. Everybody knew, of course. When he was the way he was, they thought it was a punishment. They were like that round here, then. I lived off the allowance, and what I had put by, and I couldn't manage. And then, I used to steal things, what do you think of that? I never got found out. Just once, this woman stopped me. She said: I think you have a tin of beans in your bag. I had, too, and the bill. What a red face she got. She didn't tumble the other things I'd taken and hadn't paid for. Then I had a windfall. The old man I used to work for, the butcher, he died, and he left me something. That was a real surprise. A few thousand it was. And I put it in the Society, and I draw the interest."

I walked through into the room. She had had a refill from the bottle and was stirring sugar into it.

"Do you mean Daniel's father raped you?"

"Course that's what I mean."

"And you didn't know who it was?"

"No." She drank. She was smiling slightly and licked the sugar off her lips.

"I thought you said he was a sailor."

"I never. I said he was at sea. That's what I told people. My husband's at sea. I bought myself a ring, and gave myself a different name. Besmouth. I saw it on an advertisement. Besmouth's Cheese Crackers." She laughed. "At sea," she repeated. "Or out of if.

He was mother naked, and wringing wet. I don't know where he'd left his clothes. Who'd believe you if you told them that."

"Shall I take this up to Daniel?" I said.

She looked at me, and I didn't like her look, all whisky smile.

"Why not," she said. She swallowed a belch primly. "That's where you've wanted to go all along, isn't it? 'How's Daniel?' " she mimicked me in an awful high soppy voice that was supposed to be mine, or mine the way she heard it. " 'Is Daniel Ookay?' Couldn't stop looking at him, could you? Eyes all over him. But you won't get far. You can strip off and do the dance of the seven veils, and he won't notice."

My eyes started to water, a sure sign of revulsion. I felt I couldn't keep quiet, though my voice (high and soppy?) would tremble when I spoke.

"You're being very rude. I wanted to help."

"*Ohhh* yes," she said.

"The thing that worries me," I said, "is the way you coop him up. Don't you ever try to interest him in anything?" She laughed dirtily, and then did belch, patting her mouth as if in congratulation. "I think Daniel should be seen by a doctor. I'm sure there's some kind of therapy—"

She drank greedily, not taking an apparent notice of me.

I hurried out, clutching the sandwich plate, and went along the corridor and up the stairs, perching on two wobbly sticks. If I'd stayed with her much longer, I, too, might have lost the use of my lower limbs.

Light came into the hall from the glass in the door, but going up, it grew progressively murkier.

It was a small house, and the landing, when I got

to it, was barely wide enough to turn round on. There was the sort of afterthought of a cramped bathroom old houses have put in—it was to the back, and through the open door, I could see curtains across the windows. They, too, must be boarded, as she had said. And in the bedroom which faced the back. A pathological hatred of the sea, ever since she had been raped into unwanted pregnancy beside it. If it were true. . . . Did she hate Daniel, as well? Was that why she kept him as she did, clean, neat, fed, cared for and deliberately devoid of joy, of soul—

There was a crisp little flick of paper, the virtually unmistakable sound of a page turning. It came from the room to my right: the front bedroom. There was a pane of light there too, falling past the angle of the half-closed door. I crossed the door and pushed it wide.

He didn't glance up, just went on poring over the big slim book spread before him. He was sitting up in bed in spotless blue and white pyjamas. I had been beginning to visualise him as a child, but he was a man. He looked like some incredible convalescent prince, or an angel. The cold light from the window made glissandos over his hair. Outside, through the net, was the opposite side of the street, the houses, and the slope of the hill going up with other houses burgeoning on it. You couldn't even see the cliff. Perhaps this view might be more interesting to him than the sea. People would come and go, cars, dogs. But there was only weather in the street today, shards of it blowing about. The weather over the sea must be getting quite spectacular.

When she went out, how did she avoid the sea? She couldn't then, could she? I suddenly had an idea that somehow she had kept Daniel at all times from the sight of the water. I imagined him, a sad, sub-

normal, beautiful little boy, sitting with his discarded
toys—if he ever had any—on the floor of this house.
And outside, five minutes' walk away, the sand, the
waves, the wind.

The room was warm, from a small electric heater
fixed up in the wall, above his reach. Not even weather
in this room.

He hadn't glanced up at me, though I'd come to
the bedside, he just continued gazing at the book. It
was a child's book, of course. It showed a princess
leaning down from a tower with a pointed roof, and
a knight below, not half so handsome as Daniel.

"I've brought you some lunch," I said. I felt self-
conscious, vaguely ashamed, his mother drunk in the
room downstairs and her secrets in my possession.
How wonderful to look at the rapist must have been.
Crawled away, she had said. Maybe he too—

"Daniel," I said. I removed the book gently from
his grasp, and put the plate there instead.

How much of what she said to me about my own
motives was actually the truth? There were just about
a million things I wouldn't want to do for him, my
aversion amounting to a phobia, to a state not of
wouldn't but *couldn't*. Nor could I cope with this
endless silent non-reaction. I'd try to make him react,
I was trying to now. And maybe that was wrong,
unkind—

Maybe I disliked and feared men so much I'd
carried the theories of de Beauvoir and her like to
an ultimate conclusion. I could only love what was
male if it was also powerless, impotent, virtually
inanimate. Not even love it. Be perversely aroused
by it. The rape principle in reverse.

He wasn't eating, so I bent down, and peered into
his face, and for the first time, I think he saw me.
His luminous eyes moved, and fixed on mine. They

didn't seem completely focused, even so. But meeting them, I was conscious of a strange irony. Those eyes, which perhaps had never looked at the sea, held the sea inside them. *Were* the sea.

I shook myself mentally, remembering the whisky plummeting on the gin.

"Eat, Daniel," I said softly.

He grasped the sandwich plate with great serenity. He went on meeting my eyes, and mine, of course, filled abruptly and painfully with tears. Psychological symbolism: salt water.

I sat on the edge of the bed and stroked his hair. It felt like silk, as I'd known it would. His skin was so clear, the pores so astringently closed, that it was like a sort of silk, too. It didn't appear as if he had ever, so far, had to be shaved. Thank God. I didn't like the thought of her round him with a razor blade. I could even picture her producing her father's old cutthroat from somewhere, and doing just that with it, another accident, with Daniel's neck.

You see my impulse, however. I didn't even attempt to deal with the hard practicality of supporting such a person as Daniel really was. I should have persuaded or coerced him to eat. Instead I sat and held him. He didn't respond, but he was quite relaxed. Something was going through my brain about supplying him with emotional food, affection, physical security, something she'd consistently omitted from his diet. I was trying to make life and human passion soak into him. To that height I aspired, and, viewed another way, to that depth I'd sunk.

I don't know when I'd have grown embarrassed, or bored, or merely too tired and cramped to go on perching there, maintaining my sentimental contact with him. I didn't have to make the decision. She walked in through the door and made it for me.

"Eat your sandwich, Daniel," she said as she entered. I hadn't heard her approach on this occasion, and I jerked away. Guilt, presumably. Some kind of guilt. But she ignored me and bore down on him from the bed's other side. She took his hand and put it down smack on the bread. "Eat up," she said. It was macabrely funny, somehow pure slapstick. But he immediately lifted the sandwich to his mouth. Presumably he'd recognised it as food by touch, but not sight.

She wasn't tight anymore. It had gone through her and away, like her dark tea through its strainer.

"I expect you want to get along," she said.

She was her old self, indeed. Graceless courtesies, platitudes. She might have told me nothing, accused me of nothing. We had been rifling each other's ids, but now it was done, and might never have been. I didn't have enough fight left in me to try to rip the renewed facade away again. And besides, I doubt if I could have.

So I got along. What else?

Before I went back to my room, I stood on the promenade awhile, looking out to sea. It was in vast upheaval, coming in against the cliffs like breaking glasses, and with a sound of torn atmosphere. Like a monstrous beast it ravened on the shore. A stupendous force seemed trying to burst from it, like anger, or love, or grief, orchestrated by Shostakovich, and cunningly lit by an obscured blind sun.

I wished Daniel could have seen it. I couldn't imagine he would remain unmoved, though all about me people were scurrying to and fro, not sparing a glance.

When I reached my nominative aunt's, the voice of a dismal news broadcast drummed through the

house, and the odour of fried fish lurked like a
ghost on the stairs.

The next day was Tuesday, and I went to work.

I dreamed about Daniel a lot during the next week. I
could never quite recapture the substance of the
dreams, their plot, except they were to do with him,
and they felt bad. I think they had boarded windows.
Perhaps I dreamed she'd killed him, or I had, and
the boards became a coffin.

Obviously, I'd come to my senses, or come to avoid
my senses. I had told myself the episode was finished
with. Brooding about it, I detected only some per-
verted desire on my side, and a trap from hers.
There was no one I could have discussed any of it
with.

On Wednesday, a woman in a wheelchair rolled
through lingerie on her way to the china department.
Dizzy with fright, if it was fright, I watched the omen
pass. She, Mrs. Besmouth, could get to me any time.
Here I was, vulnerably pinned to my counter like a
butterfly on a board. But she didn't come in. Of
course she didn't.

"Here," said Jill-sans-bra, "look what you've gone
and dunn. You've priced all these eight-pound slips
at six-forty-five."

I'd sold one at six-forty-five, too.

Thursday arrived, Cinema day. A single customer
came and went like a breeze from the cold wet street.
There was a storm that night. A little ship, beating
its way in from Calais, was swept over in the troughs,
and there were three men missing, feared drowned.
On Friday, a calm dove-grey weather bloomed, and
bubbles of lemonade sun lit the bay.

I thought about that window looking on the street.
He should have seen the water, oh, he should have

seen it, those bars of shining lead, and the great cool topaz master bar that fell across them. That restless mass where men died and fish sprang. That other land that glowed and moved.

Saturday was pandemonium, as usual. Angela was cheerful. Her husband was in Scotland, and this evening the extra-marital relationship was meeting her. Rather than yearn for aloneness together, they apparently deemed two no company at all.

"Come over the pub with us. Jill and Terry'll be there. And I know Ray will. He asked me if you were coming."

Viewed sober, a night of drinking followed by the inevitable Chinese nosh-up and the attentions of the writhing Ray, was uninviting. But I, as all pariahs must be, was vaguely grateful for their toleration, vaguely pleased my act of participant was acceptable to them. It was also better than nothing, which was the only alternative.

"It's nice here," said Jill, sipping her Bacardi and Coke.

They'd decided to go to a different pub, and I'd suggested the place on The Rise. It had a log fire, and they liked that, and horse-brasses, and they liked sneering at those. Number 19. Sea View Terrace was less than a quarter of a mile away, but they didn't know about that, and wouldn't have cared if they had.

Lean, lithe Ray, far too tall for me, turned into a snake every time he flowed down towards me.

It was eight o'clock, and we were on the fourth round. I couldn't remember the extra-marital relationship's name. Angela apparently couldn't either; to her he was "darling," "love," or in spritely yielding moment, "Sir."

"Where we going to eat then?" said Ray.

"The Hwong Fews's ever so nice," said Jill.

Terry was whispering a dirty joke to Angela, who screamed with laughter. "Listen to this—"

Very occasionally, between the spasms of noise from the bar, you could just hear the soft shattering boom of the ocean.

Angela said the punchline and we all laughed.

We got to the fifth round.

"If you put a bell on," Ray said to me, "I'll give you a ring sometime."

I was starting to withdraw rather than expand, the alternate phase of tipsyness. Drifting back into myself, away from the five people I was with. Out of the crowded public house. Astral projection almost. Now I was on the street.

"You know I could really fancy you," said Ray.

"You want to watch our Ray," said Angela.

Jill giggled and her jelly chest wobbled.

It was almost nine, and the sixth round. Jill had had an argument with Terry, and her eyes were damp. Terry, uneasy, stared into his beer.

"I think we should go and eat now," said the extra-marital relationship.

"Yes, sir," said Angela.

"Have a good time," I said. My voice was slightly slurred. I was surprised by it, and by what it had just vocalised.

"Good time," joked Angela. "You're coming, too."

"Oh, no—didn't I say? I have to be somewhere else by nine."

"She just wants an excuse to be alone with me," said Ray. But he looked as amazed as the rest of them. Did I look amazed, too?

"But where are you going?" Angela demanded. "You said—"

"I'm sorry. I thought I told you. It's something I have to go to with the woman where I stay. I can't get out of it. We're sort of related."

"Oh, Jesus," said Ray.

"Oh well, if you can't get out of it." Angela stared hard at me through her mascara.

I might be forfeiting my rights to their friendship, which was all I had. And why? To stagger, cross-eyed with vodka, to Daniel's house. To do and say what? Whatever it was, it was pointless. This had more point. Even Ray could be more use to me than Daniel.

But I couldn't hold myself in check any longer. I'd had five days of restraint. Vile liquor had let my personal animal out of its cage. What an animal it was. Burning, confident, exhilarated and sure. If I didn't know exactly what its plans were, I still knew they would be glorious and great.

"Great," said Ray. "Well, if she's going, let's have another."

"I think I'll have a cream sherry," said Angela. "I feel like a change."

They had already excluded me, demonstrating I would not be missed. I stood on my feet, which no longer felt like mine.

"Thanks for the drinks," I said. I tried to look reluctant to be going, and they smiled at me, hardly trying at all, as if seeing me through panes of tinted glass.

It was black outside; where the street lights hadn't stained it, the sky looked clear beyond the glare, a vast roof. I walked on water.

Daniel's mother had been drunk when she told me about the rape. Truth in wine. So this maniac was presumably the true me.

The walk down the slope in the cold brittle air

neither sobered me nor increased my inebriation. I simply began to learn how to move without a proper centre of balance. When I arrived, I hung on her gate a moment. The hall light mildly suffused the door panels. The upstairs room, which was his, looked dark.

I knocked. I seemed to have knocked on that door thirty times. Fifty. A hundred. Each time, like a clockwork mechanism, Mrs. Besmouth opened it. Hallo, I've come to see Daniel. Hallo, I'm drunk, and I've come to scare you. I've spoken to the police about your son, I've said you neglect him. I've come to tell you what I think of you. I've booked two seats on a plane and I'm taking Daniel to Lourdes. I phoned the Pope, and he's meeting us there.

The door didn't open. I knocked twice more, and leaned in the porch, practising my introductory gambits.

I'm really a famous artist in disguise, and all I want is to paint Daniel. As the young Apollo, I think. Only I couldn't find a lyre. (Liar.)

Only gradually did it come to me that the door stayed shut, and gave every sign of remaining so. With the inebriate's hidebound immobility, I found this hard to assimilate. But presently it occurred to me that she might be inside, have guessed the identity of the caller, and was refusing to let me enter.

How long would the vodka stave off the cold? Ages, surely. I saw fur-clad Russians tossing it back neat amid snowdrifts, wolves howling in the background. I laughed sullenly, and knocked once more. I'd just keep on and on, at intervals, until she gave in. Or would she? She'd had over fifty years of fighting, standing firm, being harassed and disappointed. She'd congealed into it, vitrified. I was comparatively new at the game.

After ten minutes, I had a wild and terrifying notion that she might have left a spare key, cliché-fashion, under a flower pot. I was crouching over my boots, feeling about on the paving round the step for the phantom flower pot, when I heard a sound I scarcely knew, but instantly identified. Glancing up, I beheld Mrs. Besmouth pushing the wheelchair into position outside her gate.

She had paused, looking at me, as blank as I had ever seen her. Daniel sat in the chair like a wonderful waxwork, or a strangely handsome Guy Fawkes dummy she had been out collecting money with for Firework Night.

She didn't comment on my posture, neither did I. I rose and confronted her. From a purely primitive viewpoint, I was between her and refuge.

"I didn't think I'd be seeing you again," she said.

"I didn't think you would, either."

"What do you want?"

It was, after all, more difficult to dispense with all constraint than the vodka had told me it would be.

"I happened to be up here," I said.

"You bloody little do-gooder, poking your nose in."

Her tone was flat. It was another sort of platitude and delivered without any feeling, or spirit.

"I don't think," I said, enunciating pedantically, "I've ever done any good particularly. And last time, you decided my interest was solely prurient."

She pushed the gate, leaning over the chair, and I went forward and helped her. I held the gate and she came through, Daniel floating by below.

"You take him out at night," I said.

"He needs some fresh air."

"At night, so he won't see the water properly, if at

all. How do you cope when you have to go out in daylight?"

As I said these preposterous things, I was already busy detecting, the local geography fresh in my mind, how such an evasion might be possible. Leave the house, backs to the sea, go up The Rise away from it, come around only at the top of the town where the houses and the blocks of flats exclude any street-level view. Then down into the town centre, where the ocean was only a distant surreal smudge in the valley between sky and promenade.

"The sea isn't anything," she said, wheeling him along the path, her way to the door clear now. "What's there to look at?"

"I thought he might like the sea."

"He doesn't."

"Has he ever been shown it?"

She came to the door, and was taking a purse out of her coat pocket. As she fumbled for the key, the wheelchair rested by her, a little to one side of the porch. The brake was off.

The vodka shouted at me to do something. I was slow. It took me five whole seconds before I darted forward, thrust by her, grabbed the handles of the wheelchair, careered it around, and wheeled it madly back up the path and through the gate. She didn't try to stop me, or even shout, she simply stood there, staring, the key in her hand. She didn't look non-plussed either—I somehow saw that. *I* was the star-tled one. Then I was going fast around the side of Number 19, driving the chair like a cart or a doll's pram, into the curl of the alley that ran between cliff and wall to the beach. I'm not absolutely certain I remembered a live thing was in the chair. He was so still, so withdrawn. He really could have been some kind of doll.

But the alley was steep, steeper with the pendulum of man and chair and alcohol swinging ahead of me. As I braced against the momentum, I listened. I couldn't hear her coming after me. When I looked back, the top of the slope stayed empty. How odd. Instinctively I'd guessed she wouldn't lunge immediately into pursuit. I think she could have overcome me easily if she'd wanted to. As before, she had given over control of everything to me.

This time, I wasn't afraid.

Somewhere in the alley, my head suddenly cleared, and all my senses, like a window going up. All that was left of my insanity was a grim, anguished determination not to be prevented. I must achieve the ocean, and that seemed very simple. The waves roared and hummed at me out of the invisible, unlit dark ahead. Walking down the alley was like walking into the primeval mouth of Noah's Flood.

The cliff rounded off like a castle bastion. The road on the left rose away. A concrete platform and steps went up, then just raw rock, where a hut stood sentinel, purpose unknown. The beach appeared suddenly, a dull gleam of sand. The sea was all part of a black sky, until a soft white bomb of spray exploded out of it.

The street lamps didn't reach so far, and there were no fun-fair electrics to snag on the water. The sky was fairly clear, but with a thin intermittent race of clouds, and the nearest brightest stars and planets flashed on and off, pale grey and sapphire blue. A young crescent moon, too delicate to be out on such a cold fleeting night, tilted in the air, the only neon, but not even bleaching the sea.

"Look, Daniel," I murmured. "Look at the water."

All I could make out was the silken back of his

head, the outline of his knees under the rug, the loosely lying artist's hands.

I'd reached the sand, and it was getting difficult to manoeuvre the wheelchair. The wheels were sinking. The long heels of my boots were sinking too. A reasonable symbol, maybe.

I thrust the chair on by main force, and heard things grinding as the moist sand became clotted in them.

All at once, the only way I could free my left foot was to pull my boot and leg up with both hands. When I tried the chair again, it wouldn't move anymore. I shoved a couple of times, wrenched a couple, but nothing happened and I let go.

We were about ten feet from the ocean's edge, but the tide was going out, and soon the distance would be greater.

Walking on tiptoe to keep the sink-weight off my boot heels, I went around the chair to investigate Daniel's reaction. I don't know what I'd predicted. Something, patently.

But I wasn't prepared.

You've heard the words: Sea-change.

Daniel was changing. I don't mean in any supernatural way. Although it almost was, almost seemed so. Because he was coming alive.

The change had probably happened in the eyes first of all. Now they were focused. He was looking— really looking, and seeing—at the water. His lips had parted, just slightly. The sea wind was blowing the hair back from his face, and this, too, lent it an aura of movement, animation, as though he was in the bow of a huge ship, her bladed prow cleaving the open sea, far from shore, no land in sight. . . . His hands had changed their shape. They were curiously flexed, arched, as if for the galvanic effort of lifting himself.

I crouched beside him, as I had crouched in front of the house searching for the make-believe spare key. I said phrases to him, quite meaningless, about the beauty of the ocean and how he must observe it. Meaningless, because he saw, he knew, he comprehended. There was genius in his face. But that's an interpretation. I think I'm trying to say possession, or atavism.

And all the while the astounding change went on, insidious now, barely explicable, yet continuing, mounting, like a series of waves running in through his blood, dazzling behind his eyes. He was alive— and with something. Yes, I think I do mean atavism. The gods of the sea were rising up in the void and empty spaces of Daniel, as maybe such gods are capable of rising in all of us, if terrified intellect didn't slam the door.

I knelt in the sand, growing silent, sharing it merely by being there beside him.

Then slowly, like a cinematic camera shot, my gaze detected something in the corner of vision. Automatically, I adjusted the magical camera lens of the eye, the foreground blurring, the distant object springing into its dimensions. Mrs. Besmouth stood several yards off, at the limit of the beach. She seemed to be watching us, engrossed, yet not moving. Her hands were pressed together, rigidly—it resembled that exercise one can perform to tighten the pectoral muscles.

I got to my feet a second time. This time I ran towards her, floundering in the sand, deserting the wheelchair and its occupant, their backs to the shore, facing out to sea.

I panted as I ran, from more than the exertion. Her eyes also readjusted themselves as I blundered towards her, following me, but she gave no corresponding movement: a spectator only. As I came right up to her, I lost my footing and grabbed out to steady myself, and it was her arm I almost inadvertently caught. The frantic gesture—the same one I might have used to detain her if she had been running forward—triggered in me a whole series of responses suited to an act of aggression that had not in fact materialised.

"No!" I shouted. "Leave him alone! Don't you dare take him away. I won't let you—" and I raised my other hand, slapping at her shoulder ineffectually. I'm no fighter; I respect—or fear—the human body too much. To strike her breast or face would have appalled me. If we had really tussled I think she could have killed me long before my survival reflexes dispensed with my inhibitions.

But she didn't kill me. She shook me off; I stumbled and I fell on the thick cold cushion of the sand.

"I don't care what he does," she said. "Let him do what he wants." She smiled at me, a knowing scornful smile. "You adopt him. You take care of him. I'll let you."

I felt panic, even though I disbelieved her. To this pass we had come, I had brought us, that she could threaten me with such things. Before I could find any words—they would have been inane violent ones—her face lifted, and her eyes went over my head, over the beach, back to the place where I'd left the chair.

She said: "I think I always expected it'd come. I think I always waited for it to happen. I'm sick and tired of it. I get no thanks. All the rest of them. They don't know when they're well off. When did I ever have anything? Go on, then. Go on."

I sat on the ground, for she'd knocked the strength from me. She didn't care, and I didn't care.

Someone ought to be with Daniel. Oh God, how were we going to get the wheelchair back across the sand? Perhaps we'd have to abandon it, carry him back between us. I'd have to pay for a new chair. I couldn't afford it, I—

I had been turning, just my head, and now I could see the wheelchair poised, an incongruous black cut-out against the retreating breakers which still swam in and splintered on the lengthening beach. It was like a surrealist painting, I remember thinking that, the lost artifact, sigil of stasis, set by the wild night ocean, sigil of all things metamorphic. If the chair had been on fire, it could have been a Magritte.

Initially the movement didn't register. It seemed part of the insurge and retraction of the waves. A sort of pale glimmer, a gliding. Then the *weirdness* of it registered with me, and I realised it was Daniel. Somehow he had slipped from the chair, collapsed forward into the water, and, incredibly, the water was pulling him away with itself, away into the darkness.

I lurched up. I screamed something, a curse or a prayer or his name or nothing at all. I took two riotous running steps before she grasped me. It was a fierce hold, undeniable, made of iron. Oh she was so strong. I should have guessed. She had been lifting and carrying a near grown man for several years. But I tried to go on rushing to the ocean, like those cartoon characters you see, held back by some article of elastic. And like them, when she wouldn't let me go, I think I ran on the spot a moment, the sand cascading from under me.

"Daniel—" I cried, "he's fallen in the water—the tide's dragging him out—can't you see—"

"I can see," she said. "You look, and you'll see, too."

And her voice stopped me from moving, just as her grip had stopped my progression. All I could do then was look, so I looked.

We remained there, breathing, our bodies slotted together, like lovers, speechless, watching. We watched until the last pastel glimmer was extinguished. We watched until the sea had run far away into the throat of night. And after that we watched the ribbed sands, the plaster cast the waves forever leave behind them. A few things had been stranded there, pebbles, weed, a broken bottle. But Daniel was gone, gone with the sea. Gone away into the throat of night and water.

"Best move the chair," she said at last, and let me go.

We walked together and hoistd the vacant wheelchair from the sand. We took it back across the beach, and at the foot of the alley we rested.

"I always knew," she said then. "I tried to stop it, but then I thought: Why try? What good is it?" Finally she said to me: "Frightened, are you?"

"Yes," I said, but it was a reflex.

"I'm glad," she said. "You silly little cow."

After that we hoisted the chair up the alley, to the gate of Number 19. She took it to the house, and inside, and shut the door without another word.

I walked to the bus stop, and when the lighted golden bus blew like a spaceship from the shadows, I got on it. I went home, or to the place where I lived. I recall I looked at everything with vague astonishment, but that was all. I didn't feel what had occurred, didn't recognise or accept it. That came days later, and when it did I put my fist through one of my nominative aunt's windows. The impulse came and was gone in a second. It was quite extraordinary. I didn't know I was going to, I simply did. My right hand, my painter's hand. I managed to say I'd tripped and fallen, and everything was a mistake. After the stitches came out, I packed my bags and went inland for a year. It was so physically painful for a while to manipulate a brush or palette knife, it became a discipline, a penance to do it. So I learned. So I became what now I am.

I never saw Mrs. Besmouth again. And no one, of course, ever again saw Daniel.

You see, a secret agent is one who masquerades, one who pretends to be what he or she is not. And, if successful, is indistinguishable from the society or group or affiliation into which he or she has been infiltrated. In the Magritte painting, you're shown the disguise, which is that of a human girl, but the actuality also, the creature within. And oddly, while she's more like a chess-piece horse that any human girl, her essence is of a girl, sheer girl, or rather, the sheer feminine principle don't you think? Maybe I imagine it.

I heard some rumour or other at the time, just before the window incident. The atrocious Ray was supposed to have laced my drink. With what I don't know, nor do I truly credit it. It's too neat. It accounts for everything too well. But my own explanations then were exotic, to say the least. I became convinced at one point that Daniel had communicated with me telepathically, pleaded, coerced, engineered everything. I'd merely been a tool of his escape, like a file hidden in a cake. His mother had wanted it too. Afraid to let go, trying to let go. Letting go.

Obviously, you think we murdered him, she and I.

A helpless, retarded, crippled young man, drowned in Ship Bay one late autumn night, two women standing by in a horrific complicity, watching his satin head go under the black waters, not stirring to save him.

Now I ask myself, I often ask myself, if that's what took place. Maybe it did. Shall I tell you what I saw? I kept it till the end, coup de grâce, or cherry, whichever you prefer.

It was a dark clear night, with not much illumination, that slender moon, those pulsing stars, a glint of phosphorous, perhaps, gilding the sea. But naked, and so pale, so flawless, his body glowed with its own incandescence, and his hair was water-fire, colourless, and brilliant.

I don't know how he got free of his clothes. They *were* in the chair with the rug—jeans, trunks, pullover, shirt—no socks, I remember, and no shoes. I truly don't think he could walk, but somehow, as he slid forward those three or four yards into the sea, the sight of the waves must have aided him, their hypnotism drawing off his garments, sloughing them like a dead skin.

I saw him, just for a moment. His Apollo's head, modelled sleek with brine, shone from the breakers. He made a strong swimmer's movement. Naturally, many victims of paralysis find sudden coordination of their limbs in the weightless medium of fluid. . . . Certainly Daniel was swimming, and certainly his movements were both spontaneous and voluntary.

And now I have the choice as to whether I tell you this or not. It's not that I'm afraid, or nervous of telling you. I'm not even anxious as to whether or not you believe me. Perhaps I should be. But I shan't try to convince you. I'll state it, once. Recollect, the story about Ray and the drinks may be true, or possibly the quirk was only in me, the desire for miracles in my world of Then, where nothing happened, nothing was rich, or strange.

For half a minute I saw the shape of a man, spearing fishlike through the water. And then came one of those deep lacunas, when the outgoing tide abruptly collects itself, seems to swallow, pauses. And there in the trough, the beautiful leaping of something, white as salt crystal, smoky green as glass. The hair rose on my head, just as they say it does. Not terror, but a feeling so close to it as to be untranslatable—a terror, yet without fear. I saw a shining horse, a stallion, with a mane like opals and unravelling foam, his forefeet raised, heraldic, his belly a craven bow, the curve of the moon, the rest a silken fish, a great greenish sheen of fish, like the tail of a dolphin, but scaled over in a waterfall of liquid armour, like a shower of silver coins. I saw it, and I knew it. And then it was gone.

The woman with me said nothing. She had barricaded her windows, built up her wall against such an advent. And I said nothing because it is a dream we have, haven't we, the grossest of us, something that with childhood begins to perish; to tear the veil, to see. Just for a moment, a split second in all of life. And the split second was all I had, and it was enough. How could one bear more?

But I sometimes wonder if Magritte, whose pictures are so full of those clear moments of terror, but not fear, moment on moment on moment—I sometimes wonder—

Then again, when you look at the sea, or when I look at it, especially at night, anything at all seems possible.

MONKEY'S STAGGER

Edmund, a hero, strode through the ripe green jungle-forest of Darzilla-Ny. Clad in link mail of the finest gold-washed bronze, on his hip a gold-hilted Darzillan scimitar, a selection of jewelled knives in various pouches and a frown of stern intent on his tanned and handsome face, Edmond was, nevertheless, plainly terrified. He had some cause to be.

"Whatever you do, Edmund-sir," the native villagers had intoned, with servile contempt radiating from every dusky pore, "do *not*, on no account indeed, stray from the forest path."

Edmund, with a shiver of recognising alarm, inquired: "Why not?"

"The sir should know," the natives said, "a demon dwells in an ancient shrine to the north of the forest. Whoever approaches is caught by his snares."

"Oh, just demons, eh?" said Edmund, white to the lips and trembling.

"Yes indeed, brave sir," snickered the natives. "There is great treasure in the shrine. If the sir wished a guest, of course—But he had better be warned. Of all those who have been snared by the demon, a few have outwitted him. But of these, not one was an Inglish-man."

"Oh, come," said Edmund faintly.

"Not a one," reiterated the natives stubbornly.

Edmund shut his beautiful eyes, and whispered:

"Then I'll make it my business to be the first Inglish-man who does."

Then he visited a nearby grove and threw up.

Half an hour later, he set off into the jungle-forest. The natives watched him go with much kow-towing and licking of Edmund's white bull-skin sandals. He vanished amid the trees.

"There's a brave bloody-silly sir," the natives said to each other.

Edmund's sad fate had been fixed for him long before his birth. A few hundred years prior to this event, a bizarre flying ship from a distant some-where had been wrecked on the exotic plains of Darzilla-Ny. Those who survived the crash of the ship were apparently of a race or tribe known as the Inglish, and their new environment swiftly eroded the nice uni-sexual, non-xenophobic veneer they had come down with.

Discovering a native population of primitive sort, the tribe of the Inglish seemed to recapture some ancient colonial appetite. Using a few oddments sal-vaged from the wreck, they demonstrated their supe-riority over the dusky blue Darzillans. Presently the Inglish set themselves up as lords, exacted tythes, had mansions built for themselves, furnished them with what appealed from the Darzillan culture, and settled into a happy degeneration. The Darzillans, a philosophical and canny people, accepted their lot. Occasionally recruited as slaves ("servants"), they ac-cepted that too, content to steal and exacerbate their masters with feigned foolishness, running away when they got bored. They were very adept at all forms of escape and at all forms of mockery. There were, besides, the strange demons, devils and other super-naturals who infested all Darzilla, and which only the natives understood or could properly deal with. This would lead to conversations as following: "This damned servant's spilled soup on me. Look here, no dinner for you." "If sir will not give me dinner since I spilled soup on his tunic, I am afraid I may forget, through hunger naturally indeed, the spell to keep the snake phantom from biting off sir's feet in the night." Etc:—etc:—

However, faced with such a diversity of monsters, another bit of old Inglish temperament arose. It became the thing for the second sons of the Inglish mansions to don Darzillan Warrior gear and go out to "slay dragons" (there were no dragons on Darzilla), amass riches, and rescue virgins (of whom there were very few).

At the birth of Edmund, the second son, he had been dedicated to heroic adventure. An attractive child, even so young, he had nonetheless screamed with horror, as if he understood the life he was being saddled with. As he grew older, and the ghastly day drew closer when he must leave hearth and home, he had fallen prey to fainting fits. It wasn't any use at all. Even as he lay in a swoon on his twenty-first birthday, they had buckled on his sword and carried him carefully out on to the lawn of the family estate, next bolting the doors against him from inside.

Having no choice, Edmund did his best. As an Inglish hero he was recognisable to all. For in those modern times, only the Inglish went about dressed as archaic Darzillan warriors. And an Inglish hero's duty and desire was to respond to the slightest breath of danger by flinging himself rapidly forward to meet it. Edmund secretly suspected the natives took pleasure in slinking to his side as he rested in the mauve shade of a flowering fire-tree, and mouthing about a mad lion-devil who was terrorizing the village that Edmund might enjoy slaying, or a ghost in the well that ate men's ears that Edmund might be interested in exorcising. Altogether, Edmund was pretty sure they just liked upsetting him, because none of these tales was ever true. And despite his ultimate courage—for he was so scared by now, even getting up in the morning had become an act of supreme valour—Edmund was beginning to think of dyeing his blond hair indigo and his tanned skin dusk-blue, and going native. The only trouble was, of course, he couldn't speak the language. Another mark of the Inglish lords was their utter determination to keep pure their own tongue by never learning anyone else's. Apparently there had been a machine in their ridiculous flying ship which had done all that for them. That it had ended up as a heap of molten slag they seemed to take as an omen. No, in order to communicate, the Darzillans must learn Inglish. Being clever, they did so. Even the demons, it appeared, could speak Inglish. Even this demon in the jungle-forest, for the villagers had assured Edmund that the creature would speak to a man in whatever tongue was his own.

On the matter of this forest demon to be sure Edmund, returning from the grove, had asked a few further questions.

The questions had been of this nature:

"How big is the demon? What does it look like?"

The villagers' replies were ambiguous.

"It has many forms."

To Edmund's reminder that, according to the village, certain persons had escaped the demon, and if so, why was that? The villagers had merely said: "It is because they were not Inglish."

"Well," cried Edmund in despair, "have any of you ever met it?"

"No, not at all," they smiled.

"But last night," Edmund blurted, suddenly remembering something, "you told me a story of a holy man who lived in these parts and had power over demons—Ish or Bish or something."

The villagers bowed.

"Clever sir is right. The holy man, Kwua Iss. But he has been dead as many years as wise sir could count on his hairs."

"Oh," said Edmund. "But aren't there some relics of his somewhere?"

The villagers became very excited—acting?—and babbled about earth spirits, and the energy of a man's hand giving strength to a relic when he held it. Then they pronounced the demon too awful, and advised him again not to go near it, thereby sealing Edmund's doom.

Thus Edmund came to be striding through the jungle-forest, dressed to kill and half dead of fright.

The large warm sun of Darzilla-Ny got higher, and the leaves and fronds dappled the forest floor with green coins of light. No demon had manifested itself, and Edmund began to nurture a foolish hope that possibly the tale was another lie. Just then a large yellow tiger emerged from the undergrowth and fixed Edmund with a pair of malignant sapphire eyes.

The blood rushed from Edmund's head and heart. He tottered, and saw three more tigers coming up on his right. He knocked a fifth one flying as he fell on it in a dead faint.

*   *   *

Edmund came to himself with the delicate sound of Darzillan wind-chimes in his ears, a sweet smell of incense in his nostrils, a soft rare light above and a wonderfully soothing touch on his forehead. As his long eyelashes untangled themselves farther, Edmund was able to perceive he lay in a gorgeous garden-courtyard. All about, flowers and plants were blooming among curious statuary; above, a canopy shielded him from the afternoon sun; his head lay on a cushion. Edmund looked behind him, gave a hoarse cry and attempted to rise. But the man seated at his back gently pressed him down again on the cushions, and resumed the soothing of Edmund's fevered brow.

He sat cross-legged, this man, and was nearly naked, which gave a view of his magnificent physique and a skin bluer and more burnished than any Edmund had ever beheld. Moreover, the man's hair was not dark, but of a fiery amber that surrounded his head and shoulders like a sunburst. His eyes, like those of the tigers, were sapphire. He was extraordinarily handsome, overpoweringly so. His cruel face was radiant with confidence and a wicked sort of tenderness as he smiled down on Edmund and stroked him. The nails of the stroking hand, were long and pointed, and the seducer's mouth almost, but not quite, concealed the two extended dog teeth, like sickle moons. Clearly, this was the demon.

"Don't get up," said the demon in faultless Inglish, with just the slightest trace of fascinating accent.

"I believe," said Edmund, "that I would rather."

"Have it your own way," said the demon.

Edmund scrambled to his feet, and retained them, swaying. The demon arose more leisurely, flexing his splendid musculature as he did so. Arrived, he towered over Edmund by at least a foot.

"Have a little wine," said the demon. "It will revive you. Old chap," he added lasciviously.

Edmund's blood was already in turbulent motion. He blushed and averted his eyes to stare about the garden-court instead.

"Is this the court of the ancient shrine?" he asked nervously.

The demon took his arm with a sensual touch, and led Edmund to a lacquer table where golden wine stood ready-poured in a gemmed cup.

"It is the shrine. Once it belonged to another. Now, I am the master here, and you are my guest."

Edmund, who felt he could do with a drink, still hesitated. Just then, a small yellow monkey leapt on the table, took the cup and held it out to Edmund.

"Oh, I say—" Edmund was captivated. He accepted the cup, and imbibed a large swallow. And choked. The demon clapped him on the back. "Strong!" gasped Edmund.

"Yes," said the demon lovingly, "but you needn't drink any more. One mouthful is sufficient to bind you in this place which is now mine. You cannot escape."

Edmund didn't bother to object to this on the grounds that a hero had no wish to escape from any peril. Whether it was necessary or not, he had another drink from the cup.

"Isn't there a treasure here?" he asked presently, looking at the demon obliquely.

"Oh, yes indeed," cried the demon. "A most valuable treasure! It is your one chance to elude me." He gave a sonorous laugh, which showed off his sickle teeth to perfection. "But don't trouble your head with it, old boy. Many have come to my home," the demon went on, taking the empty cup from Edmund's unresisting hand, "but none so alluring as yourself. I swear to you, there's no need to be afraid of me. Or rather, not yet. When the sun goes down, admittedly, there is a change in my amiable nature."

"In what way?" hiccupped Edmund, who felt rather improved by the wine.

"In this way," murmured the demon, "that I shall rip the beauteous golden flesh from your sculptured ivory bones, tear the silver hair from your deliciously modelled skull. . . . And so on. Such a pity," the demon said, tickling Edmund's neck.

Even the wine was not proof against such statements of intent.

"How long before the sun goes down?" was Edmund's not surprising question.

"An hour or two. Time enough for us to become friends."

The demon was really quite irresistible, but already a rosy glaze was on the sky, the prologue to a Darzillan sunset.

"Look here," said Edmund querulously.

"Where?" asked the demon with mild interest.

"I mean," said Edmund, "are you going to play fair and tell me what this one chance is I have to escape you and find the treasure?"

"I am bound to tell you," said the demon, "and, when the darkness comes, bound also to permit you space to seek it out—the time it takes an hour-candle to burn down. Such was laid on me by the Presence in this shrine."

Edmund's pulse galloped.

"Then—what is it I must seek?"

The demon laughed again. His teeth clashed.

"Adorable Inglish-man," he said, "I will tell you. In order to escape me, you must seek the monkey's stagger."

Edmund's eyes enlarged.

"The *what?*"

The demon was convulsed, his amusement sublime.

"The monkey's stagger."

"But—"

"Yes, yes, monkey's stagger," declared the demon, pyrotechnic with mirth.

"The monkey's stagger," said Edmund flatly.

"You do not understand?" queried the demon, clasping Edmund to him exuberantly. "It is quite plain. Unlike you, my dear fellow."

Edmund turned his head in a desperate attempt to discover, somewhere in the vicinity, a staggering monkey, and failed.

Then his senses reeled at the glory of supernatural ravishment.

The sun dived into the jungle-forest on flamingo wings. A blue evening, lit by the electric brilliance of thickly clustered Darzilla-Nyan stars, took its place in the sky.

Edmund stirred voluptuously, yawned, focussed his eyes, and saw—

A squat candle on a spike burning at the centre of the garden-court. The light wind had not blown it out, nor would it, and a few minutes of the precious hour had already trickled with the wax down its stem.

"Oh Kryst," said Edmund. He tried to pull himself together. It was difficult. What had gone before had been abrupt, and climactic in many senses. Edmund blushed as he put on his link-mail in the starlight. Then paled as he discovered his scimitar and knives had been removed.

However, panic was slow in coming. Or, at least, slower than usual. His recent experience seemed to have drained him of agitation, good or bad, and anaesthetised him slightly to dread, for the moment. Besides, it was rather odd to suppose that, having been the object of such veneration, he would later be torn limb from limb. Perhaps he might get round the demon a second time? A unique, if unsteady, vitality imbued his spirits.

Anyway, he had the clue, he thought, and he had the best part of an hour to find out what it was.

A staggering monkey.

Oh, well.

Edmund stared round the garden-court, and suddenly recalled the yellow monkey which had handed him the wine. Patently, the monkey was the key to the whole absurd thing. Did it stagger? Perhaps it had had a limp. Edmund hadn't noticed at the time. And now where was the little beast?

Edmund searched the garden thoroughly, poking behind the statuary and among the woven stalks of flowers. Above, the star-gilded roofs of the shrine went up around the court. Of course, the monkey might be anywhere, even aloft, tittering in its sarcastic paws at Edmund. He must find an enticement that would draw it to him: Food. Which meant, in turn, he must locate the shrine kitchens.

He faced the double doors that led from the court into the shrine, wavered, then marched forward.

Fronting the garden-court was a large chamber, the temple-hall of the building. It was lit by tapers in porphyry dishes of oil. No other attention had been paid it, save one. Where the religious pictures were painted on the columns or inset in the walls, something had scratched them over with a steel rake—or with long pointed steely claws. Edmund began to shake from head to foot, and made haste to vacate the area, having first armed himself with one of the

dished-tapers against the pitch black beyond the hall—
not prudence, more a hysterical fear of the dark.

A succession of closets opened from the temple-
hall, the tiny cells of the priests who had once dwelt
there. These were littered by musty books and
mouldering parchments. When steps led downward,
he took them hopefully, through skeins of cobwebs
and festoons of dust, trusting he would be led into
the kitchens or store of the shrine. At every movement of his sandals on the stairs, weird echoes whirred
up. Otherwise the shrine was as quiet as what Edmund found himself thinking more and more of—a
grave.

At length he stumbled into a square refectory of
broken benches and tables, and, in a side chamber,
was a store and cookhouse. It was not as he had
wished. Beetles clanked about the floor, and spiders
swung acrobatically through the air. From the only
uncracked bin, when Edmund raised its lid, huge
clouds of mildew flew up to set him coughing, sneez-
ing and cursing. When he had recovered, he saw, by
the flicker of his wretched light, the monkey seated
on the cold hearth, chewing a bit of parchment and
regarding him with interest.

Repressing a yell, Edmund began to coax the
monkey.

"Nice monkey, pretty monkey, come to Edmund—
oh, damn!" This, as the monkey sprinted past him.
"Oh, damn and blast it to hell," Edmund elaborated
as, pursuing the monkey, he witnessed it bouncing
crazily over the broken benches. One thing was sure,
it hadn't got a limp. With one gargantuan bound it
catapulted itself out through a door at the far end of
the refectory. Wildly, Edmund catapulted himself
after it.

The door gave on stairs that wound upwards. It

must be a route back to the topmost storeys of the building. The monkey cavorted up the stairs, occasionally glancing over its shoulder to ascertain if Edmund was still in tow. Demonstrably, the monkey thought this was a game. Edmund assured the monkey it was not. The monkey chittered and dashed on.

At last the stairway ended in a corridor.

Edmund was gasping for breath by now; in contrast, the monkey was at the peak of its performance. Navigating the final stair, Edmund missed his footing, reeled and brought up against the wall of the corridor. As he slumped there, panting, he had an idea. Perhaps it was not that the monkey *did* stagger, but that it *would*, some time in the future. No doubt there was some prophecy involved, such as: *When the monkey staggers, the demon will die.* And though the animal was agile, even its mercurial feet might be betrayed, as Edmund's had on the stair. Or even—he cast a sharp glance at the simian, which was riotously somersaulting on a carved rafter—could it be that he, Edmund, was supposed to stagger it personally? Thereby causing some obscure magic to be released and vanquish the forces of evil. Then again, the demon had told him the treasure had to do with this staggering process. (For a wistful moment, Edmund visualized getting enough treasure to bribe a Darzillan to teach him the lingo, so he could really go native. . . .) Then the monkey was off again, and had disappeared in the black beyond the taper.

Edmund plunged after. A series of the priests' cells opened along the far wall, such as he had seen before and, having lost his quarry, he ran into each of these, searching for it. He glimpsed the usual webs and broken furniture, and the usual litter of rotting papers and unvaluable knick-knacks. But in the ultimate wall-cell of the corridor, he found him-

self face to face with an open window which looked
out on to the garden-court below. He hurried to the
window and glared straight down from it to where
the candle burned on its spike, marking Edmund's
hour of grace. And, even as he glared, the candle
sank, fluttered and went out.

Shrinking back in icy horror, Edmund turned madly
to the doorway—and confronted the monkey, who
poised there, grinning at him malevolently. Edmund
put on a lunatic burst of speed, raced for the monkey,
which successfully dodged him, and collided with the
upright of the doorway. He saved the taper, but part
stunned himself. All was surely now lost.

Then two things swimmingly occurred to him.

The simian pest had fled on up the corridor to
where a last cell stood in the adjacent wall, present-
ing a kind of cul-de-sac. From there it seemed the
beast had no farther avenue it could take to evade
him. Had he got it cornered? The second revelation
was what he had slammed his hand on, when he
crashed into the doorway. It was a rusty old knife in a
sheath of green scabby leather, and hung from a peg
fastened through the upright. Certainly, it was not as
fine as one of his own blades—bright from disuse—
but definitely it was good enough and weighty enough
to sling at a monkey and make it stagger.

Edmund unhooked the knife. The monkey was
crouched in the opening of the cul-de-sac cell. Edmund faltered.

Only a second, he faltered. The Inglish had a
reputation for a rather unrealistic and generally flawed
concern for animals. Though in a case like this, self
preservation should have triumphed—

The second proved decisive.

The monkey, as if it read Edmund's mind, not to

mention his flamboyantly upraised knife-clutching hand, rocketted into the cell, out of range.

Edmund, toting the fungoid-sheathed weapon, pelted after the monkey into the cell. And stopped with a cry.

For there, majestic and amberly luminous in the gloom, towered the handsome demon, no longer quite as handsome as before.

"Ah, my beloved Inglish-man," said the demon, half closing his sapphire eyes, half opening his appalling mouth, "you have come to meet me, and so eagerly, too."

The monkey squealed, shot itself through a convenient hole in the wall and away over the roofs of the shrine. Edmund longed to emulate it, but foresaw no opportunity. He tried to smile winsomely at the demon, therefore, and lifted his hands in supplication. At which point, something unprecedented happened. The demon's lazy eyes widened and his jaw sagged. Under his luxuriant blueness, he now blanched to the colour of an Inglish summer sky. Then, as pearly beads of sweat dappled his flesh, he burst into a flood of Darzillan, quite incomprehensible to Edmund.

Edmund's puzzlement in this direction was next augmented from another. A tingling and throbbing sensation made him glance down. He nearly dropped the knife, but somehow was prevented. Rusty no more, and with the decayed sheath sloughed from it, it was giving off a fierce white glow and singing like a kettle on the hob.

"What the?" said Edmund.

The demon cascaded to his knees.

"How did you know?" the demon muttered. "It was my joke—my genius that turned the safeguard of the shrine into its bane. Ugh, you Inglish-man—

how did you think to search for the Kwua Iss-a
Sharm?"

"Look," said Edmund, "is it this knife-thing that's
got you in a state?"

"Yes," said the demon, lying now at Edmund's
feet, and chuckling bitterly amidst his sunburst of
hair. "What else but that? A few have overcome me
by means of it, but they were my own people, of
Darzilla. The Inglish heroes—*never*! Oh, how did
you realise, Inglish-man, you must search for the
dagger of Iss?"

Edmund checked.

"You mean this knife's one of the relics of the holy
man—Ish?"

"Iss," corrected the demon feebly.

"Iss, then. It's one of the relics and it conveys
power over demons—what did the natives say—from
the energy of a man's hand giving strength to it."

"Yes," said the demon, in a fading voice. "The
Dagger of Kwua-Iss. In your hand it renders me
helpless before you."

"It does? Oh. Well, then. Where's the treasure?"

"You have it. What other treasure do you need?
You are free to leave the shrine, no spell of mine can
detain you now. And if you take the Dagger with
you, no other demon can withstand you any more
than I. For Kwua Iss had power over us all and the
relics likewise."

"If it's that effective," objected the sceptical Edmund,
"why didn't anyone else take it away who found it?"

"Those that escaped through its application were
Darzillan. Darzillans do not seek such an all-embracing
hold over their demons. They are able to answer our
riddles, for there have always been safeguards set on
us by priests, clues we are obliged to give, which a
Darzillan can comprehend. But not the damned

Inglish!" howled the demon, frustratingly grinding his teeth and claws on the floor. "The Inglish can never outwit us, because they don't speak our language."

"I do wish you'd explain," said Edmund, but with an ounce or two of affection in his tone, for he was safe, and after all, the demon had rather endeared himself to Edmund previously.

After some elaborate prompting, the demon did explain. It gave Edmund considerable food for thought.

Edmund didn't bother to collect his scimitar and knives. He didn't think he would require much else besides the Daggar of Kwua Iss. He bade the demon farewell, almost with regret, but when he stroked the demon's amber hair, the demon said, in Darzillan, a particular sentence that plainly meant *push off*, or words to that effect. Nothing daunted, for once, Edmund strode out of the shrine and into the world, with a hitherto unknown bravura in his step. And when the sun rose, he did not feel his accustomed sinking of the heart at another day of terrors begun.

Edmund became famous, as a tamer of demons, naturally, but also as the first Inglish hero to press for the Inglish families on Darzilla to learn the Darzillan tongue—even though it meant allocating vast portions of their wealth towards bribing the natives to tutor them.

"I survived the demon's shrine," he would modestly recount, "through pure luck. I found the Dagger of Iss by chance, not even aware I should be looking for it. A Darzillan speaking Darzillan would have known from the start."

As Edmund went on to say, centuries before, Iss had laid a spell on the shrine which forced the demon to inform his victims that their single hope of survival was in finding the Kwua Iss-a Sharm. However, if the victim were not a Darzillan but a foreigner who only spoke another language, the demon had to translate the words concerning the clue of the Dagger exactly into that language, so the foreign victim should grasp as fully as a native where his promise of rescue lay. Which probably worked very well in a hundred languages, but not in Inglish The demon himself soon got the ironic point of the jest, and doubtless installed the relevant beast on the premises in order further to mislead.

It was this way, as Edmund was fond of relating. In the Darzillan tongue 'Sharm' meant Dagger, and Iss-a was simply the possessive version of the name— Iss apostrophe, or Iss'. However, the precise translation of 'Kwua' in Inglish was Monk. Every Inglish hero who entered the shrine thought he was being instructed to seek the Monkey's Stagger. But, in fact, of course, it was the Monk Iss' Dagger.

Statistics show that the Inglish on Darzilla are now bi-lingual, and the demons have retired underground.

dock to see what had come in, and to talk with some
of the captains. He is a handsome young man, blond
as Apollo, and with the easy gracious manner of the
true nobleman, and a natural charm, capable of cap-
tivating anyone he has a mind to. His father lets him
do much as he pleases, for Lysias never yet did
anything in the city to send trouble or dishonour on
the house. His friends are of the best, his pleasures
intellectual and athletic bring him credit, and if other
pleasures are indulged, then these are carried on
with discretion and good taste. A model son, and no
harm in that. There are enough fathers in the city
with sound reason to curse fortune on this score. For
myself, the family has always been good to me.
Generally, I am treated as freeman more than slave.
Being myself old and grizzled and childless, nor likely
ever to get a child, having passed the age for such
inclinations, I admit I love my Master's boy, as if he
were in part a son of mine. And I, too, have taken a
pride in him, from the day he cut his first man's
tooth, to the day he rode back from his first hunt, a
man indeed. And I know my Master says to someone,
if ever Lysias has done some extra thing of merit, as
when he took the prize for the chariot-racing, last
spring, "Go tell old Tohmet. It will please him."

As we went by the slave-market, then, the men
were calling out the virtues of the wares, as usual.
Noise, and a smell of perfumes and sweats washed
round me, but I was figuring amber accounts on my
slate as I rode, and looked nowhere else. Until Lysias
said quietly to me: "Look, Toh. Look at that."

Then I looked. So I saw. About ten paces from us,
Skiro, who styles himself The Traveller, was selling
off a troop of girls. They were all shapes and sizes
and complexions, and some I felt sorry for, wilting
and weeping in the hot sun. But foremost, as my

eyes came round to her, was one not like the others. I have seen the blood now and then, and knew it before I remembered its name, and first I took her for an Egyptian, though she was too little. For she was short; she would stand no higher than my chin, and as I later saw, the top of her head reached only to my Young Master's heart, and only so far in high Samian sandal heels. But despite her lack of stature, she was well-made, though not slender—her breasts were full and her hips wide, yet her waist, made all the smaller by its contrast, looked narrow as a stem. Like a sand-glass she was, and her skin was olive, but very pale, and round her to her feet, which were long and slim and pretty, poured thick-curling hair of the bluest-black. The sort of hair which is called The Hyacinth, for its blue tinting, and its little curls that resemble clustered petals. Out of the hair looked a face of exquisite beauty that no man, even an old man such as I, would not glance at a second time, and maybe keep his eyes on her much longer. And in this face, two large eyes, staring away beyond us all, so for a moment, I wondered if she were blind.

Skiro, The Traveller, noting Lysias had stopped, now began to bow and call winningly to him.

"Beautiful sir, come closer. Let me show you a rare wonder."

Lysias smiled, and half turned as if to ride on, and it seemed he could not. Abruptly, he swung off his horse, threw the rein to me, and went over to where Skiro was grinning and nodding.

"Only touch her," said Skiro. "Her flesh is like a lily, her hair is like silk, her mouth—"

"Is like a rose. Yes, Skiro, I know," said Lysias good naturedly. But he did put out one hand, gently— his courtesy extends to all—to smooth a strand of her hair.

"But if you would behold something wonderful," said Skiro, "look in her eyes."

"Seas to drown the senses?" hazarded Lysias.

"An enticing phrase. May I use it? But no, this is something unique. This is a mark of the gods. Bend close, and look."

So Lysias leaned near her, and looked at her eyes. And presently he exclaimed softly.

"Tohmet, come see this."

A child on the look-out for coins had run up, so I gave the reins to him, got off my donkey and went over. It seemed a curious matter to make a business of, a woman's eyes, and again I pondered my notion of blindness.

When I was near enough, my Young Master stepped aside, and Skiro leeringly invited me. The girl stood quiet and still, but she blinked once, and I realized after all she could see me. When I put my face near hers, as I must to see the odd phenomenom, whatever it might be, I experienced a vague yet physical feeling I could neither locate nor put a name to, nor could I tell if it were pleasant or otherwise. Next instant, I found what Lysias had exclaimed over. Sometimes, I have seen strange marks in the eyes, frecklings, or differing colours, and once I knew a man in whose right eye the dark centre was cloven in two parts. But in the girl there was a stranger thing. For her eyes were both like two flowers of dark blue petals, raying out from the black centre. Nor was this an uncertain effect, but very clearly drawn. The coloured portion, which in all others I have ever seen, man or woman, is round, was in her, split, in each eye the same, into seven petal-like segments. One must go close to see, but being close, it was not to be missed.

I straightened slowly, staring, and she staring back

and through me and away beyond me, and the market, and beyond the world it almost seemed. And I knew in that moment I did not care for her eyes, or for her, and the feeling I felt at her nearness to me I did not like, either, and I stepped back three or four paces from her.

"Well, Toh. You're the scholar in our house. What does such a thing mean?"

My Young Master was obviously entranced. As I fumbled, Skiro replied: "It is the sign of Aphrodite, of Ishtar—the morning star, like a flower. The sign of Love."

Lysias laughed.

"Which means, you ask a high price."

"Sir, she is not merely lovely, but accomplished. She can play upon the Egyptian harp, the Lydian lyre."

"And does she sing, too?"

"That she does not do."

Something prompted me, and I said to Skiro:

"With my Master's permission, I'd ask you if she has a voice at all?"

Skiro faltered.

"Well, sir," he said to Lysias, appealingly, "she does not speak languages. She has no Greek, though she understands it. Her native tongue—"

"She's dumb," I said.

Skiro scowled at me.

"*Not* dumb," he said. He looked at the girl and said, "utter, Sirriamnis, so the beautiful young lord, and his doubting slave, may hear you have a voice."

At that, she turned and looked at Lysias. Her lips, which were delicately-shaped if rather thin, parted. She made at him a low, liquid crooning. She must have been schooled to it. It was the kind of sound a woman makes in bed. When she did it, the skin prickled on my neck and scalp, alerting me. But I beheld that Lysias was roused another way. He had never owned a woman before, but his father would certainly not disallow it, rather it was the tradition of the noble houses, for paid hetairas in such a port as Crenthe are not always of the best.

And I, why did I dislike her? Her odour was fresh and pleasing. Even her breath was sweet. And yet my aversion was physical. Could it be, foolish old man, I had grown jealous of my Young Master's new interest?

I listened as Lysias haggled aristocratically over the price. He did not try very hard to beat Skiro down, for it would have been bad manners for a rich man to do so. In a few minutes it was settled, Skiro to expect payment by noon, my Master's house to take the girl in at sunset.

As we rode away up the street, Lysias was very silent. For myself, I made so many mistakes with my accounting that I gave over until we got home.

When the smoky redness of the sunset filled the house, and they began to light the lamps, one of Skiro's boys brought the slave to the gate. I watched her as she crossed the courtyard, and as she passed beneath the fig tree which grows there, its shadow turned her all a velvet black, and I shuddered and called myself an idiot.

That night, my Master, Lysias' father, had her in to play during dinner. We do not keep the Latin custom here, and the women of the house do not eat with the men, would think themselves insulted to be asked. The only female company during supper is that of a singer or dancer, although this is usually when there are guests and I am not present. Seated in the thick golden light of the lamps, the gold flying off the strings of the tall Egyptian harp with the well-wrought notes, her hair flooding about her, and dressed with white flowers, she was clearly an asset to the household. I could tell, Lysias thought himself very cunning, and my Master was not displeased, saying things such as: "When Kaimon comes to dine, I will borrow her from you," and so on. Another time, I would have been tickled, but not now. And when my Master turned to me, and said something about her beauty, I had to lie for wisdom's sake, a thing I have seldom had to do in this house.

I do not know if Lysias had already lain with her, but I do not think so. To snatch the sweet before supper would have had little propriety, and no finesse. But he went off early to sleep, and my Master chuckled, and called me to stay with him for a game of Jackal and Dog on the painted board.

"These young men, eh, Toh? The blood is hot. We must have some thoughts of marriage, next year, and it's a hard fact, there are few eligible girls bred to the looks of such as that Egyptian hussy."

"I think she may not be an Egyptian, sir."

"Is that so? Now you mention that, it comes to me the harp was not quite of the Egyptian fashion."

I considered the harp, when I should have been considering my first move of the game, and after a while it came to me there had been a bar across the lower body of the harp. It was more like the kinnor of the east—and then I remembered Skiro had mentioned Ishtar in his praises, the Semitic Venus.

"Where is she from then, Toh?" My Master asked me, when I had made my very poor pass with my jackal. "You can name races and a man's blood better than any other I ever knew."

"I am thinking of Assyria," I said. Yet that, too,

was not exactly the geography I sensed in her lines, her aura, if you will.

"Assyrian? No wonder she will not talk. Their speech is like the hissing of snakes, the cackling of geese. She'll never get her tongue round honest Greek. They never can get it right."

We played on, and I lost. Nor was it from politeness.

After midnight, I walked out on the roof of the house in the cool. I could not sleep, or think of sleep. I looked at the stars, the dark buildings under me, the dark city, its lamps mostly out, and far away the wink of starlight and a thin moon on the sea. My eyes are still very good, though I have paid for my years in teeth.

My Young Master's window is away at the end of the courtyard, looking upon the fig tree and the marble cistern. I was a little embarrassed to find my eyes had strayed to that window. The hour was a late one. Most probably by now he had had his fill and put her out. He was to go hunting tomorrow, and would need to be awake before dawn. But some fixed, though unexplained, idea kept my eyes on the unlit slot of the window, and suddenly something moved there. My heart started, my tough old heart that is one of the soundest parts of me. At first I could not make out what it was at the window, and I had a weird fancy it was some sort of bird beating its wings up and down there. Then sense came to me, and I deciphered. Pushed through the slim holes of the ornamental grille, were two forearms, two wrists, two hands. It could be none but she, the slave-girl Sirriamnis. Though wide-hipped, full-breasted, her ankles and her wrists were slender, and her hands narrow. What then were the motions she made, as if she signalled to someone out in the night? I looked swiftly beyond the west wall of the house. A wild

garden grows there, about a ruined shrine which is
no longer tended. Could it be some illicit lover lurked
down there, looking for signals from the house? But
no one stirred in the garden, or in the alley beyond.
There was, else, only the sky she might make her
gestures to, the sky and the young moon. When I
had thought that, I grew uneasy, uneasy upon
uneasiness. Girls who reverence Artemis are often
dubious, since she prizes virginity and dislikes most
mortal love, unless it be between woman and woman,
man and man. But then I recalled Skiro's talk of
Ishtar, who is also a goddess of moon and morning
star, but is a voluptuary for all that.

The hands at the window went on and on, tirelessly
dancing to the moon over the sea, as they had tirelessly skimmed the kinnor at supper. And the conviction began oddly to grow on me, that though her
race was Semitic, its location was not in the east, or
no longer, and the lunar deity she worshipped was
not Ishtar, the Courtesan. And then, between one
breath and another, it came to me, her origin and
her blood. Her land lay over westward, on the African coast. The hub of her land was that trader city,
Cartago, in the Latin tongue—Carthage, the port of
blue-red dyes and ivory, proud genius of the seas,
birthed out of the colonies of Tyre. And the goddess
there, the Lady of the City, who ruled the moon and
the star, ruled also darker things and older things,
the daughter of that ancient god who drank the
blood of small children, or else mouthed them in
fire. Not Ishtar, but Tanit.

Her hands had stopped, as if she heard my
thoughts. Perhaps, in some formless way, she did. I
was glad she could not get her face by the iron
lattice, which is there to prevent robbers. She could
not get her face by it, and so see me, this Phoenician

slave with her star-flower eyes, who worshipped the moon-witch and the darkness.

Next morning, I had some business to see to in the library, and was on my way there when I met young Mardian, who is Lysias' body-slave. Mardian is a handsome youth, of farm-stock, but with the eye-catching Persian strain in him, and more than half in love with his master; I believe he would die for Lysias if the need arose. But he has a free tongue, has Mardian, for, being beautiful, he has seldom had it checked. Stopping me between the pillars in the shade-walk, he said slyly:

"Lysias made fine music last night, with the Egyptian. And no, I did not listen, but saw the evidence with my eyes this morning."

"What evidence?" I demanded sternly.

Mardian laughed, and lowered his lashes like a girl.

"When I dressed him at sun-up for the hunt, I saw she had scored him all down the back, with her nails."

I told Mardian to keep such bawdy news to himself, and went to brood over the accounts amid the scrolls in the library. But having finished there, I could not rest, and wandered, listening closely to the gossip of the house. I know very well it is sometimes the fashion for lovers to mark each other, in the eastern way, but I did not think it proper for a slave so to mark her lord, and I wondered he had let her, and not punished her. A slight punishment would have done, to be sure, but even small reprimands are spoken of, and all I heard of her, aside from Mardian's tale, was that she bided in the women's quarters, and that the other girls, those that had no household duties, were glad of her for she played music all day, and so

entertained them—all but one who had a child at
suck, and said the foreign melodies soured her milk.
"But Kryse is envious of any new girl. And the Egyptian will be playing so she can dream of her home,"
said the cook, as he sliced oranges and livers for the
evening meal. Everyone of them now called her the
'Egyptian', even my Master, who thought her Assyrian.
Only I knew better.

Lysias came home from the hills in the afternoon,
covered in dust and blood—the beast's, not his own,
though I never like to see it, and many do not, for it
is like an omen. He gave only a few words to me: "A
bad day's work. Two dogs killed, Toh." He had lost
none of his own, at least, for the three of them
trotted in at his horse's heels, though their tails were
down like wooden handles. Lysias called for the bath
and went off to it, but presently, when I looked
about for him in the shade-walk, where usually he is
to be found with some of his friends at that time of day,
when he is home, there he was not. And I did not
really need Mardian, slipping by, to say to me, "You
cannot discuss the price of amber with him now. He
is with *her*."

I began now to be angry with myself. I could see
Mardian was jealous of the slut, and I accused myself
of something of the same kind. A powerful and
unpleasant mood was growing on me, like the heaviness some feel before a storm. Come, old man, I
thought. He will do as he wishes. She is new and she
stirs him, and that is good, for he is young and
strong, and would you have him otherwise? What
does it matter if she acts moon-rites? In her country,
that is religion, and perhaps it is to her credit that
she is pious. But such musing did not comfort me.
The memory of her hands at the window drove me,
after a while, to the kitchen, which has a small walled

courtyard, and in the wall a wicket gate which gives on the wild garden, and thus the alley.

To my surprise, I found one of the hounds there before me, eagerly sniffing at the gate. It is the entrance to which traders come, and in the kitchen court sometimes there is slaughtering. I thought a piece of offal must have been dropped, and was astonished the dog wanted it, for they are well fed after hunting, and trained not to be greedy.

When I had the wicket open, however, the dog shot through like a spear, ignored the worn path in from the alley, and plunged among the dry tall grasses of the garden. With my sense of heaviness and dread absurdly increasing, I walked after the dog.

A low, broken wall bounds most of the garden. Tamarisk trees stand there, which some nights are strung with glowing necklets of fire-flies. The shrine itself is little more than rubble, the plaster roof having fallen in more than a hundred years ago. The dog ran among the stones and the hedge of tamarisk and vanished. At that, I began to call to him, and he did not come out, though he is normally obedient. Then, when I, too, had come among the tamarisk shadow, I saw him again, pawing at a piece of stone, growling softly, his tongue lolling and spit running off it—and for a moment I checked, wondering if he had the madness, for there was surely nothing there. "Gently, Achilles," I said to him, as I came up. "Are you growing as stupid as I, and you a tenth my age?" And then I looked where Achilles pawed, and there was something there after all, of a sort.

The stone had a flat top, smoothed by weather, and it was drawn all over with a crowd of little signs. There were those which were like the crescent moon, and others by them that were circular as the moon at full. There were also stars of four, six and seven points. And another sign, like a human figure with its arms outstretched. But in the centre of the stone was a hand print, a small, narrow hand, the thumb and the little finger stretched outward in an unnatural way, the three middle fingers almost together: the print of a hand like the distorted form of a lotus. . . . These things were bizarre, and I did not care for them, but even less did I care for the ink she had used to write her symbols. It was brown now, as old blood always is. No astonishment then that the dog had snuffed at it, though his excitement still puzzled me. I had a vision of her as I stood there. I saw her stealing forth in the hour before dawn, after Lysias had sent her away. I saw her steal into the garden, passing through the tall grasses like a ghost in the twilight. The previous deity of the shrine would mean nothing to her, but that it had been holy ground, perhaps that might. Often there is something bloody to be found in a kitchen. She had dipped her hand in it before she went out, or caught some in a vessel and taken it with her. I did not relish such thoughts, and went back, calling the dog roughly. This time, he came.

When I came into the main courtyard, Mardian was sitting under the fig tree, burnishing Lysias' hunting spears. As soon as I saw Mardian, a horrible thought came to me, with no warning at all. I paused for several heartbeats, arguing with myself, gathering myself, before I could go up to him and say, "Mardian, do you recall what you told me of, this morning?"

"What did I tell you, Tohmet? That you are waxing fat? Was I so saucy as to say such a thing?"

"I will box your slim ear with my fat fist," I said, as a matter of course. Then: "You told me the slut had clawed her master's back."

"Oh ho," said Mardian, smiling his velvet smile, "so that spices you, does it?" Then he took in my face, and said, "What is it, Toh? I only joked. Why do you look sick?"

"Only tell me this," I said. "Had she drawn blood?"

"Blood? Yes, and to spare. And so had he. There was blood on the covers. She was a virgin, the Egyptian, and my Master the first to have her."

I dropped back when he said that, not sure if I was relieved, or if this made things darker. For she had surely used her own maiden's blood to paint the stone.

"Best go in, out of the sun, Tohmet," said Mardian.

Overhead, beyond the fig tree branches, beyond the lattice, there came a low, wordless moan, a woman's sound. Both Mardian and I turned at it. He blushed and lowered his eyes. I went cold to my bones. I had heard the sound, or others like it, often enough. But I thought of the marks her hands had left, of the hands themselves thrust through the lattice, and I was afraid, with no true reason. But I knew I would rise early tomorrow, and the morrow after, every morrow if I must. I would wait in the kitchen yard. I would spy on her, if she returned that way, and certainly she would. I would find out her purpose, beyond paintings in blood. There would be one.

She did not make music that evening at supper, though my Master asked for her. Lysias turned and said something quietly to him, and my Master replied, "Sometimes, a young man with his first female slave may be too lenient. She is not your wife, to earn this consideration." Lysias reddened, a thing he does not often do. I did not know if it was from anger or shame.

I did not sleep, even for three breaths that night. When the dawn twilight began to come, I went out and waited in the kitchen yard, in the shadow of two walls' corners.

The world was very still in that place, though at the edges of my hearing I could make out the city astir below. Yet it seemed that here there was a lacuna where no sound came, or where no sound meant anything or had any power. And with the stillness and the grey-blue light, I began to feel a horrid icy dread, far worse than any dread I had felt the day before. I do not think I could have moved, either to follow her if she had come, or to run away. Then I noted the dawn star hanging like a blurred jewel, low down in the sky. And I commenced superfluously to pray for the sunrise, for the warmth and the light of day. It seemed to me, the Phoenician had summoned something from the night and from the twilight, and also from herself, something which had never touched this spot before. But now it had come there, walked there, *dwelled* there.

The sun did come up, at last, without my encouragement. Shivering, I went back into the house. I was angry with myself once more, and berated myself for an elderly child, falling into imagining things, and calling up horrors for himself. The girl was no magician, simply strange, as in some peoples it is racially usual to be strange. But I had no need to join her in her antics. I would keep an eye out for her, that was wise. But to creep round the chill corners of the house in the dawn, and sense coldness creeping from the ether, that was to become her accomplice.

But I did not get far with myself. And when I met with Mardian that day, I hastened by, nervous of what he might tell me, this time.

Many days went by then, many days, and their sistering nights. There is little to note of them. Perhaps no other but I could have seen any change in the house. Indeed, none but I seemed conscious of it. For the rest, they treated affairs separately, as they affected only themselves. The cook sulked that Lysias no longer ate heartily of his carefully prepared dishes. One of Lysias' closer companions, a very noble young man whose father is of high standing, came with his slave to inquire after Lysias' health, and Lysias sent him off with a courteous joke or two, but did not go with him. My Master even, remarked, "I shall be glad when this Egyptian-Assyrian torch has burned itself out," but no more.

And the girls of the house were sorry that Lysias no longer flirted with them. And even his sisters had discreet, cruel words to trade about the slave-girl. In the women's quarters, the women had now all apparently grown jealous of her, nor did she play music for them any more. The girl Kryse's baby was sick, and she had begun to mutter. An Egyptian trader who came to the house about this time, and from whom all the ladies of the house bought unguents and ornaments, remarked we should have trouble among the women soon, from that one bitter orange on the tree. For sure, *he* knew she was not of his people.

Then one morning Mardian was weeping in the shade-walk. Trying to conceal his tears in indignation, he blurted to me: "He beat me."

"Then you will have been negligent and deserved it," I said, though without much conviction, for in the matter of his master, Mardian is always diligent.

"No," he said now, "I had not deserved it. He was at his bath, and I saw the bitch had clawed him again. I said: I did not know you had gone hunting lions. And he turned and struck me. And when he came from the bath, he beat me with the rod. Five blows. I shall be scarred for ever."

He showed me the stripes, and they were light enough. His fine flesh would not be scarred at all. Yet having reassured him, I was myself perturbed. For Lysias had never before corrected any offence with the rod, though it is his right. And though Mardian had been insolent I have overheard these two, who though master and slave are much of an age, exchange badinage of a rougher sort, when no other was by.

Perturbed then, not amazed. Indeed, not amazed, though I have no doubt my grey head grew more grey. Least of all, did I like the way Lysias had become in himself. It was not that he was sick, nor that he looked sick, nor pale, not that he had become listless or tired swiftly; only his appetite seemed less, which in a young man generally so active was uncommon. No, it was nothing singular, or particular. And yet, something in his stride, which no longer had any spring to it. In his manner of reclining, of standing, even in such small things as these. . . . It seemed to me he moved now without the quick urgency of youth, as if all his eagerness had centred solely upon one object, and that was Sirriamnis. His eyes also were changed. They had begun to have a far-off look in them as if he gazed away into some other landscape, dimly seen beyond this one—*her* look, almost like blindness. I wondered he had come back sufficiently, from whatever weird country she was leading him to, that he should think to beat Mardian.

And then again, there was the sense of some other thing, some dark bloom upon the house, and only I felt it. Mostly at night it would steal upon me, and I would not let myself get up and walk about, knowing where my steps would lead me. I did not know what she did, or if she did anything at all, but if I should sleep, and I did not often sleep at that time, then I would dream of shadows. Shadows which slid down a wall into a courtyard, slid through the house, slid from the kitchen wicket into the garden of the ruined shrine. Curious, these shadows were, for they were very small, smaller by far than a woman, even a woman so little in stature as the Phoenician. And once or twice I think I dreamed of that old god who drank the blood of children, and I would see a moon white hand, held awkwardly in the form of a lotus, and blood ran down its fingers to the wrist. And always there was foreboding in me, growing, day and night, like a vine of ivy, stifling me. Until that afternoon, following Mardian's beating, when, going in the library, I found Lysias there before me.

It had become a rule that if he was at home, he would be with the woman in his chamber. He looked up and saw my expression before I could smooth it, and he laughed. For the moment of a moment, then, he was Lysias once more, and then the uncanny difference drew over him again, like a wave.

"It startles you to see me here, Toh. That says little for my studious nature."

"Excuse me, sir. I had thought—"

"Had thought I would be occupied. There are days when the gods insist on abstinence. I'm afraid my temper has been short today, and I beat poor Mardian. I do not think I marked him. It would be a pity if I had. He's as proud of his skin as a girl."

"No, sir, you have not marked him."

Lysias smiled, and we spoke of the dialogue in the scroll he was reading. All the while I was thinking: There is only one reason he would abstain from her.

It is her woman's time. And this made me shiver, and I could not have said why, except for the dreams of blood and shadow, and the blood she had used to draw on the stone. It was not until supper time, when I saw the moon come up over the hills beyond Crenthe, that I recollected it was at its first night of fullness—the same night that she was purged of her fullness of female blood.

That evening at supper, I could eat little. My Master asked how I did, seeing me wave plates aside without selecting from them. I told some tale or other. Meanwhile, as I pecked and played with the food, my Young Master, for once, ate as heartily as if after a hunt.

Later, when I had taken myself to my bed, I lay and the thoughts came and went.

Eventually I rose as if I must, and went out quietly into the heart of the night. I could smell the scent of jasmine, of the day-burned walls cooling, and of the figs ripening on the tree. The stars shone, the moon had moved over towards the west, but her bloodless rays struck hard on everything, as if to suck the life from it. I had never been aware before, of that nature of the moon's, which is like that of a cold, white sun. The sun's other self, perhaps, the sun of the dead. Such fancies I hid as I stole across the courtyard.

I went swiftly to the second yard, by the kitchen. I had awaited her there before, and she had not come. Yet tonight I knew that she would. How did I know? Because she was a worshipper of Tanit, that lady of dark things and of the darkness' eye, the moon, now at full. And because her condition kept her from my Young Master's bed, which left her free to wander the night as she willed. Logic therefore instructed me. Yet I think I would have gone to that place to wait, to feel of the night, if I had been blind and not seen the moon, if I had been deaf and did not know she was not to be with Lysias. It was my skin which saw, my bones which heard, and both quaked, yet I walked to the spot and stood there in the shadow between two walls' corners, still unsure if I should have the strength to follow her, or to fly from her—and presently, like a spirit, Sirriamnis passed.

It was like my dreams of her, though much darker than in my dreams. Her black hair mantled her, and some black cloak she had wrapped herself in. No sooner was she through the wicket, than she slunk aside among the grasses and the tamarisks. And she vanished, blackness into blackness.

I, on stiff, numbed limbs, had set about following her, despite my fears. If she had turned about at any point, however, I cannot say what I should have done. But it did not seem likely. I had glimpsed something of her face as she went by me, and it was the face of one who is not wholly in the body, the face of the tranced, or the possessed. I had expected nothing else, though I had thought it horrible enough.

On her vanishing, I hesitated, then pressed on, through the tamarisks, reckoning to find her the far side of them and taking pains with my stealth. I ventured first to look out from among the boughs. There, not seven paces before me, stood the tumbled, flat-topped stone where she had drawn. About stood others, none much higher than the back of a dog. Beyond was the ruined shrine, roofless and hollow. But nowhere in the vista could I discover the woman. There was no place for any grown creature to conceal itself, save they lay down on the ground, and even this would be poor cover, for the grasses were thinner here, and the moon itself pierced through and through them, like a blade through water. Truly, then, it seemed she had disappeared, a sorceress. And my chilled blood ran more lethargically, as if I were near to death.

And then—and then I saw a little quiver of movement in the grass. So, she crawled on her belly after all. What game was this, or did she know I spied on her, and sought to elude or confuse me?

Should I challenge her now, or keep still? Idle question. My tongue was swollen, my throat closed. And all the while the maddening sense of horror grew in me, and grew, and had no name.

And suddenly the eddy of motion flickered straight as invisible fire through the grass to the edge of the alley, and there it was gone. I did not see what made that rush, but certainly it was not the Phoenician. Some small night beast, it must be, or scavenging cat, perhaps. But she, *where then was Sirriamnis?*

Wretched in my dilemma, I hardly knew what I did. Nor do I properly recapture it now. But it seems I dragged myself away, groaning, I think, under my oppression and fright, and so into the courtyard where the fig tree grew. And there I crept into the shades of the branches, and sat on the rim of the marble cistern, trembling. I suppose I may have stayed a long while there, not knowing what I was at. I know that when the moon was lower, I heard a little noise, like a dry leaf blown about the court. And then, I suspect that I fathomed it, if not the heart, at least the manner of the spell, but I could not force myself to turn about and see.

When at long last I shifted myself, the court yard, of course, was empty, save for the ultimate moonlight lying in shattered plates on the walls and in the lowest branches of the tree above.

I remember I thought, most clearly, This is not your business, Tohmet. Let it alone, whatever it should be. For it is stronger than you, and older even than you, old man. Old as the moon, maybe, old as the night itself.

And thinking this, I felt myself give in, and a sort of relief came to me, as at a fever's breaking. I went back to my bed, and slept.

"Toh. There are black hairs in my Master's bed," said Mardian next afternoon.

I cursed him, being in a poor humour.

"Why tell me such a thing? They will be the woman's, will they not?"

"She was not with him. And these hairs are not hers, they are short and coarse. I did not dare say a word to him about it, for fear he'd beat me again."

"Why trouble *me*?"

Mardian came close. His face was pale and his dark eyes large and anxious.

"You do not like her, Toh. Or trust her. And—I think there is a bewitchment that has followed her. I woke in the night, in the outer room where I sleep, and there was something at the foot of my pallet, for I partly saw it—and then it was gone."

"A dream," I said.

"No dream. I smelled it."

"What smell then had this demon?" I demanded scornfully, tapping my stylus on my knee to show I had other tasks than to listen to his nightmares.

"A smell of the hills. Of grass and herbs and night."

"A smell of terror indeed."

"I heard its claws scrape on the floor."

"And its shape?"

"Small and crouching, like a frog—yet it had long straight horns. I would have cried out, but no sound would come. I could not move. When it was gone I lay awake an hour or more, rigid with fear, and thought I might die. It was an unnatural thing. It put stone on my limbs and my heart beat sluggishly. My mother told me once, before I was sold from the farm, of night things that come and go, that suck the strength from men, that eat their souls—"

I rose and shook my fist at him, and he fled.

And then I sank down, and saw night overlaid on day, the amber shadows turned to purple, the golden sun to a leprous whiteness. I thought of the Phoenician, and how she vanished among the tamarisks, of the grasses running as if with fire, of a noise like a dry leaf. . . .

I went to the kitchen. The cook was active with a goose, and feathers flew like foam. The cook was bursting with gossip, as ever. He soon spoke of Sirriamnis. "She sleeps all day through, the lazy slut, even when she has not been called to his bed. The women are afraid of her, and will not say why. They would like to harm her, but too scared of Lysias' anger to do it. Kryse's baby has a long scratch on its neck. Kryse mutters. The women blame the cat, but the cat has run away. We shall have trouble if she does not return. How will you fancy a nice plump mouse pie? I've heard in Rome it's a delicacy."

Lysias had gone riding with his friend, the noble young man who had called to inquire for him previously. Nor did Lysias come back at lamplighting, but was off at some supper in the friend's house. I thought this good. Yet I stayed abroad until midnight, and at midnight Lysias came home. Under the glare of the great moon, which again had risen in her pride, his face was pale as Mardian's. And when I rose to greet him, he went straight by me, unseeing, he who never passed without notice, and some kind word.

I had given it up, but not it seemed with my whole

heart. I sat and worried over it as a dog at a bone. What was my life, old and used, the life of a slave, against that young shining vigorous life? His father had missed it. Did I, who dared think myself almost a father to him, did I mean to leave go the thread that might decide Lysias' fate?

An hour after, I had nerved myself enough I went up silently into the lobby that opens on Lysias' sleeping room. There I woke up Mardian, nearly terrifying him from his wits.

"Hush, brat," said I. "I know you too scared to sleep, despite your snores, audible from the floor below. I've come to share the watch with you."

"It is you, Toh, who snore, not I," he said. But he had seized my hand. Awake, I saw he was indeed still afraid, and glad to have me by. But we could not light a lamp for fear of disturbance, and soon Mardian, regardless of his fears, in or in some way because of them, fell asleep again. And so I let him slumber, for it seems old men require less of this balm than the young.

I sat alone, then, by the pallet, on the floor, feeling a sort of horror at myself, and as cold as the marble. Quickly enough the moon slid sideways in through the lattice grille, and scattered patterns on the floor. I stared at these patterns, and it seemed to me I saw pictures in them, of white hands and lotuses. Then, my head nodded. I dozed in an icy, drug-like stupor, just as Mardian did, afraid, yet unable to resist the tide of sleep which somehow fastened on the tide of fear and came in with it.

In a while, I felt it pass like a breeze along the floor.

I felt, too, that it looked at me, and in some way I saw the light caught, low down, in its eyes, flat and colourless. And then it had gone by. My relief at its

going was very great, for now I might sleep safe
from harm. But then I dimly recalled where it would
be proceeding—the chamber of my Young Master.
The curtain rings whispered at just that instant, and
I knew it had slipped by the curtain and was in the
room with him. Ah, but it was no business of mine.
For what were they to me, these lords of the house, I
their slave, and considered less than a man, a clever
animal that could do sums. . . . But then I heard him
moan, just once, but frantic and deep, my boy, my
Lysias, and I came alert as if I had been struck in the
face. Those thoughts I had been having, they came
from the enchantment, the air-borne night-borne
poison of her spell. I shook them from me, and I got
to my feet as if I raised myself through clinging
mud, and I went towards the curtain as the little
thing had done.

I have heard men say that to be often in great
pain, as from an old wound, is in the end to grow
accustomed to such pain, and thus, while suffering
from it, to continue with other deeds in full concen-
tration. And so it had come to be with me, I think.
That dreadful clinging horror, which I had now felt
so often, and which I felt at this hour as if my life's
blood ran out of me, did not halt me, did not prevent my taking hold of the curtain and quietly step-
ping through. Nor did I flinch at standing there in
the full glare of the moon's eye, a glare eased only by
the window grille and the branches of the fig tree
which came between yet could not stop the light
from seeping through, like some deadly corrosive,
into the room. And so I stood, unarmed by any
weapon, as generally a slave will not be armed, or by
any sorcery of my own. And this, in the white wild
light, is what I saw.

Lysias lay out on the bed, naked and fine-made as

any bronze of a sleeping youth, for sleep it seemed
he did, though now and then he turned his head,
and his hands clenched and loosened, yet he did not
wake; it appeared only that he dreamed. Along his
ribs was a thin dark glistening line like a narrow
ribbon, but it was a narrow scratch some thin honed
implement had made, a little blade, or a long claw,
and it bled. At first, I took the heap of darkness for
the bunching of the cover, or some trick of shadow,
but it was neither of these, for all at once there came
again that flat glowing of the two discs which were its
eyes, and slowly, slowly, like the petals of a flower, I
beheld the two straight horns rising upward until
vertical upon its head.

I believe my heart did pause. To add fresh fear to
the old was quite impossible, I seemed rather to
disintegrate, to crumble, or maybe to petrify instead,
as men did who faced the gorgon Medusa. And
then—then my senses came back in a dazzling race,
and I almost cursed aloud. For I saw, at last, what
the thing was which was crouched on my Young
Master's body. It was a hare.

Black as night, and smooth as velvet, its eyes gleaming soullessly and its two tall ears, that were not
horns at all, raised up on its head to catch the sound
of me. There was another sound, too. Very soft, a
tiny modest mouthing sound, as of a child at suck.
And at this sound, I froze again, and my eyes, which
were already starting, strained wider.

I thought an instant that, having scratched him,
the black hare drank from the trickling cut, milking
Lysias of his blood. But quickly I saw the milking was
of another order. Crouched against his groin, it had
taken the organ of his manhood into its mouth, and
worked on it, like some terrible uncanny harlot.

If I had kept motionless till then, if I had been

petrified, now I gained a new layer of stone. The teeth of a hare, though square and uncarnivorous, are sharp as razors from the vegetation it must feed on. Now it mouthed him. But if it should bite—it would make a eunuch of him for sure, and most likely kill him too.

And so I must stand, and must oversee the foul, unnatural act, afraid to move either into the room or out of it. Though I would have wished to run forward and seize the monstrous beast and crush its neck in my hands. And so I stood, and so I watched, like the pimp who regards his whore and her customer from behind the screen, getting his delight by what is done by them. Though I had no delight in it. Rather I shook all over and nausea came in my throat, but I thrust it down, frightened even to retch lest I cause those two square fangs to close on what they fondled.

And for Lysias, in his charmed sleep, doubtless he dreamed of some wholesome pleasure. Presently his quickened breathing broke and his back arched upward from the bed. The hare, which had never taken its eyes from me, did not take them from me now but I saw the swift movements of its throat.

As the spasm left him, Lysias fell back with a long sigh. I held my breath, waiting on what the beast would do now it had had its vampire's drink. I think I gave a quavering sob as the long mouth opened, letting go of him. The hare reared upward on its two hind limbs, and its round cold eyes seemed to flash, like two exploding moons, and then went black. Even as I staggered forward to grab for it, it sprang straight by me, and dashed through the curtain and was gone.

I did not wait for anything, not even to go to my Young Master—one glance had assured me he was unmaimed, indeed relaxed and peaceful now, and yet asleep. I stumbled out and through the lobby, not even calling to Mardian, for I did not reckon he could answer. I alone must pursue the demon, as before. For its name I knew well enough. It could be none other than Sirriamnis, and this her sorcery, which was transmogrify, the oldest and most sinister magic known to human kind. And that she had lapped his virility, his man's strength, this I knew also, for she had forced the vital fluid from him, which in the male creates the miracle of life, just as those fluids expended from the womb of the female are negative and waste.

Though far from young, I am sound in heart and wind, nor do my joints fail me. So I ran through the house and out into the courtyard, the way I knew the creature had gone. I knew also where it would be going next, in a sort of madness, I knew it, recalling how Mardian, child of farm stock that he is, had noted the smell of open hills and night-blooming herbs. The hills beyond Crenthe, that was the way it would take, the way it must have gone firstly the night before, and returned to work its obscene will in the house.

I hesitated only once, to fetch two of the hunting dogs from their sleeping place. It never occurred to me, frantic as I was, that what I did was stupid and against the laws of men. I had no mind in me but the mind which would hunt her down before the sun came and made her back into what she was not, a woman I might not slay.

The dogs were eager. They had had hares now and then, and knew the scent gladly. Usually they will harken to my whistle, so I let them run ahead. Old Tohmet trotted behind, and I am sure my eyes were as hers had been, the look of one asleep or possessed.

It was very late that white night, the city closed and silent, save for the odd riot of a drinking house by the harbour, and the occasional solitary glimmer of a lamplit window, where someone kept awake from much sickness or much health.

The dogs' feet pattered on the stones or on the hard earth of the streets, and my sandalled feet padded soft as theirs. The quarry I no longer saw, but I knew she was before us, that bitch-beast, running under the auspice of Tanit's moon, to reach some haven in the hills. As I went, a strangely pragmatic brooding came on me, and I pondered Skiro, who called himself The Traveller, and if he knew that the girl might shape-change, or if she had not had the knack till her virginity was gone, or if she might resist the shape of the hare when she deemed it not expedient—but all this was theoretical to me. I cared only for my task as her executioner.

Over on Crenthe's east side, the wall is in bad repair, with many exits and entrances, but in these times of peace the rebuilding is slow, and slight watch is kept there. This would be the way she had taken, and the way I took with the dogs. Far off on a ride, a sentry leaned on a tree, and from the look of him he slept.

The moon was almost down now, and the hills, exactly before me, darkening, but the dawn star was up, and the dawn could not be so far behind her. I had come a great way, yet felt no weariness, such is the power of hatred in a man. But now I began to despair of our coming up with her before sunrise, such a fleet thing she had become.

But even a hare may tire. As we climbed through the coarse grass and the wild flowers of the hills, clouds rose in the west and blotted up the sinking moon. Suddenly the dogs began to whine and grunt, and all at once they launched themselves towards the top of the slope, frenzied as when the quarry first starts.

I was by now weary enough I could not, despite my hating strength, put on myself any extra burst of speed. But abruptly, against the dimly lightening eastern vault of sky, I saw something running in silhouette along the topmost slant of the hill. It was the hare, and after it the dogs went pelting, yipping and snarling, their mouths stretched to rend.

I believe I, too, tried to run then, to reach them and see it done. And as I did my foot caught in a tussock of matted grass and I fell, hard and heavy, winding myself with my own brought-down bulk. As I sprawled there, it was all I could do to lift my head, but so I did. And so I witnessed the last event of that evil night, to which, if it were necessary, I would swear on the altar of any decent god.

The dogs were almost level with the hare, and knowing it, the beast leapt about. There was one moment then when I saw the hare, drawn black on the melting sky, the morning star above its long-eared head like a glistening dagger in the air. The dogs checked a second, as they will with anything at bay, but they slavered and I heard them growling. Then the growling changed to an awful whimpering noise, the kind a dog will give when he has been beaten, or torn in the hunt. Bewildered, yet I felt a sinking in my very soul. Next instant I learned that to the accustomed music or horror that hate had lulled, there could yet be added some new notes.

The hare rose up on its hind limbs, but having done as much, continued to rise up, and *continued*. I saw then a being which, if I must translate, was the

interim condition of Sirriamnis' transmogrify, that
state between beast and woman, and yet, too, was
some other thing.

I think it had a woman's body, what I could see of
it, and the long hair showered round it—yet it had a
bestial face, still, though bloated up to human size,
and the ears lifted from the head, and the hands
were blunted paws, and from these sprayed the tre-
mendous digging claws of the hare. While from its
deformed mouth came, with its black tongue, a hideous hissing, quite unlike the hissing of snake or cat.
The dogs cowered with their bellies flattened to the
hill. For me, it was as if a million ants ran over my
skin. My fear caused me to choke and shortly I lost
my senses.

The red sky of dawn was in my eyes and a leather
flask of wine to my lips, when I recovered myself. It
was none other than that guard I had taken to be
asleep on the rise. Apparently wide awake he had
seen me go by, and being speculative, when the
dawn watch relieved him, he left his place and followed me, and found me on the hill, the two dogs
cowering in the grass beside me. Of any other there
was no sign.

"Up now, ancient one, if you are able," said my
benefactor. He was a soldier, rough but not unkind,
as the wine-flask showed. He had excellent eyesight
too, and had spotted my slave-ring. "You never
thought to run off, did you? You'd not get far on
foot. And to take the dogs, too, that was a silly thing,
was it not? You're a bit simple, I expect. Nevermind
it. I think I know your house," and he named it, and
my Master. "He'll be just. Come along. I'll see you
home. You're too full of years to be sleeping on the
ground."

I did not disillusion him as to my wits. Indeed, I
had been a veritable fool, and now I saw it. For sure,
I was very shaken, too, and needed the support the
young soldier gave me through the morning streets.
He brought me direct to the gate, at which the dogs
ran in on their own. But he would not have anything
but that he should speak to my Master himself. Most
respectfully, then, the soldier offered his tale, and
handed me over to my Master like an idiot child,
adding, "I am certain you'll be understanding, sir,
for I'm sure he meant no harm."

My Master bore it all with equanimity, and even
gifted the fellow with some money, which of course
had been his hope all along. But when he had gone
whistling back to his barracks, my Master set his
hand on my shoulder and said: "Tohmet, are you
such a fool indeed? You know the law better than I
do, I should say. And to take the dogs—What were
you thinking of? Did you mean to abscond?"

"No, sir." I had been puzzling all the way back
what I should say to excuse myself, for I knew I
could not, nor would I, tell him the fantastic truth of
why I had gone out and what I had seen. That
would have made him, civilised as he is, suppose me
insane for sure.

"Come, Toh. If you've a reason, I will have it
now."

I said, "A fox, or some other beast, had come
down from the hills and was in the garden by the
shrine. The dogs made a fuss, and I took a notion to
let them out and see if they could catch it. Then they
ran off and would not answer the whistle. And I,
anxious they would be lost, went after them."

He frowned very long and hard at me, and then
he said,

"Well, I'll accept your word for that. But I never

heard a dafter tale in all my life. I would think you out after woman, if you were younger and I did not know you better." Then he took a turn over the floor, and said with his back to me, "Here is the black part of it, Tohmet. That boy from the garrison knows the house and will spread the story. The household slaves will also catch the gossip from the one that let you in at the gate. I have no choice, this being the case, but to chastise you, or they may all be—taken with a notion. Do you see how it is, Tohmet?"

I could see how it was, and that my Master had no other course; also that he was sorry for it. But I had been unwise, and like many an unwise man, had brought trouble on more than myself.

I told him I understood the matter. He answered that he must use the whip on me, according to the law, and in the courtyard where they might all see, but that he would make it three stripes rather than the number which are customary in like circumstances.

In my boyhood I had been whipped now and then, and knew the process well enough not to relish making its acquaintance again. But it was only justice, and besides, being a good deal fatter now than then, the thong would have more padding to strike on.

Nevertheless, it was a nasty time I had of it, the three brief blows seeming to go on for ever, and the pain, which grows worse as the numbing shocks of the blows themselves wear off, sickened me.

I felt my shame very keenly, too, to stand stripped to my drawers in the court, obese, elderly and a clot, fit only to be whipped. I deserved no better.

Afterward, my Master sent one of the women to see to my stripes, and a good job she made of her work, being gentle, and skilled with herbs. I was a little feverish, but I asked her, presently, if the black-haired slave was in the women's quarters. The girl answered with some surprise that certainly the Egyptian was in the house, and did I think that sly snake as addled as I to try sneaking off after foxes. It seemed Sirriamnis had made better speed home than I.

When the girl had gone, I lay on my belly, and I own I wept. It was weakness and pain, and it was anger, too. I knew well enough who was truly to blame for my beating, but I did not see how I could come near the witch anymore, to be rid of her.

I had the fever two days, but on the evening of the third, I was well enough to be sitting out in the shade walk for the cool air. As I sat, Lysias came walking between the pillars and stopped when he saw me. His face was grey and his eyes were very bright, as if he had suffered my sickness with me.

"How are you, Toh?"

"I am well, sir."

"My father had no call to lash you," he said in a low and bitter voice.

"Every call, I regret, sir. He could hardly do otherwise."

"Nonsense, man. To take the whip to one of your years and standing in the house? Never. He was wrong, and I have told him so. There have been hot words between us."

I remonstrated, reminding him of the law, and his duty to his father. Yet I could hardly help being glad too. All the while, my eyes roved about him. The nights of the moon's fullness were done, but I feared for him still as I never feared another thing all my life. Yet he looked as fine as ever he did, but for his pallor. As he went away I saw his eyes were moist, and my vanity was greatly uplifted by that, as it turned out with no cause. For when my nurse came to see to me an hour after, she brought a piece of news that almost set me fainting.

Soon after the noon meal, the Egyptian, as they still called her, and still do when they speak of her, had been overcome by a dreadful bout of vomiting. A physician was summoned, but his verdict came as no surprise. No one, judging by her symptoms, doubted she had been poisoned. Soon enough the facts emerged to light. The girl Kryse, who, more than all others thought the Phoenician a sorceress, and feared some bane had been put on her child by the witch, had obtained particular cosmetics from the Egyptian trader who had earlier come to the house. And a portion of these cosmetics, which if swallowed are invariably lethal, she had crushed and dropped in Sirriamnis' food. At sunset, wracked by ghastly contortions, and spewing blood, Sirriamnis had died.

My head spun, and I must have looked near death myself, for my nurse made a huge fuss. What I myself felt was a grim and burning joy. And with that, as I came to myself more, an urge to laugh. For I had laboured so mightily to be rid of her, and in the end it had taken only a woman's malice to see to it. And then I mused, and reasoned that maybe, since it was the shadow-magic of a female god, it would have needed another woman to accomplish the task, where a man must fail.

Lysias was not himself for a long while. He mourned his slave in private, yet as intensely as if she had been his lawful wife, the mother of his heir, one he loved as he loved himself. But he was young and healthy, and in the end they brought him round, his father and his friends, and he laughed and joked and chose spears for the hunt, and went to suppers and came home from them a little drunk, though not dishonourably so, and with flowers in his hair. And by the year's end, his father had seen to things, and Lysias was married.

She is a sweet child, his wife, with soft fair hair that falls to her waist when it it unbound, so he tells me. She loves and honours him, as a wife should, and he is very fond of her. But they have been wed well into the second year now, and still there are no children, and no promise of any.

It is general to blame the woman in such a pass. It might be the girl is barren, though her married sisters have each several sons to their credit. But, when I think of it, it is as if a cold wind blows by me, I smell the scent of the wild grass on the hills, and the three fading scars on my back flare up as if kissed with flame. I remember, nor shall I ever forget, what I saw in Lysias' sleeping chamber, the beast which crouched on him and did him that service of the harlot's, and which drank down his seed thirstily and to the last drop. It is a dream to haunt me, though only I know of it, the dream of the black hare, and the moon's blind white eye, and an eye which is a flower, and a flower which is a hand, and that mysterious goddess of the African coast, daughter to a god who only drank blood.

Nor is the house quite free of her. It is nothing I could put into words, as I have all the rest, nothing to which I could give a name. But sometimes, on the nights of the moon's fullness, or when the dawn star gathers itself in the east like a molten tear, then I would not be down by the wicket gate, nor in the courtyard by the fig tree. I keep to my bed, and though I invariably wake, I do not rise, I do not listen, I do not look, and I practice not to consider.

But I do not think she is quiet, that goddess who has been invoked here. I cannot tell myself she is appeased.

Kryse was sold as a whore for what she had done, and her child kept here, for it is a boy. So she lost it, for all she had done to keep it with her. That was her punishment, and it was harsh. And I, for my part, was whipped, but I hazard it was not punishment enough for what I tried to do.

Maybe some night I will, after all, be drawn out into the darkness, and walk into that old garden and to the stone which Sirriamnis painted with her blood. I do not like to meditate upon such things, nor to believe in them. But there are matters so dark, so deep, so ancient and so abiding, that believe them or not, still, they Are. And will Be, until the sun dies and only the moon is left in the sky, and that demon creature which surely is in all women, however gracious or kind, rises up to destroy us all.

BECAUSE OUR SKINS ARE FINER

In the early winter, when the seas are strong, the grey seals come ashore among the islands. Their coats are like dull silver in the cold sunlight, and for these coats of theirs men kill them. It has always been so, one way and another. There were knives and clubs, now there are the guns, too. A man with his own gun and his own boat does well from the seals, and such a man was Huss Hullas. A grim and taciturn fellow he was, with no kin, and no kindness, living alone in his sea-grey croft on the sea rim of Dula, under the dark old hill. Huss Hullas had killed in his time maybe three-hundred seals, and then, between one day and the next, he would not go sealing any more, not for money and surely not for love.

Love had always been a stranger to him, that much was certain. He had no woman, and cared for himself as any man can in the islands. And once a month he would row to the town on the mainland, and drink whisky, and go upstairs with one of the paid girls. And row back to Dula in the sunrise, no change to be seen in him for better or worse. Then one time he went to the town and there was a new girl working at the bar. Morna was her name. Her hair was black as liquorice, and her skin was rosy. As the evening drew to a close, Huss Hullas spoke to Morna, but not to order whisky. And Morna answered him, and he got to his feet and went out and banged the bar door behind him. It seemed she would not go with him as the other girls would. She had heard tell of him, it seemed. Not that he was rough, or anything more than businesslike in bed, but he was no prince either, with no word to say and no laugh to laugh, and not even a grunt to show he had been gladdened. "I will not go upstairs with a lump of rock, then," she said. "There are true men enough who'll pay me."

Now love was stranger to him but so was failure. And though this was a small prize to fail at the winning of, yet he did not like to fail. If he would eat a rabbit or bird for his meal, he would find and shoot one. If he baked bread it would rise. If he broke a bone, he could set it himself, and it would mend. Only the sea had ever beaten him, and that not often, and he is a foolish man will not respect the sea, who lives among her isles. Even the Shealcé, the Seal People, dropped down before Huss Hullas' gun obediently. And since he had never yet asked a free woman to take him, he had never yet been refused, till Morna did it.

When he went again to town, he went before the month was up, and when Morna came by his table, he said she should sit down and drink whisky with him. But Morna stepped sharply away. "I will not do that, neither."

"What will you do then," said Huss Hullas, "will you be got the sack?"

"Not I," said she. "The rest like me. They have cause."

"I will give you a pound more," he said.

Morna smiled. "No."

"How much, then?"

"Nothing, then." And she was gone, and presently so was he.

When he came back the next month, he brought her a red lacquer comb that had been his mother's.

"What now," she said, "is it wooing me, you are?"

"Learning your price, then," he said.

"Well, I'll not go with you for an old comb."

"It's worth a bit."

"I have said."

"For what then?"

Morna frowned at him angrily. It must be made clear, he was not a bad-looking man for all the grim way he had with him, which had not altered, nor his stony face, even as he offered her the comb. And his eyes, dark as the hill of Dula, said only: *You will do it. This is just your game.* And so it was.

It was winter by then, and all along the shore the oil-lamps burned where the electricity had not yet been brought in, and the seals were swimming South like the waves, as they had swum for hundreds of years.

"Well," said Morna. "Bring me a sealskin for a coat, and I'll go upstairs with you. That is my promise. It shall keep me warm if you cannot, you cold pig of a man."

"Ah," said Huss Hullas, and he got up and went out of the bar to find another woman for the night, on Fish Street.

The seals came that month and beached on all the islands west of Dula. They lay under the pale winter sun and called to each other, lying on the rocks where the sea could find them. On some of these bleak places it might seem men had never lived yet in the whole world, but still men would come there.

One or another rowed over to Dula and hammered on Huss Hullas' door, and he opened it with a rod and a line he was making in one hand.

"The seals are in. Are you ready, man?"

"I am."

"We shall be out at dawn tomorrow, with the tide to help us."

"I'll be there."

"So you will, and your fine gun. How many will you get, this winter?"

"Enough."

"And one for her on the mainland."

"We'll say nothing of that," said Huss Hullas, and the man looked at him and nodded. Grim and hard and black, the eyes in Huss Hullas' head could have put out fires, and his fists could kill a man, as well as a seal.

In the first stealth of the sunrise, Huss Hullas rowed away from Dula with his gun and his bullets by him. He rowed to where the ocean narrows and the rocks rise up to find the air. In the water over westward, dark buoys bobbed in the blushing water that were the neads of seals. Tarnished by wet they lay, too, on the ledges of the isles, shelf on shelf of them, and sang in their solemn unhuman way. not knowing death approached them.

There was some ice, and here and there a seal lay out on the plates of it. They watched the men in the shadowy boats from their round eyes. The Shealcé is their old name, and still they are named so, now and then, the Seal People. who have a great city down under the sea.

When the guns spoke first, the Shealcé looked

about them, as if puzzled, those that did not flop and loll and bleed. When the guns spoke again, the rocks themselves seemed to move as shelf upon shelf slid over into the water and dived deep down. The guns shouted as if to call them back, the pink water smoked and blood ran on the ice. Men laughed. It is not the way, any more, to know what you kill is a living thing. It was different once, in the old times, very different then, when you would know and honour even the cut-down wheat. Men must live, like any other creatures, and it is not always a sin to kill, but to kill without knowledge may well be a sin, perhaps.

Huss Hullas had shipped his oars, and let the current move him through the channels. He knew the islands and their rocks as he knew his own body, their moods and their treacheries, and the way the water ran. He drifted gently in among the panic of the seals, and slew them as they hastened from the other men towards him, along the ice.

Each one he killed he knew, and would claim after. Every man marked his own.

Then, as Huss Hullas' boat nosed her way between the rocks, the sun stood up on the water. In the rays of it he saw before him, on a patch of ice, one loan seal, but it was larger by far than all the others, something larger than any seal Huss Hullas had ever seen. Plainly, it was a bull, but young, unscarred and shining in the sunlight. It had a coat on it that, in the dawn, looked for sure more gold than grey. And even Huss Hullas could not resist a little grimace that was his smile, and he raised the gun.

As he did so the seal turned and looked at him with its circular eyes, blacker than his own.

Yes, now, keep still, the man thought. For to blunder in the shot and spoil such fur would be a grave pity.

Huss Hullas was aiming for one of the eyes, but at

the last instant the great golden seal lowered its head, and the bullet, as it speared away, struck it in the brain. It seemed to launch itself forward, the seal, in the same instant, and the dull flame of its body hit the water beyond the ice. Huss Hullas cursed aloud and grabbed up one of his oars. Already dead, the seal clove the water in a lovely arching dive—and was damned against Huss Hullas' wooden rower.

His strong arms cracking and his mouth uttering every blasphemy known among the islands—which is many and varied—Huss Hullas held the seal, first with the oar, next with his hands, and as the boat roiled and skewed and threatened to turn herself over in the freezing sea, he struggled and thrust for the nearest edge of rock. Here, by some miracle, he dragged the dead-weight of the seal, the boat, himself, aground, his hands full of blood and fur and the oar splintering.

He stood over the seal, until another boat came through the narrows. Frost had set the seal's dead eyes by then, as he towered over it, panting and cursing it, and the golden fur was like mud.

"That is a rare big beast, Huss Hullas. It should fetch a good price at the sheds."

"This is not for the sheds."

Taking out his knife then, he began to skin the great seal.

When he was done, he tossed the meat and fat and bones away, and took the heavy syrupy skin into the boat with him. After the other seals had been seen to, he left his share with the rest of the men. They saw the oar was ailing, and they knew better than try to cheat him.

He rowed back to Dula with the skin of the one seal piled round him, and the oar complaining.

*   *   *

The remainder of that day, with the skin pegged up in the outhouse, Huss Hullas sat fishing off Dula, like a man who has no care on Earth, and no vast joy in it, either. If he looked forward to his next visit to the town you could not have said from the manner of him. But he caught a basket of fish and went in as the sun was going out to clean and strip them and set them to cook on the stove.

The croft was like a dozen others, a single room with a fire-place in one wall and a big old bed on another. Aside from the stove there was a cupboard or two, and tackle for the boat or for the fishing stacked about, some carpentry tools, and some books that had been his father's that Huss Hullas never read. A couple of oil-lamps waited handy to be lit. Often he would make do with the light of the fire. What he did there in his lonliness, sitting in his chair all the nights of the months he did not go drinking and whoring, was small enough. He would clean his gun, and mend his clothing and his boots; he would repair the leg of a stool, cook his food and eat it, and throw the plate into a pan of water for the morning. He would brew tea. He would think to himself whatever thoughts came to him, and listen to the hiss and sigh of the sea on the rim of Dula. In the bed he would sleep early, and wake early. While he slept he kept his silence. There rose up no comfortable snoring from Huss Hullas, and if he dreamed at all, he held the dreaming to himself. And two hours before the sun began, or before that, he would be about. He could stride right across Dula in a day, and had often done so and come back in the evening, with the stars and the hares starting over the hill.

This night though, as the fish were seething and

the sun going down into the water on a path of blood, he walked back to the outhouse, and took a stare at the sealskin drying on its pegs. In the last sunglare, the fur of the pelt was like new copper. It had a beautiful sheen to it, and no mistake. It was too good to be giving away. But there, he had made his bargain—not to the girl, but to himself. Set in his ways, he had not the tactics to go back on his word. So with a shrug, he banged shut the outhouse door. and went to eat his supper in the croft.

It was maybe an hour after the sunset that the wind began to lift along the sea.

In a while, Huss Hullas put aside the sleeve he was darning, and listened. He had lived all his life in sight and sound of the ocean, and the noise of water and weather were known to him. Even the winds had their own voices, but this wind had a voice like no other he had ever heard. At first he paid it heed, and then he went back to his darning. But then again he sat still and listened, and he could not make it out, so much any could tell, if they had seen him. At last, he got to his feet and took the one oil-lamp that was burning on the mantlepiece, and opened the door of the croft. He stood there, gazing out into the darkness, the lamp swinging its lilt of yellow over the sloping rock, and beyond it only the night and the waves. There was nothing to be found out there. The sea was not even rough, only a little choppy as it generally would be at this season of the year. The sky was open and stars hung from it, though the moon would not be over the hill for another hour or more.

So there was no excuse for the wind, or the way it sounded. No excuse at all. And what had caught Huss Hullas' attention in the croft was five times louder in the outer air.

It was full of crying, the wind was, like the keening of women around a grave. And yet, there was nothing human in the noise. It rose and fell and came and went, like breathing, now high and wild and lamenting, now low and choked and dire.

Huss Hullas was not a superstitious man, and he did not believe any of the old tales that get told around the fires on winter nights. He had not enough liking for his own kind to have caught their romancing. Yet he heard the wind, and finding nothing he went inside again and bolted the door.

And next he took a piece of wood and worked on it, sawing and hammering it, while the kettle sang on the hob and the fire spat from a dose of fresh peat. The wind was not so easily heard in this way. Nor anything much outside. Though when the knock came sharp on his bolted door, Huss Hullas heard it well enough.

In all the years he had lived on Dula, there had only been one other time someone had knocked on the door by night. There are some two hundred souls live there, and no phone and not even a vet. One summer dark with a child of his ailing, a man came to ask Huss Hullas to row him over to the mainland for a doctor. Huss Hullas refused to row, but for three pounds he let the man hire his boat. That was his way. Later that night the doctor was operating for appendicitus over the hill on a scrubbed kitchen table. The child lived; the father said to Huss Hullas: "Three pounds is the worth you set on a child's life." "Be glad," was the answer, "I set it so cheap."

Money or no, Huss Hullas did not like to be disturbed, and perhaps it was this made him hesitate, now. Then the knocking came again, and a voice called to him out of the crying of the wind.

"Open your door," it said. "I see your light under it."

And the voice was a woman's.

Maybe he was curious and maybe not, but he went to the door at last and unbolted it and threw it wide.

The thick dull glow of the lamp left on the mantlepiece fell out around him on to the rock. But directly where his shadow fell instead, the woman was standing. In this way he could not see her well, but he made a guess she was from one of the inland crofts. She seemed dressed as the women there were dressed, shabby and shawled, and her fashion of talking seemed enough like theirs.

"Well, what is it?" he said to her.

"It's a raw night," she said. "I would come in."

"That's no reason I should let you."

"You are the man hunts the seals," she said.

"I am."

"Then I would come in and speak of that."

"I've nothing to sell. The skins are in the sheds across the water."

"One skin you have here."

"Who told you so?"

"No matter who told me," said the woman. "I heard it was a fine one. Beautiful and strangely coloured, and the size of two seals together."

"Not for sale," said Huss Hullas, supposing suddenly one of the other sealers had jabbered, though how news had got to Dula he was not sure, unless he had been spied on.

"It is a love gift, then?" said the woman. "You are courting, and would give it to her?"

At this, his granite temper began to stir.

"This skin is mine, and no business of yours," he said. "Get home."

When he said this the wind seemed to swell and break on the island like a wave. Startled, he raised his head, and for a moment there seemed to be a kind of mist along the water, a mist that moved, swimming and sinuous, as if it were full of live things.

"*Get home*," the woman repeated softly. "And where do you think my home to be?"

When he looked back at her, she had turned a little and come out of his shadow, so the lamp could reach her. She was not young, but neither was she old, and she was handsome, too, but this is not what he saw first. He saw that he had been mistaken in the matter of the shawl, for she was shawled only in her hair, which was very long, streaming round her, and of a pale ashy brown uncommon enough he had never before seen it. Her eyes, catching the lamp, were black and brilliant, but they were odd, too, in a way he could not make out, though he did not like them much. Otherwise she might have seemed normal, except her hair was wet, and her clothing, which was shapeless and seemed torn, ran with water. Perhaps it had rained as she walked over the hill.

"Your home is nothing to me," he said. "And the skin is not for sale."

"We will speak of it," she said. And she put out her hand as if to touch him and he sprang backwards before he knew what he did. Next moment she came in after him, and the door fell shut on the night, closing them in the croft together.

In all his life, Huss Hullas had never feared anything, save the ocean, which was more common sense than fear. Now he stood and stared at the woman with her wet dress and her wet hair, knowing that in some way fear her he did, but he had not the words or even the emotion in him to explain it to himself, or what else he felt, for fear was not nearly all of it.

He must have stood a long while, staring like that, and she a long while letting him stare. What nudged him at length was another thing altogether. A piece of peat barked on the fire, and in the silence after, he realized the wind had dropped, and its eerie wailing ceased.

"Your name is Huss Hullas," the woman said in the silence. "Do not ask me how I learned it. My name, so we shall know each other, is Saiuree."

When she told him her name, the hair rose on his neck. It did not sound human, but more like the hiss the spume would make, or the sea through a channel, or some creature of the sea.

"Well," he said harshly. "Well."

"It shall be well," she agreed, "for I'll have the skin from your shed. But I'll pay you fairly for it, whatever price you have set."

He laughed then, shortly and bitterly, for he was not given to laughter, he did it ill and it ill-became him.

"The price is one you would not like to pay, Missus."

"Tell it me, and I shall know."

"The price," he said brutishly, "is to spill between a woman's spread legs."

But she only looked at him.

"If that is what you wish, that is what I can give you."

"Ah," he said. "But you see, it's not you I want."

"So," she said, and she was quiet a while. He felt an uneasy silly triumph while she was, standing there in his own croft with her and he unable to show her the door. Then she said, "It is a black-haired girl on the mainland you would have. Her name is Morna."

His triumph went at that.

"Who told you?" he said.

"You," said she.

And he understood it was true. She smiled, slow and still, like a ripple spreading in a tide pool.

"Oh, Huss Hullas," said she, "I might have filled this room up with pearls, and not have missed them, or covered the floor with old green coins from the days before any man lived here. There is a ship sunk, far out, and none knows of it. There are old shields rotting black on the sides of it and a skeleton sits in the prow with a gold ring on his neck, and I might have brought you that ring. Or farther out there is another ship with golden money in boxes. Or I could bring you the stone head with stone snakes for hair, that was cast into the sea for luck, and made you rich. But you will have your bar girl and that is your price."

Huss Hullas sat down in his chair before the fire and wished he had some whisky by him. At the woman who called herself Saiuree, he snarled: "You're mad, then."

"Yes," she said. "Mad with grief. Like those you heard in the wind, crying for the sea they have lost and the bodies they have lost, so they may not swim any more through the waterworld, or through the towered city under the ocean."

"I've no interest in stories," he said.

"Have you none."

"No. But you'll tell me next you are one of the Shealcé, and the skin you seek is your own."

"So I am," she said. "But the skin is not mine. It is the skin of my only son, Connuh, that you shot on the ice for his beauty and his strength as the dawn stood on the water."

Huss Hullas spat in the fire.

"My mother had a son, too. There's no great joy in sons."

"Ah," she said, "it's that you hate yourself so much you can never come to love another. Well, we are not all of your way. Long before men came here, the Seal People held this water and this land. And when men came they took the fish from us and drove us out. And when, in passing then, we paused to rest here, they killed us, because our skins are finer than their own. How many of this People have you slain, man? Many hundreds is it not? And today with your gun you slew a prince of this People. For he was of the true Shealcé, from whom all the Shealcé now take their name. But still even we do not give hate for hate, greed for greed, injustice for injustice. I'll pay your price. Look in my eyes and see it."

"I'll not look in your eyes."

"So you will," she said.

She came close. No steam rose from her nor was she dry. Her dress was seaweed, and nothing else. Her hair was like the sea itself. He saw why he had misliked her eyes. About their round bright blackness there was no white at all. Even so, he looked at them and into them and through them, out into the night.

Above, the night sea was black, but down, far down where the seal dives, it was not black at all. There was a kind of light, but it came from nothing in the sea. It came from the inside of the eyes of the ones who swam there, who had seen the depths of the water in their own way, and now showed it to the man. If Huss Hullas wished to see it who can say? Probably he did not. A man with so little life-love in him he was like one without blood, to him maybe to see these things he saw was only wasted time. But if he had only walled himself in all these years against his own thought and his own dreams, then maybe there was a strange elation in the seeing, and a cold pain.

At first then, only the darkness through which he saw as he went down in it, like one drowning, but alive and keeping breath, as the seals did, on land or in ocean both. Then there began to be fish, like polished knives without their hafts, flashing this way and that way. And through the fish, Huss Hullas began to see the currents of the water, the milky strands like breezes going by. All around there were, too, the dim shadows of the Shealcé, each one graceful and lovely in that gentle shape of theirs, like dancers at their play, but moving ever down and down, and ever northwards.

They passed a wreck. It was so old it was like the skeleton of a leaf, and in the prow a human skeleton leaned. It had a gold torc round its bone throat, while the shields clung in black bits and flakes to the open sides of the vessel, just as Saiuree had said. It was a Wicing long-boat of many many hundred years before.

The seals swam over and about the wreck, and then away, and Huss Hullas followed them.

And it began to seem to him then that he felt the silk of the water on his flesh, and the power and grace of the seal whose body he seemed to have come to inhabit, but he was not sure.

Shortly beyond the wreck there was a space of sheer blackness, that might have been a wall of rock. But here and there were openings in the black, and one by one the seals ebbed through with the water, and Huss Hullas after them. On the further side was the city of the Shealcé.

Now, there are many tales told of that spot, but this was how he saw it for himself.

It must in part have been a natural thing, and this is not to be wondered at, for the Shealcé have no hands in their water form with which to build, whatever figure they may conjure on the land. Above would be islets, no doubt, where they might bask in the sun of summer. But here the cold-sea coral had grown, pale greyish-red and sombre blueish-white, and rose in spines and funnels all about. It seemed to Huss Hullas like a city of chimneys, for the curious hollow formations twisted and humped and ascended over each other, but all went up—in places ten times the height of a man and more—and at their tops they smoked and bubbled, and that was from the air brought down into them by the Shealcé themselves, in their chests and in their fur, which gradually went up again and was lost in the water.

So he beheld these pastel spires, softly smoking, and glittering too. For everywhere huge clusters of pearls had been set, or those shells which shine, or other ornaments of the sea, though nothing that had come from men, not silver or gold, nor jewels.

But strangest of all, deep in the city and far away, there were a host of faint lights, for all the world like vague-lit windows high in towers. And these yellow eyes beamed out through the water as if they watched who came and who departed, but if the Shealcé had made and lit them he did not know. Nor did he think of it then, perhaps.

For all the seals swam in amid the chimnied city and he with them, and suddenly he heard again that dreadful hopeless crying, but this time it was not in the wind he heard it, but in his own brain. And this time, too, he knew what it said. He saw, at last, the shapes about him were shadows for sure, were wraiths, the ghosts only of seals, who swam out this final

journey before their lamenting memory should die
as their bodies had already died from the bullets of
men.

Oh, to be no more, to be no more, the seals were
crying. *To be lost, to be lost. The hurt of the death was less,
far less, than the hurt of the loss. Where now are we to go?*

If he felt the hurt they cried of he did not know
himself, most likely. But he was close to it as generally no man comes close to anything, and rarely to
his own self.

And then one of the yellow-eyed towers was before him, and he swam up into the light and the
light enclosed him—

—and he was in the corridor above the mainland
bar with Morna opening a door.

Then they were in the bedroom, and she was not
sulky or covetous, but smiling and glad. And she
took her stockings off her white legs and bared her
rosy breasts and combed her liqorice hair with her
hands. He forgot the seals that moment, and the
water and the crying. "Lie down with me, sweetheart,"
said Morna, and took him to her like her only love.
And he had something with her that hour he never
had had with any woman before, and never would
have again so long as he lived.

A while before dawn, just as the sky was turning
grey under the hill, he woke up alone in his bed in
the croft. That he thought he had been dreaming is
made nothing of by the fact he came instantly from
the covers, flung on his clothes and went to the door.
He meant to go and look in the outhouse, doubtless,
but he had no need. What he sought lay on the
rocky edge of Dula, less than twenty strides below
him.

The whole sky was higher, with the darkness going fast. He had a chance to see what he was staring at.

There by the ocean's brink a woman knelt, mourning over a thing that lay along the rock and across her lap. Her showering hair covered what remained of this thing's face, and maybe Huss Hullas was thankful for it. But from her hair there ran away another stream of hair that was not hers, richer and more golden, even in the tweenlight. And beyond the hair stretched the body of a young man, long-limbed and wide in the shoulder, and altogether very large and well-made, and altogether naked. At least, it would seem to be a body, but suddenly you noticed some two or three shallow cuts of a knife, and then you would see the body had no meat to it and no muscle and no bone—it was an empty skin.

There came some colour in the sky within the grey, and the woman, with a strange awkward turn, slipped over into the water, and dragged the human skin with her, and both were gone.

And then again, as the sun came up over the hill of Dula, and Huss Hullas was still standing there, he saw the round head of a seal a half mile out on the water, with an odd wide wake behind it as if it bore something alongside itself. He did not go to fetch his gun. He never shot a seal from that day to this. Nor did he go drinking or to find women in the town. Indeed, he went inland, over the hill, to live where he might not heed the noise of the sea. He kept away from his own kind; that did not change.

Do you think it was guilt then that turned him from his outward ways, deeper into those inner ways of his? Perhaps only he saw the seal tracks on the rock and sand, or found a strip of seawrack in between the covers of the bed, and knew what he had lain with, even if it had passed for rosy Morna. The

QATT-SUP

He had been out in the woods, actually in hopeless pursuit of the cat, when it happened.

It was getting on for sunset, the sun right down in the lower valleys, among the trees there, making golden haze. It was beautiful, and he had picked out the cabin here for just such beauty, and for peace, but right then he was blind to one and sadly lacking in the other. It was, of course, irrational to get in such a rage at a 'dumb animal', but there, the heck with it, he was. When the cat had first shown up he had tabbed it as belonging to one of the two or three sprawling farms over towards the river. That being the case, he reckoned it wouldn't need feeding, only the occasional complimentary bowl of water or tinned milk. For the rest it would catch birds, and clean out the mice that—legacy of a previous idiot owner—had taken over the cabin's out-house. Yes, in the beginning he had thought the cat would be very useful, and he liked the idea of an animal around sometimes, something as independent as a cat, which would look after itself and impose no ties, but be there for his admiration and aesthetic pleasure, like the woods, the river and the clean sky.

However, the cat had other ideas. It was an accomplished thief. Rather than get rid of the mice, it began to steal small things, with an extraordinary cunning, from the traps he had set. Worse, it took off with articles of food from the cupboards—things a cat shouldn't want—a slab of cheese, a bag of cookies, and ate them too, for a litter of paper, smears and crumbs had been scattered (deliberately?) for him to find, along with the illicit bones, by the big maple in the clearing. Even an opened bottle of Mary-May's Own Cat-Sup had been pilfered. The ironic pun left him cold. The fridge door was faulty, too, and the cat had gotten wise to the fact. Now, the two fine fish he had caught for supper were gone, the last damn straw, leaving him flat and furious, with the prospect of a bread and beans dinner, or the long drive to the greasy diner in town—a trip he made as seldom as possible.

As he headed for the maple, he was dreaming of revenge, not really believing though the cat would be such a fool as to be there, not even sure what he would do if it was.

He had just come out on to the up-slope of the clearing, the fiery tree above him and the sun-sheen under it, when a most peculiar sensation swept over him. It affected his ears, his head, his eyes, even the surface of his skin, and his first thought was that he'd worked himself into too much of a lather and was about to keel over in a faint. But then, he began to realize that the humming and throbbing, the tingling, the thickening of the light, might also be external. It was instinct to look up. Spielberg's Law.

And up there was a reddish cloud, and out of the cloud dropped an emptying of sentient nothingness that caught him, spun him, and threw him down.

The last contact he had with Earth was that of his face in the soil and fallen leaves.

When he came to, he was no longer anywhere near
Earth, and instinctively, with a pang of terrified
excitement, he knew it.

As his head cleared he opened his eyes, and let
them look about. He was in a sort of filmy pristine
bubble, resting soft, and not tied down. There was a
scent in the air, fresh and delightful. He felt well. No
after-effects then, to the ultra-scientific drug they
had used on him. He sat up slowly.

Though he was, naturally, afraid and very shocked,
yet there was something exhilarating about this
adventure. And he was not a prisoner, no one had
harmed him. He felt rather cherished. It went through
his mind, a fantasy he was powerless to avoid, that
he, the chosen one, was about to encounter alien
beings, an alien and superior technology, and maybe
the far-flung worlds which burn in the imagination
of men like jewels and flames. It was one thing to
escape the rat-race and the pollution in the precari-
ous innocence of the woods. But this—the ultimate
escape—*To boldly go*—But he must hang on to himself,
here. Not get drunk on the rich and strange. After
all, they'd want to talk to him, and he would need to
be coherent.

Just then part of the bubble misted over, cleared,
and two of the most elegant, beautiful. . . . Two alien
creatures moved quietly into the space with him.
They regarded him with their large liquid eyes, the
nearest thing to corundum he had ever seen that
wasn't sapphire, and he stared back at them.

My God, and they *were* beautiful. Serene, calm,
looking at him with a still patience and understanding.
He felt himself shiver at their perfection. Their culture must be a wondrous one, if they were its
proponents.

In the end, he couldn't stand it another minute. He blurted: "Is it possible for me to speak to you?"

The briefest pause. Then, "Oh, yes," one of them replied. He didn't know—or for the moment care—how it was done; telepathy or hidden circuits making translation, or maybe he himself had been given a crash-course, hypnotic-wise, in their language while unconscious, and was now only rationalising that they spoke to him in pure Amerenglish. "Yes. It's perfectly possible for us to speak together. We'd like to talk to you for a while. To tell you how it will be."

"Especially that," said the second, just the same. "It pleases us to extend the truth. It is our actual pleasure to do so."

He relapsed, gratified, flattered, almost in love. They were so *beautiful*. Gender was something he couldn't make out. But their sleekness, the articulation, the grace—and those glorious optics—And now they had come softly near to him, and he caught a scent from them, fresh and charming as that other perfume in the air. Gods and men, he thought with proud humbleness. And tears filled his eyes.

"You see," the first one said, "it's your blood that we want. What we shall enjoy. The dermis, the meat—these, too, but they're of secondary value."

A little silence.

"What?" he said.

"Your blood," said the second. "We realize it must amaze you, a thing so inferior to ourselves, to learn that you can provide us with joy. But we assure you, you really can."

"Yes, truly," said the other. " It will be so lovely. To drain, to squeeze you dry."

Then they told him, bending near, their eyes smiling, how they would draw the blood, and from

where, and he forgot his fantasies and began screaming.

"Not too loud," they cautioned then, "we'd like
you to be able to cry out as much as you need to, we
enjoy that, also, a great deal. But too much noise at
the start could be a little inconvenient. Isn't it feasible for you simply to emote your fear? We promise,
you won't be letting us down at all, if you emote fear,
it will make us just as happy. And you're doing it
very well in any case."

But he couldn't restrict himself to emoting and he
went on shrieking very loudly, and tried to run across
the slippery surface of the bubble. He had only gone
a few feet when they caught him.

He was very angry. Of course, he knew it was foolish
to react in this way, but he had had such hopes for
his little freelance expedition and the treasures it
would garner. And this wasn't the first time, either.

Trying to relax, he stretched his long body, winding his several legs around the cushioned props. The
ship was making excellent time towards what, in the
parlance of the last planet, was known as 'Andromeda.' But to keep that excellent timing intact, he
was unable now to turn back for another specimen.
And it had seemed rather interesting anyway, the
first one, with some (rather limited) but amusing
potential. The trouble was that damnable storage
capsule and the faulty entry-mechanism. Which those
two wretches had figured out how to by-pass. He
had taken them on for company, he admitted, and
to keep an eye out for the—the rough equivalent of
the word and species is 'mice'—that tended to infest
any low-budget vessel such as his own. But hang it
all, they hadn't done a thing about the 'mice'. *Oh* no.
To get hold of the valuable specimens, that was their

trick. And this was the fourth time the pair of them had done it.

The problem was, he always forgave them. Aesthetically, they turned him on. So beautiful, these pets of his, whose name in the parlance of earth might be an equivalent of 'cat', but only if spelled very, very differently. But their independence, he liked that so much, even their lawlessness—to be honest, though the loss pained him, he kind of admired their robbery. . . .

And it was certainly too late now for recriminations. One glance at the remains in the capsule told him that. He would just have to find some way to fix that confounded door. Otherwise, he was going to get home with nothing to show at all.

Heaving a scented bluish vapour of sigh, the alien intelligence rose, and poured out two bowls of *mhurlk*, and left them there on the floor for his *qatts*.

DRACO, DRACO

You'll have heard stories, sometimes, of men who
have fought and slain dragons. These are all lies.
There's no swordsman living ever killed a dragon,
though a few swordsmen dead that tried.

On the other hand, I once travelled in company
with a fellow who got the name of 'dragon-slayer'

A riddle? No. I'll tell you.

I was coming from the North back into the South, to
civilisation as you may say, when I saw him, sitting by
the roadside. My first feeling was envy, I admit. He
was smart and very clean for someone in the wilds,
and he had the South all over him, towns and baths
and money. He was crazy, too, because there was
gold on his wrists and in one ear. But he had a sharp
grey sword, an army sword, so maybe he could de-
fend himself. He was also younger than me, and a
great deal prettier, but the last isn't too difficult. I
wondered what he'd do when he looked up from his
daydream and saw me, tough, dark and sour as a
twist of old rope, clopping down on him on my
swarthy little horse, ugly as sin, that I love like a
daughter.

Then he did look up and I discovered.

"Greetings, stranger. Nice day, isn't it?"

He stayed relaxed as he said it, and somehow you knew from that he really could look after himself. It wasn't he thought I was harmless, just that he thought he could handle me if I tried something. Then again, I had my box of stuff alongside. Most people can tell my trade from that, and the aroma of drugs and herbs. My father was with the Romans, in fact he was probably the last Roman of all, one foot on the ship to go home, the rest of him with my mother up against the barnyard wall. She said he was a camp physician and maybe that was so. Some idea of doctoring grew up with me, though nothing great or grand. An itinerant apothecary is welcome almost anywhere, and can even turn bandits civil. It's not a wonderful life, but it's the only one I know.

I gave the young soldier-dandy that it was a nice day. I added he'd possibly like it better if he hadn't lost his horse.

"Yes, a pity about that. You could always sell me yours."

"Not your style."

He looked at her. I could see he agreed. There was also a momentary idea that he might kill me and take her, so I said, "And she's well known as mine. It would get you a bad name. I've friends round about."

He grinned, good-naturedly. His teeth were good, too. What with that, and the hair like barley, and the rest of it—well, he was the kind usually gets what he wants. I was curious as to which army he had hung about with to gain the sword. But since the Eagles flew, there are kingdoms everywhere, chiefs, war-leaders, Roman knights, and every tide brings an invasion up some beach. Under it all, too, you can feel the earth, the actual ground, which had been measured and ruled with fine roads, the land which had been subdued but never tamed, beginning to quicken. Like the shadows that come with the blowing out of a lamp. Ancient things, which are in my blood somewhere, so I recognise them.

But he was like a new coin that hadn't got dirty yet, nor learned much, though you could see your face in its shine, and cut yourself on its edge.

His name was Caiy. Presently we came to an arrangement and he mounted up behind me on Negra. They spoke a smatter of Latin where I was born, and I called her that before I knew her, for her darkness. I couldn't call her for her hideousness, which is her only other visible attribute.

The fact is, I wasn't primed to the country round that way at all. I'd had word, a day or two prior, that there were Saxons in the area I'd been heading for. And so I switched paths and was soon lost. When I came on Caiy, I'd been pleased with the road, which was Roman, hoping it would go somewhere useful. But, about ten miles after Caiy joined me, the road petered out in a forest. My passenger was lost, too. He was going South, no surprise there, but last night his horse had broken loose and bolted, leaving him stranded. It sounded unlikely, but I wasn't inclined to debate on it. It seemed to me someone might have stolen the horse, and Caiy didn't care to confess.

There was no way round the forest, so we went in and the road died. Being summer, the wolves would be scarce and the bears off in the hills. Nevertheless, the trees had a feel I didn't take to, sombre and still, with the sound of little streams running through like metal chains, and birds that didn't sing but made purrings and clinkings. Negra never baulked or complained—if I'd waited to call her, I could have done it for her courage and warm-heartedness—but she couldn't come to terms with the forest, either.

"It smells," said Caiy, who'd been kind enough not to comment on mine, "as if it's rotting. Or fermenting."

I grunted. Of course it did, it was, the fool. But the smell told you other things. The centuries, for one. Here were the shadows that had come back when Rome blew out her lamp and sailed away, and left us in the dark.

Then Caiy, the idiot, began to sing to show up the birds who wouldn't. A nice voice, clear and bright. I didn't tell him to leave off. The shadows already knew we were there.

When night came down, the black forest closed like a cellar door.

We made a fire and shared my supper. He'd lost his rations with his mare.

"Shouldn't you tether that—your horse," suggested Caiy, trying not to insult her since he could see we were partial to each other. "My mare was tied, but something scared her and she broke the tether and ran. I wonder what it was," he mused, staring in the fire.

About three hours later, we found out.

I was asleep, and dreaming of one of my wives, up in the far North, and she was nagging at me, trying to start a brawl, which she always did for she was taller than me, and liked me to hit her once in a while so she could feel fragile, feminine and mastered. Just as she emptied the beer jar over my head, I heard a sound up in the sky like a storm that was not a storm. And I knew I wasn't dreaming any more.

The sound went over, three or four great claps, and the tops of the forest reeling, and left shuddering. There was a sort of quiver in the air, as if sediment were stirred up in it. There was even an extra smell, dank, yet tingling. When the noise was only a memory, and the bristling hairs began to subside along my body, I opened my eyes.

Negra was flattened to the ground, her own eyes rolling, but she was silent. Caiy was on his feet, gawping up at the tree-tops and the strands of starless sky. Then he glared at me.

"What in the name of the Bull was that?"

I noted vaguely that the oath showed he had Mithraic allegiances, which generally meant Roman. Then I sat up, rubbed my arms and neck to get human, and went to console Negra. Unlike his silly cavalry mare she hadn't bolted.

"It can't," he said, "have been a bird. Though I'd have sworn something flew over."

"No, it wasn't a bird."

"But it had wings. Or—no, it couldn't have had wings the size of that."

"Yes it could. They don't carry it far, is all."

"Apothecary, stop being so damned provoking. If you know, out with it! Though I don't see how you can know. And don't tell me it's some bloody woods demon I won't believe in."

"Nothing like that," I said. "It's real enough. Natural, in its own way. Not," I amended, "that I ever came across one before, but I've met some who did."

Caiy was going mad, like a child working up to a tantrum.

"*Well?*"

I suppose he had charmed and irritated me enough I wanted to retaliate, because I just quoted some bastard non-sensical jabber-Latin chant at him:

Bis terribilis—
Bis appellare—
Draco! Draco!

At least, it made him sit down.

'What?" he eventually said.

At my age I should be over such smugness. I said,
"It was a dragon."

Caiy laughed. But he had glimpsed it, and knew
better than I did that I was right.

Nothing else happened that night. In the morning
we started off again and there was a rough track,
and then the forest began to thin out. After a while
we emerged on the crown of a moor. The land
dropped down to a valley, and on the other side
there were sunny smoky hills and a long streamered
sky. There was something else, too.

Naturally, Caiy said it first, as if everything new
always surprised him, as if we hadn't each of us, in
some way, been waiting for it, or something like it.

"This place stinks."

"Hn."

"Don't just grunt at me, you blasted quack doctor.
It does, doesn't it. Why?"

"Why do you think?"

He brooded, pale gold and citified, behind me.
Negra tried to paw the ground, and then made herself desist.

Neither of us brave humans had said any more
about what had interrupted sleep in the forest, but
when I'd told him no dragon could fly far on its
wings, for from all I'd ever heard they were too
large and only some freakish lightness in their bones
enabled them to get air-borne at all, I suppose we
had both taken it to heart. Now here were the valley
and the hills, and here was this reek lying over
everything, strange, foul, alien, comparable to nothing,
really. Dragon smell.

I considered. No doubt, the dragon went on an
aeriel patrol most nights, circling as wide as it could

to see what might be there for it. There were other things I'd learnt. These beasts hunt nocturnally, like cats. At the same time, a dragon is more like a crow in its habits. It will attack and kill, but normally it eats carrion, dead things, or dying and immobilised. It's light, as I said, it has to be to take the skies, but the lack of weight is compensated by the armour, the teeth and talons. Then again, I'd heard of dragons that breathed fire. I've never been quite convinced there. It seems more likely to me such monsters only live in volcanic caves, the mountain itself belching flame and the dragon taking credit for it. Maybe not. But certainly, this dragon was no fire-breather. The ground would have been scorched for miles; I've listened to stories where that happened. There were no marks of fire. Just the insidious pervasive stench that I knew, by the time we'd gone down into the valley, would be so familiar, so soaked into us, we would hardly notice it any more, or the scent of anything else.

I awarded all this information to my passenger. There followed a long verbal delay. I thought he might just be flabbergasted at getting so much chat from me, but then he said, very hushed, "You truly believe all this, don't you?"

I didn't bother with the obvious, just clucked to Negra, trying to make her turn back the way we'd come. But she was unsure and for once uncooperative, and suddenly his strong hand, the nails groomed even now, came down on my arm.

"Wait, Apothecary. If it *is* true—"

"Yes, yes," I said. I sighed. "You want to go and challenge it, and become a hero." He held himself like marble, as if I were speaking of some girl he thought he loved. I didn't see why I should waste experience and wisdom on him, but then. "No man ever killed a dragon. They're plated, all over, even the underbelly. Arrows and spears just bounce off—even a pilum. Swords clang and snap in half. Yes, yes," I reiterated, "you've heard of men who slashed the tongue, or stabbed into an eye. Let me tell you, if they managed to reach that high and actually did it, then they just made the brute angry. Think of the size and shape of a dragon's head, the way the pictures show it. It's one hell of a push from the eye into the brain. And you know, there's one theory the eyelid is armoured, too, and can come down faster that *that*."

"Apothecary," he said. He sounded dangerous. I just knew what he must look like. Handsome, noble and insane.

"Then I won't keep you," I said. "Get down and go on and the best of luck."

I don't know why I bothered. I should have tipped him off and ridden for it, though I wasn't sure Negra could manage to react sufficiently fast, she was that edgy. Anyway, I didn't, and sure enough next moment his sword was at the side of my throat, and so sharp it had drawn blood.

"You're the clever one," he said, "the know-all. And you do seem to know more than I do, about this. So you're my guide, and your scruff-bag of a horse, if it even deserves the name, is my transport. Giddy-up, the pair of you."

That was that. I never argue with a drawn sword. The dragon would be lying up by day, digesting and dozing, and by night I could hole up someplace myself. Tomorrow Caiy would be dead and I could leave. And I would, of course, have seen a dragon for myself.

After an hour and a half's steady riding—better once I'd persuaded him to switch from the sword to poking a dagger against my ribs, less tiring for us both—we came around a stand of woods, and there was a village. It was the savage Northern kind, thatch and wattle and turf banks, but big for all that, a good mile of it, not all walled. There were walls this end, however, and men on the gate, peering at us.

Caiy was aggrieved because he was going to have to ride up to them pillion, but he knew better now than to try managing Negra alone. He maybe didn't want to pretend she was his horse in any case.

As we pottered up the pebbled track to the gate, he sprang off and strode forward, arriving before me, and began to speak.

When I got closer I heard him announcing, in his dramatic, beautiful voice,

"—And if it's a fact, I swear by the Victory of the Light that I will meet the thing and kill it."

They were muttering. The dragon smell, even though we were used to it, sodden with it, seemed more acid here. Poor Negra had been voiding herself from sheer terror all up the path. With fortune on her side, there would be somewhere below ground, some cave or dug out place, where they'd be putting their animals out of the dragon's way, and she could shelter with the others.

Obviously, the dragon hadn't always been active in this region. They'd scarcely have built their village if it had. No, it would have been like the tales. Dragons live for centuries. They can sleep for centuries, too. Unsuspecting, man moves in, begins to till and build and wax prosperous. Then the dormant dragon wakes under the hill. They're like the volcanoes I spoke of, in that. Which is perhaps, more than habitat, why so many of the legends say they breathe fire when they wake.

The interesting thing was, even clouded by the

dragon stink, initially, the village didn't seem keen to admit anything.

Caiy, having made up his mind to accept the dragon—and afraid of being wrong—started to rant. The men at the gate were frightened and turning nasty. Leading Negra now, I approached, tapped my chest of potions and said:

"Or, if you don't want your dragon slain, I can cure some of your other troubles. I've got medicines for almost everything. Boils, warts. Ear pains. Tooth pains. Sick eyes. Womens' afflictions. I have here—"

"Shut up, you toad-turd," said Caiy.

One of the guards suddenly laughed. The tension sagged.

Ten minutes after, we had been let in the gate and were trudging through the cow-dung and wild flowers—neither of which were to be smelled through the other smell—to the head-man's hall.

It was around two hours after that when we found out why the appearance of a rescuing champion-knight had given them the jitters.

It seemed they had gone back to the ancient way, propitiation, the scape-goat. For three years, they had been making an offering to the dragon, in spring, and at midsummer, when it was likely to be most frisky.

Anyone who knew dragons from a book would tell them this wasn't the way. But they knew their dragon from myth. Every time they made sacrifice, they imagined the thing could understand and appreciate what they'd done for it, and would therefore be more amenable.

In reality, of course, the dragon had never attacked the village. It had thieved cattle off the pasture by night, elderly or sick cows at that, and lambs that were too little and weak to run. It would have

taken people, too, but only those who were disabled
and alone. I said, a dragon is lazy and prefers carrion,
or what's defenceless. Despite being big, they aren't
so big they'd go after a whole tribe of men. And
though even forty men together undoubtedly couldn't
wound a dragon, they could exhaust it, if they kept
up a rough-house. Eventually it would keel over and
they could brain it. You seldom hear of forty men
going off in a band to take a dragon, however. Dragons are still ravelled up with night fears and spiritual
mysteries, and latterly with an Eastern superstition
of a mighty demon who can assume the form of a
dragon which is invincible and—naturally—breathes
sheer flame. So, this village, like many another, would
put out its sacrifice, one girl tied to a post, and leave
her there, and the dragon would have her. Why not?
She was helpless, fainting with horror—and young
and tender into the bargain. Perfect. You never could
convince them that, instead of appeasing the monster,
the sacrifice encourages it to stay. Look at it from the
dragon's point of view. Not only are there dead
sheep and stray cripples to devour, but once in a
while a nice juicy damsel on a stick. Dragons don't
think like a man, but they do have memories.

When Caiy realized what they were about to do,
tonight, as it turned out, he went red then white,
exactly as they do in a bardic lay. Not anger, mind
you. He didn't comprehend any more than they did.
It was merely the awfulness of it.

He stood up and chose a stance, quite uncon-
sciously impressive, and assured us he'd save her. He
swore to it in front of us all, the chieftain, his men,
me. And he swore it by the Sun, so I knew he meant
business.

They were scared, but now also childishly hopeful.
It was part of their mythology again. All mythology

seems to take this tack somewhere, the dark against the light, the Final Battle. It's rot, but there.

Following a bit of drinking to seal the oath, they cheered up and the chief ordered a feast. Then they took Caiy to see the chosen sacrifice.

Her name was Niemeh, or something along those lines.

She was sitting in a little lamplit cell off the hall. She wasn't fettered, but a warrior stood guard beyond the screen, and there was no window. She had nothing to do except weave flowers together, and she was doing that, making garlands for her death procession in the evening.

When Caiy saw her, his colour drained away again.

He stood and stared at her, while somebody explained he was her champion.

Though he got on my nerves, I didn't blame him so much this time. She was about the most beautiful thing I ever hope to see. Young, obviously, and slim, but with a woman's shape, if you have my meaning, and long hair more fair even than Caiy's, and green eyes like sea pools and a face like one of the white flowers in her hands, and a sweet mouth.

I looked at her as she listened gravely to all they said. I remembered how in the legends it's always the loveliest and the most gentle gets picked for the dragon's dinner. You perceive the sense in the gentle part. A girl with a temper might start a ruckus.

When Caiy had been introduced and once more sworn by the sun to slay the dragon and so on, she thanked him. If things had been different, she would have blushed and trembled, excited by Caiy's attention. But she was past all that. You could see, if you looked, she didn't believe anyone could save her. But though she must have been half dead already of

despair and fright, she still made space to be courteous.

Then she glanced over Caiy's head straight at me,
and she smiled so I wouldn't feel left out.

"And who is this man?" she asked.

They all looked startled, having forgotten me. Then
someone who had warts recalled I'd said I could fix
him something for warts, and told her I was the
apothecary.

A funny little shiver went through her then.

She was so young and so pretty. If I'd been Caiy
I'd have stopped spouting rubbish about the dragon.
I'd have found some way to lay out the whole village,
and grabbed her, and gone. But that would have
been a stupid thing to do too. I've enough of the old
blood to know about such matters. She was the sacrifice and she was resigned to it; more, she didn't
dream she could be anything else. I've come across
rumours, here and there, of girls, men too, chosen
to die, who escaped. But the fate stays on them.
Hide them securely miles off, across water, beyond
tall hills, still they feel the geas weigh like lead upon
their souls. They kill themselves in the end, or go
mad. And this girl, this Niemeh, you could see it in
her. No, I would never have abducted her. It would
have been no use. She was convinced she must die,
as if she'd seen it written in light on a stone, and
maybe she had.

She returned to her garlands, and Caiy, tense as a
bowstring, led us back to the hall.

Meat was roasting and more drink came out and
more talk came out. You can kill anything as often as
you like, that way.

It wasn't a bad feast, as such up-country things go.
But all through the shouts and toasts and guzzlings,
I kept thinking of her in her cell behind the screen.

hearing the clamour and aware of this evening's sunset, and how it would be to die. . . . as she would have to. I didn't begin to grasp how she could bear it.

By late afternoon they were mostly sleeping it off, only Caiy had had the sense to go and sweat the drink out with soldiers' exercises in the yard, before a group of sozzled admirers of all sexes.

When someone touched my shoulder, I thought it was warty after his cure, but no. It was the guard from the girl's cell, who said very low, "She says she wants to speak to you. Will you come, now?"

I got up and went with him. I had a spinning minute, wondering if perhaps she didn't believe she must die after all, and would appeal to me to save her. But in my heart of hearts I guessed it wasn't that.

There was another man blocking the entrance, but they let me go in alone, and there Niemeh sat, making garlands yet, under her lamp.

But she looked up at me, and her hands fell like two more white flowers on the flowers in her lap. "I need some medicine, you see," she said. "But I can't pay you. I don't have anything. Although my uncle—"

"No charge," I said hurriedly.

She smiled. "It's for tonight."

"Oh," I said.

"I'm not brave," she said, "but it's worse than just being afraid. I know I shall die. That it's needful. But part of me wants to live so much—my reason tells me one thing but my body won't listen. I'm frightened I shall panic, struggle and scream and weep—I don't want that. It isn't right. I have to consent, or the sacrifice isn't any use. Do you know about that?"

"Oh, yes," I said.

"I thought so. I thought you did. Then. . . . Can you give me something, a medicine or herb—so I shan't feel anything? I don't mean the pain. That doesn't matter. The gods can't blame me if I cry out then, they wouldn't expect me to be beyond pain. But only to make me not care, not want to live so very much."

"An easy death."

"Yes." She smiled again. She seemed serene and beautiful. "Oh, yes."

I looked at the floor.

"The soldier. Maybe he'll kill it," I said.

She didn't say anything.

When I glanced up, her face wasn't serene any more. It was brimful of terror. Caiy would have been properly insulted.

"Is it you can't give me anything? Don't you have anything? I was sure you did. That you were sent here to me to—to help, so I shouldn't have to go through it all alone—"

"There," I said, "it's all right. I do have something. Just the thing. I keep it for women in labour when the child's slow and hurting them. It works a treat. They go sort of misty and far off, as if they were nearly asleep. It'll dull pain, too. Even—any kind of pain."

"Yes," she whispered, "I should like that." And then she caught my hand and kissed it. "I knew you would," she said, as if I'd promised her the best and loveliest thing in all the earth. Another man, it would have broken him in front of her. But I'm harder than most.

When she let me, I retrieved my hand, nodded reassuringly, and went out. The chieftain was awake and genial enough, so I had a word with him. I told him what the girl had asked. "In the East," I said, "it's the usual thing, give them something to help them through. They call it Nektar, the drink of the gods. She's consented," I said, "but she's very young and scared, delicately-bred too. You can't grudge her this." He acquiesced immediately, as glad as she was, as I'd hoped. It's a grim affair, I should imagine, when the girl shrieks for pity all the way up to the hills. I hadn't thought there'd be any problem. On the other hand, I hadn't wanted to be caught slipping her potions behind anyone's back.

I mixed the drug in the cell where she could watch. She was interested in everything I did, the way the condemned are nearly always interested in every last detail, even how a cobweb hangs.

I made her promise to drink it all, but none of it until they came to bring her out. "It may not last otherwise. You don't want it to wear off before—too early."

"No," she said. "I'll do exactly what you say."

When I was going out again, she said, "If I can ask them for anything for you, the gods, when I meet them. . . ."

It was in my mind to say: Ask them to go stick—but I didn't. She was trying to keep intact her trust in recompence, immortality. I said, "just ask them to look after you."

She had such a sweet, sweet mouth. She was made to love and be loved, to have children and sing songs and die when she was old, peacefully, in her sleep.

And there would be others like her. The dragon would be given those, too. Eventually, it wouldn't just be maidens, either. The taboo states it had to be a virgin so as to safeguard any unborn life. Since a virgin can't be with child—there's one religion says different, I forget which—they stipulate virgins. But in the end any youthful woman, who can reasonably be reckoned as not with child, will do. And then they go on to the boys. Which is the most ancient sacrifice there is.

I passed a very young girl in the hall, trotting round with the beer-dipper. She was comely and innocent, and I recollected I'd seen her earlier and asked myself, Are you the next? And who'll be next after you?

Niemeh was the fifth. But, I said, dragons live a long while. And the sacrifices always get to be more frequent. Now it was twice a year. In the first year it had been once. In a couple more years it would happen at every season, with maybe three victims in the summer when the creature was most active.

And in ten more years it would be every month, and they'd have learned to raid other villages to get girls and young men to give it, and there would be a lot of bones about, besides, fellows like Caiy, dragon-slayers dragon slain.

I went after the girl with the beer-dipper and drained it. But drink never did comfort me much.

And presently, it would be time to form the procession and start for the hills.

It was the last gleaming golden hour of day when we set off.

The valley was fertile and sheltered. The westering light caught and flashed in the trees and out of the streams. Already there was a sort of path stamped smooth and kept clear of undergrowth. It would have been a pleasant journey, if they'd been going anywhere else.

There was sunlight warm on the sides of the hills, too. The sky was almost cloudless, transparent. If it hadn't been for the tainted air, you would never have thought anything was wrong. But the track wound up the first slope and around, and up again, and there, about a hundred yards off, was the flank of a bigger hill that went down into shadow at its bottom, and never took the sun. That underside was bare of grass, and eaten out in caves, one cave larger than the rest and very ·black, with a strange black stillness, as if light and weather and time itself stopped just inside. Looking at that, you'd know at once, even with sun on your face and the whole lucid sky above.

They'd brought her all this way in a Roman litter which somehow had become the property of the village. It had lost its roof and its curtains, just a kind of cradle on poles, but Niemeh had sat in it on their shoulders, motionless, and dumb. I had only stolen one look at her, to be sure, but her face had turned mercifully blank and her eyes were opaque. What I'd given her started its work swiftly. She was beyond us all now. I was only anxious everything else would occur before her condition changed.

Her bearers set the litter down and lifted her out. They'd have to support her, but they would know about that, girls with legs gone to water, even passed out altogether. And I suppose the ones who fought and screamed would be forced to sup strong ale, or else concussed with a blow.

Everyone walked a little more, until we reached a natural palisade of rock. This spot provided concealment, while overlooking the cave and the ground immediately below it. There was a stagnant dark pond caught in the gravel there, but on our side, facing the cave, a patch of clean turf with a post sticking up, about the height of a tall man.

The two warriors supporting Niemeh went on with her towards the post. The rest of us stayed behind the rocks, except for Caiy.

We were all garlanded with flowers. Even I had

had to be, and I hadn't made a fuss. What odds? But Caiy wasn't garlanded. He was the one part of the ritual which, though arcanely acceptable, was still profane. And that was why, even though they would let him attack the dragon, they had nevertheless brought the girl to appease it.

There was some kind of shackle at the post. It wouldn't be iron, because anything fey has an allergy to stable metals, even so midnight a thing as a dragon. Bronze, probably. They locked one part around her waist and another round her throat. Only the teeth and claws could get her out of her bonds now, piece by piece.

She sagged forward in the toils. She seemed unconscious at last, and I wanted her to be.

The two men hurried back, up the slope and into the rock cover with the rest of us. Sometimes the tales have the people rush away when they've put out their sacrifice, but usually the people stay, to witness. It's quite safe. The dragon won't go after them with something tasty chained up right under its nose.

Caiy didn't remain beside the post. He moved down towards the edge of the polluted pond. His sword was drawn. He was quite ready. Though the sun couldn't get into the hollow to fire his hair or the metal blade, he cut a grand figure, heroically braced there between the maiden and Death.

At the end, the day spilled swiftly. Suddenly all the shoulders of the hills grew dim, and the sky became the colour of lavender, and then a sort of mauve amber, and the stars broke through.

There was no warning.

I was looking at the pond, where the dragon would come to drink, judging the amount of muck there seemed to be in it. And suddenly there was a reflection in the pond, from above. It wasn't definite, and it was upside down, but even so my heart plummeted through my guts.

There was a feeling behind the rock, the type you get, they tell me, in the battle lines, when the enemy appears. And mixed with this, something of another feeling, more maybe like the inside of some god's house when they call on him, and he seems to come.

I forced myself to look then, at the cave mouth. This, after all, was the evening I would see a real dragon, something to relate to others, as others had related such things to me.

It crept out of the cave, inch by inch, nearly down on its belly, cat-like.

The sky wasn't dark yet, a Northern dusk seems often endless. I could see well, and better and better as the shadow of the cave fell away and the dragon advanced into the paler shadow by the pond.

At first, it seemed unaware of anything but itself and the twilight. It flexed and stretched itself. There was something uncanny, even in such simple movements, something evil. And timeless.

The Romans know an animal they call Elephantus, and I mind an ancient clerk in one of the towns describing this beast to me, fairly accurately, for he'd seen one once. The dragon wasn't as large as elephantus, I should say. Actually not that much higher than a fair-sized cavalry gelding, if rather longer. But it was sinuous, more sinuous than any snake. The way it crept and stretched and flexed, and curled and slewed its head, its skeleton seemed fluid.

There are plenty of mosaics, paintings. It was like that, the way men have shown them from the beginning. Slender, tapering to the elongated head, which is like a horse's, too, and not like, and to the tail, though it didn't have that spade-shaped sting they put on them sometimes, like a scorpion's. There were spines, along the tail and the back-ridge, and the neck and head. The ears were set back, like a dog's. Its legs were short, but that didn't make it seem ungainly. The ghastly fluidity was always there, not grace, but something so like grace it was nearly unbearable.

It looked almost the colour the sky was now, slatey, bluish-grey, like metal but dull; the great overlapping plates of its scales had no burnish. Its eyes were black and you didn't see them, and then they took some light from somewhere, and they flared like two flat coins, cat's eyes, with nothing—no brain, no soul— behind them.

It had been going to drink, but had scented something more interesting than dirty water, which was the girl.

The dragon stood there, static as a rock, staring at her over the pond. Then gradually its two wings, that had been folded back like fans along its sides, opened and spread.

They were huge, those wings, much bigger than the rest of it. You could see how it might be able to fly with them. Unlike the body, there were no scales, only skin, membrane, with ribs of external bone. Bat's wings, near enough. It seemed feasible a sword could go through them, damage them, but that would only maim, and all too likely they were tougher than they seemed.

Then I left off considering. With its wings spread like that, unused—like a crow—it began to sidle around the water, the blind coins of eyes searing on the post and the sacrifice.

Somebody shouted. My innards sprang over. Then I realized it was Caiy. The dragon had nearly missed him, so intent it was on the feast, so he had had to call it.

Bis terribilis—Bis appellare—Draco! Draco!

I'd never quite understood that antic chant, and the Latin was execrable. But I think it really means to know a dragon exists is bad enough, to call its name and summon it—call twice. twice terrible—is the notion of a maniac.

The dragon wheeled. It—*flowed*. Its elongated horse's-head-which-wasn't was before him, and Caiy's sharp sword slashed up and down and bit against the jaw. It happened, what they say—sparks shot glittering in the air. Then the head split, not from any wound, just the chasm of the mouth. It made a sound at him, not a hissing, a sort of *hroosh*. Its breath would be poisonous, almost as bad as fire. I saw Caiy stagger at it, and then one of the long feet on the short legs went out through the gathering dark. The blow looked slow and harmless. It threw Caiy thirty feet, right across the pond. He fell at the entrance to the cave, and lay quiet. The sword was still in his hand. His grip must have clamped down on it involuntarily. He'd likely bitten his tongue as well, in the same way.

The dragon looked after him, you could see it pondering whether to go across again and dine. But it was more attracted by the other morsel it had smelled first. It knew from its scent this was the softer more digestible flesh. And so it ignored Caiy, leaving him for later, and eddied on towards the post, lowering its head as it came, the light leaving its eyes.

I looked. The night was truly blooming now, but I could see, and the darkness didn't shut my ears; there were sounds, too. You weren't there, and I'm not about to try to make you see and hear what I did. Niemeh didn't cry out. She was senseless by then, I'm sure of it. She didn't feel or know any of what it did to her. Afterwards, when I went down with the others, there wasn't much left. It even carried some of her bones into the cave with it, to chew. Her garland was lying on the ground since the dragon had no interest in garnish. The pale flowers were no longer pale.

She had consented, and she hadn't had to endure it. I've seen things as bad that had been done by men, and for men there's no excuse. And yet, I never hated a man as I hated the dragon, a loathing, deadly, sickening hate.

The moon was rising when it finished. It went again to the pond, and drank deeply. Then it moved up the gravel back towards the cave. It paused beside Caiy, sniffed him, but there was no hurry. Having fed so well, it was sluggish. It stepped into the pitch-black hole of the cave, and drew itself from sight, inch by inch, as it had come out, and was gone.

Presently Caiy pulled himself off the ground, first to his hands and knees, then on to his feet.

We, the watchers, were amazed. We'd thought him dead, his back broken, but he had only been stunned, as he told us afterwards. Not even stunned enough not to have come to, dazed and unable to rise, before the dragon quite finished its feeding. He was closer than any of us. He said it maddened him—as if he hadn't been mad already—and so, winded and part stupefied as he was, he got up and dragged himself into the dragon's cave after it. And this time he meant to kill it for sure, no matter what it did to him.

Nobody had spoken a word, up on our rocky place, and no one spoke now. We were in a kind of communion, a trance. We leaned forward and gazed at the black gape in the hill where they had both gone.

Maybe a minute later, the noises began. They were quite extraordinary, as if the inside of the hill itself were gurning and snarling. But it was the dragon, of course. Like the stink of it, those sounds it made were untranslatable. I could say it looked this way comparable to an elephantus, or that way to a cat, a horse, a bat. But the cries and roars—no. They were like nothing else I've heard in the world, or been told of. There were, however, other noises, as of some great heap of things disturbed. And stones rattling, rolling.

The villagers began to get excited or hysterical. Nothing like this had happened before. Sacrifice is usually predictable.

They stood, and started to shout, or groan and invoke supernatural protection. And then a silence came from inside the hill, and silence returned to the villagers.

I don't remember how long it went on. It seemed like months.

Then suddenly something moved in the cave mouth.

There were yells of fear. Some of them took to their heels, but came back shortly when they realized the others were rooted to the spot, pointing and exclaiming, not in anguish but awe. That was because it was Caiy, and not the dragon, that had emerged from the hill.

He walked like a man who has been too long without food and water, head bowed, shoulders drooping, legs barely able to hold him up. He floundered through the edges of the pond and the sword trailed from his hand in the water. Then he tottered over the slope and was right before us. He somehow raised his head then, and got out the sentence no one had ever truly reckoned to hear.

"It's—dead," said Caiy, and slumped unconscious in the moonlight.

They used the litter to get him to the village, as Niemeh didn't need it any more.

We hung around the village for nearly ten days. Caiy was his merry self by the third, and since there had been no sign of the dragon, by day or night, a party of them went up to the hills, and, kindling torches at noon, slunk into the cave to be sure.

It was dead all right. The stench alone would have verified that, a different perfume than before, and all congealed there, around the cave. In the valley, even on the second morning, the live dragon smell was almost gone. You could make out goats and hay and meade and unwashed flesh and twenty varieties of flowers.

I myself didn't go in the cave. I went only as far as the post. I understood it was safe, but I just wanted to be there once more, where the few bones that were Niemeh had fallen through the shackles to the earth. And I can't say why, for you can explain nothing to bones.

There was rejoicing and feasting. The whole valley was full of it. Men came from isolated holdings, cots and huts, and a rough looking lot they were. They wanted to glimpse Caiy the dragon-slayer, to touch him for luck and lick the finger. He laughed. He hadn't been badly hurt, and but for bruises was as right as rain, up in the hay-loft half the time with willing girls, who would afterwards boast their brats were sons of the hero. Or else he was blind drunk in the chieftain's hall.

In the end, I collected Negra, fed her apples and

told her she was the best horse in the land, which she knows is a lie and not what I say the rest of the time. I had sound directions now, and was planning to ride off quietly and let Caiy go on as he desired, but I was only a quarter of a mile from the village when I heard the splayed tocking of horse's hooves. Up he galloped beside me on a decent enough horse, the queen of the chief's stable, no doubt, and grinning, with two beer skins.

I accepted one, and we continued, side by side.

"I take it you're sweet on the delights of my company," I said at last, an hour after, when the forest was in view over the moor.

"What else, Apothecary? Even my insatiable lust to steal your gorgeous horse has been removed. I now have one of my very own, if not a third as beautiful." Negra cast him a sidelong look as if she would like to bite him. But he paid no attention. We trotted on for another mile or so before he added, "and there's something I want to ask you, too."

I was wary, and waited to find out what came next.

Finally, he said, "you must know a thing or two in your trade about how bodies fit together. That dragon, now. You seemed to know all about dragons."

I grunted. Caiy didn't cavil at the grunt. He began idly to describe how he'd gone into the cave, a tale he had flaunted a mere three hundred times in the chieftain's hall. But I didn't cavil either, I listened carefully.

The cave entry-way was low and vile, and soon it opened into a cavern. There was elf-light, more than enough to see by, and water running here and there along the walls and over the stony floor.

There in the cavern's centre, glowing now like filthy silver, lay the dragon, on a pile of junk such as dragons always accumulate. They're like crows and magpies in that, also, shiny things intrigue them and they take them to their lairs to paw possessively and to lie on. The rumours of hoards must come from this, but usually the collection is worthless, snapped knives, impure glass that had sparkled under the moon, rusting armlets from some victim, and all of it soiled by the devil's droppings. and muddled up with split bones.

When he saw it like this, I'd bet the hero's reckless heart failed him. But he would have done his best, to stab the dragon in the eye, the root of the tongue. the vent under the tail, as it clawed him in bits.

"But you see," Caiy now said to me, "I didn't have to."

This, of course, he hadn't said in the hall. No. He had told the village the normal things, the lucky lunge and the brain pierced, and the death-throes, which we'd all heard plainly enough. If anyone noticed his sword had no blood on it, well. it had trailed in the pond, had it not?

"You see," Caiy went on, "it was lying there comatose one minute, and then it began to writhe about, and to go into a kind of spasm. Something got dislodged off the hoard-pile—a piece of cracked-up armour, I think, gilded—and knocked me silly again. And when I came round, the dragon was all sprawled about, and dead as yesterday's roast mutton."

"Hn," I said. "*Hn*n."

"The point being," said Caiy, watching the forest and not me, "I must have done something to it with the first blow, outside. Dislocated some bone or other. You told me their bones have no marrow. So to do that might be conceivable. A fortunate stroke. But it took a while for the damage to kill it."

"Hn*n*."

"Because," said Caiy, softly, "you do believe I killed it, don't you?"

"In the legends," I said, "they always do."

"But you said before that in reality, a man can't kill a dragon."

"One did," I said.

"Something I managed outside then. Brittle bones. That first blow to its skull."

"Very likely."

Another silence. Then he said:

"Do you have any gods, Apothecary?"

"Maybe."

"Will you swear me an oath by them, and then call me 'dragon-slayer'? Put it another way. You've been a help. I don't like to turn on my friends. Unless I have to."

His hand was nowhere near that honed sword of his, but the sword was in his eyes and his quiet, oh-so-easy voice. He had his reputation to consider, did Caiy. But I've no reputation at all. So I swore my oath and I called him dragon-slayer, and when our roads parted my hide was intact. He went off to glory somewhere I'd never want to go.

Well, I've seen a dragon, and I do have gods. But I told them, when I swore that oath, I'd almost certainly break it, and my gods are accustomed to me. They don't expect honour and chivalry. And there you are.

Caiy never killed the dragon. It was Niemeh, poor lovely loving gentle Niemeh who killed it. In my line of work, you learn about your simples. Which cure, which bring sleep, which bring the long sleep without awakening. There are some miseries in this blessed world can only end in death, and the quicker death the better. I told you I was a hard man. I couldn't save her, I gave you reasons why. But there were all those others who would have followed her. Other Niemeh's. Other Caiy's, for that matter. I gave her enough in the cup to put out the life of fifty strong men. It didn't pain her, and she didn't show she was dead before she had to be. The dragon devoured her, and with her the drug I'd dosed her with. And so Caiy earned the name of dragon-slayer.

And it wasn't a riddle.

And no, I haven't considered making a profession of it. Once is enough with any twice-terrible thing. Heroes and knights need their impossible challenges. I'm not meant for any bard's romantic song, a look will tell you that. You won't ever find me in the Northern hills calling "Draco! Draco!"

LA REINE BLANCHE

The white queen lived in a pale tower, high in a shadowy garden. She had been shut in there three days after the death of her husband, the king. Such a fate was traditional for certain of the royal widows. All about, between the dark verdures of the dark garden, there stared up similar pale towers in which similar white queens had for centuries been immured. Most of the prisoners were by now deceased. Occasionally, travellers on the road beneath claimed to have glimpsed or to have thought that they glimpsed—a dim skeletal shape or two, in senile disarray, peering blindly from the tall narrow windows, which were all the windows these towers possessed, over the heads of the trees, towards the distant spires of the city.

The latest white queen, however, was young. She was just twenty on the day she wed the king, who was one hundred and two years of age. He had been expected to thrive at least for a further decade, and he had left off marrying until absolutely necessary. But he had gone livid merely on seeing her. Then, on the night of the nuptial, stumbling on his wife's pearl-sewn slippers lying discarded in the boudoir— symbol of joys to come—the king was overwhelmed.

He expired an hour later, not even at the nude feet
of his wife, only at the foot of the bridal bed. Virgin,
wife and widow, the young queen was adorned in a
gown whiter than milk, and on her head, milk-white-
coifed like that of a nun, was placed the Alabaster
Crown of mourning. With a long-stemmed white
rose in her hand, she was permitted to follow her
husband's bier to the mausoleum. Afterwards, she
was taken by torchlight to the shadowy garden beyond
the city, and conducted into a vacant tower. It contained a suite of rooms, unmistakably regal, but nevertheless bare. She was to commune with no one,
and would be served invisibly. Such things as she
might need—food and wine, fuel, clean linen—were
to be brought by hidden ways and left for her in
caskets and baskets that a pully device would raise
and lower at a touch of her finger.

Here then, and in this way, she would now live
until she died.

A year passed. It might have been fifty. Spring
and summer and autumn eschewed the garden,
scarcely dusting it with their colours. The shadow
trees did not change. The only cold stone blossoms
the garden had ever put forth were the towers
themselves. When winter began, not even then did
the trees alter. But eventually the snow came. Finding the unaltered garden, the snow at last covered it
and made it as white as the gown of the young
queen.

She stood in her window, watching the snow. Nothing else was to be seen, save the low, mauvened sky.
Then a black snow-flake fell out of the sky. It came
down in the embrasure of the window. A raven
looked at the young queen through the glass of her
casement. He was blacker than midnight, so vividly

different that he startled her and she took half a step away.

"Gentle Blanche," said the raven, "have pity, and let me come in."

The white queen closed her eyes.

"How is it you can speak?" she cried.

"How is it," said the raven, "you can understand what I say?"

The white queen opened her eyes. She went back to the narrow window pane.

"The winter is my enemy," said the raven, "he pursues me like death or old age, a murderer with a sword. Fair Blanche, shelter me."

Half afraid, half unable to help herself, the white queen undid the window catch and the terrible cold thrust through and breathed on the room. Then the raven flew in, and the window was shut.

The raven seated himself before the hearth like a fire-dog of jet.

"My thanks," he said.

The white queen brought him a dish of wine and some cold meat left on the bone.

"My thanks again," said the raven. He ate and drank tidily.

The white queen, seated in her chair, watched him in awe and in silence.

When the raven had finished his meal, he arranged his feathers. His eyes were black, and his beak like a black dagger. He was altogether so black, the white queen imagined he must be as black inside as out, even his bones and blood of ebony and ink.

"And now," said the raven, "tell me, if you will, about yourself."

So the white queen—she had no one else to talk to—told the raven how she came to be there, of her wedding, and her husband one hundred and two years old, and of following his cadaver with her white rose, and the torchlit journey here by night, and how it was since the torches went away. It had been so long. Fifty years, or one interminable year, unending.

"As I supposed," said the raven, "your story is sad, sinister and interesting. Shall I tell you, in turn, what I know of the city?"

The white queen nodded slowly, trembling.

The raven said, "There is still a king in the palace. He has had the walls dyed and the turrets carved with dragons and gryphons and swans. He loves music, dancing, and all beautiful things. He himself is young and handsome. He has been many months looking for a wife. Portraits and descriptions were brought from neighbouring kingdoms. None will do. The girls are too plump or too thin, too tall, too short, not serious enough, too serious. He sends back slighting messages and breaks hearts. There have been suicides among the rejects. He himself painted an image of the girl he wants. Slender and pale, with a mouth made to smile and eyes that have held sorrow in them like rain in the cups of two cool flowers. I have seen this portrait," said the raven. "It is yourself."

The queen laughed. She tossed a pinch of incense on the fire to make the room sweet, and so console her.

"How cruel you are," she said, "when I have tried to be kind."

"Not at all. In seven hours it will be midnight. Do you not guess I am the cousin of midnight? It can therefore sometimes be made to do things for me. And you, as you say, have been kind. I am warmed and fed. May I sleep now by your hearth, fair Blanche?"

The white queen sighed her assent.

Beyond the casement the snow-dusk deepened, and on the hearth the fire turned dense and gave off great heat. The raven seemed to melt into a shadow there. Soon his hostess thought she had dreamed it all, though the empty dishes still stood, dull-shining in the twilight.

At midnight she woke, perhaps from sleep, and she was no longer in the tower. For a year of years it had contained her, all the world she knew. Now she was free—but how?

She walked over the snow but did not feel the cold through her slim thin shoes. A moon, the condemned white widow-queen of heaven, blazed in the west, and lit the way beyond the walls of the garden, on to the straight road that led to the city. Although the gates were obscured, Blanche passed directly through the mortared stones of the wall. So she knew. "This is only a dream." And bitterly, wistfully, she laughed again. "All things are possible to a dreamer. If this is the raven's gift, let me be glad of it."

Even at these words, she made out a vehicle on the road, which seemed waiting—and for whom but herself? As she stepped closer, she saw it was a beautiful charrette, draped with white satin, and with silver crests on the doors that were like lilies or maybe carved plumes or feathers. White horses in gilded caparison with bells and tassels drew the carriage, but there was no man to drive or escort it.

Nevertheless, the white queen entered and sat down. At once the carriage started off.

Presently, shyly, she glanced at herself. Her mourning garments were gone. The white silk of her gown was figured and fringed by palest rose and sapphire. Her slippers were sewn with pearls. Her hair flowed

about her, maiden's hair, heavy, curled and per-
fumed with musk and oleander. A chaplet of pastel
orchids replaced the Alabaster Crown of widowhood
and living death.

"And there are moonstones at my throat, silver
bands on my fingers. And how the bells ring and
sing in the cold night air."

They came into the city, through the gates, un-
challenged, through dark slight streets, and broad
boulevards where torches flashed and lamps hung
like golden fruit from wide windows and bird-cage
balconies.

Along this same route Blanche had been driven to
her marriage. They had warned her from the beginning the king was old, and not easy, but even that
had not put out her pride or pleasure. Until she met
him on the mountainous stair and gave up her hand
to his of gnarled wood and dry paper. He had glared
at her in terrified lust, fumbling at his throat to
breathe. But now she wished to forget and she forgot.
Everything was novel and fresh.

In the courtyard, the charrette stopped still. Blanche
left the carriage. She looked and saw the wonderful
gryphons and swans and dragons new-made on the
turrets where the banners of the king floated out
like soft ribbons. Every window was bright, an or-
chard of windows, peach and cherry and mulberry.

The guards on the stair blinked but did not check
or salute her as she went up between them. Some
gasped, some gazed, some did not see her. And
some crossed themselves.

The doors glanced open without a sound. Or else
she thought that they did. She came across several
lamplit rooms into a moon-tinctured walk where only
glow-worms and fountains flickered, and nightin-
gales made music like the notes of the stars. At the

end of the walk, Blanche the white queen saw a golden salon where candleflames burned low. She had known the way.

As she entered, she found the young king of whom the raven had told her. He was dark as she was pale, his own hair black as the branch of a tree against the snow. He was handsome, too. And she felt a pang of love, and another of dismay, though not surprise.

He caught sight of her at once, and started to his feet.

"Are you real?" he said. His voice was musical and tensed between delight and anger.

"No," said Blanche. "I am a dream. Mine, or yours."

"You are a painting come to life."

Blanche smiled. The raven, who surely was to be her tormentor, had spoken the truth to her. Or else, for now, it was the truth.

"I would," he said, "have waited all my life for you. And since you may not be real, I may have to wait, still. Having seen you, I can hardly do otherwise. Unless you consent to stay."

"I think I may be permitted to stay until sunrise. It seems to be I am in league with darkness. Until dawn, then."

"Because you are a ghost."

Blanche went to him across the golden gloom and put her hand in his outstretched hand.

"You are living flesh," said the king. He leaned foward and kissed her lips, quietly. "Warm and douce and live. Even though a dream."

For an hour, they talked together. Musicians were summoned, and if they saw or feared her, or whatever they thought, they played, and the young queen and the young king danced over the checkered floor. And they drank wine, and walked among roses and sculptures and clocks and mysteries, and so came eventually to a private place, a beautiful bedroom. And here they lay down and were lovers together, splendidly and fiercely and in rapture, and in regret, for it was a dream, however sweet, however true.

"Will you return to me?" he said.

"My heart would wish it. I do not think I shall return, to you."

"I will nevertheless wait for you. In case it chances you put on mortal shape. For this is too lovely to believe in."

"Do not," said Blanche, "wait long. Waiting is a prison." But she knew these words were futile.

Just then a bird sang far away across the palace gardens. It was not a nightingale.

"Let me go now, my beloved," said Blanche. "I must leave instantly. I am partly afraid of what the sun may do to me before your eyes."

"Alas," he said.

He did not hinder her.

Blanche quickly drew on her garments, even the chaplet of orchids which showed no sign of withering. She clasped her jewels about her throat. A frosty sheen lay on the window-panes that the stars and the sinking moon had not put there. "Adieu," she said. "Live well. Do not, do not remember me."

Blanche fled from the chamber and away through the palace, the rooms all darkling now, the silent fountain walk, the outer salons, the stair. In the courtyard the charrette and its horses remained, but it was half transparent. This time, none of the guards had seen her pass. As she hastened on she realized that she had after all forgotten her pearl-sewn slippers. She felt only smooth cobblestones under her feet— there was no snow, and now it came to her that there had been none, in any corner of the city or the palace that she had visited.

The carriage started off. It flew like the wind, or a bell-hung bird, into the face of the dawn. And when the dawn smote through, the carriage fell apart like silver ashes. The sun's lilting blade pierced her heart. And she woke alone, seated in her chair before the cold hearth, in the pale tower, in the shadowy garden. As she had known she would.

"Cruel raven," said the white queen, as she sprinkled crumbs of meat and bread along the embrasure of her window. She was full of pain and stiffness, and even to do so much made her anxious. Nor did she think he would come back. The winter day had passed, or had it been the whole of the winter which was gone? The snow faded between the shadow trees. The white queen looked from her narrow window and pulled her breath into her body without ease. "Spring will come," she said. "But not any spring for me."

She turned and went back to her chair. Within the white coif, under the Alabaster Crown, her face was like a carved bone, the eyes sunk deep, the cheeks and lips. Her hands were like slender bundles of pale twisted twigs. As she sat, her limbs creaked and crackled, paining her. Tears welled in the sunken pools of her eyes. They were no longer two flowers holding rain.

"I am old," said the white queen. "In one night, I grew to be so. Or were they fifty nights, or a hundred nights, that seemed only one?" She recalled the young king, and his hair black as a raven. She wept a little, where once she would have laughed at the bitter joke. "He would despise me. No magic now and no demoiselle of dream. I should revolt him now. He would wish me dead, to be free of me." She closed her eyes. "As I wished my own aged husband dead, for I thought even this pale tower could be no worse than marriage to such a creature."

When the white queen opened her eyes, the raven stood in the opened window like a blot of ink.

"Gentle Blanche," said the raven, "let me come in."

"You are in," she said. "My heart is full of you, you evil magician. I gave you food and drink and shelter and you did harm to me, and perhaps to another. Of course you did."

"Also you, my lady, told me a story. Now I," said the raven, "will tell one to you.

"Long ago," said the raven, "there was a maiden of high birth. Her name was Blanche. She might have made a good marriage among several of the great houses, to young men who were her peers. But it was told to her that she might also make a marriage with the king and rule the whole kingdom. He was old, decaying and foolish, she was warned of this. But Blanche did not care. Let me agree, he will die soon, thought Blanche. Then I will be regent to any who come after, and still I will rule the land."

"Oh," said the white queen, "I remember."

"However," said the raven, sitting on the hearth like a gargoyle of black coal, "when Blanche was given to the king and saw and touched him, her courage failed her. By then it was too late. They were lighted to their bed and priests blessed it. As he had come from his disrobing, the king had stumbled on Blanche's discarded slippers, and called out, and fallen. As he was revived by his servitors, the aged monarch muttered. He had dreamed of a girl like Blanche eighty years before. Or else it was a spirit who visited him. The girl of his dreams had been his wife for one night, and he had worshipped her ever since, refusing to marry, looking only for his lover to return to him. In his youth he had been mad, ten whole years, following the uncanny visitation, wandering the earth in search of his ghost bride. He had even unearthed tombs and dug up embalmed corpses, to see if any of them might be she. All his life, even when the madness left him, he waited. And it seemed that Blanche, whom he had now wedded, was the image of the ghost-bride and, like her, had left her pearl-sewn slippers lying behind her."

"Yes," said the white queen, "I recall." She leaned her head on her hand, on her sore wrist thin as a stick.

"However," said the raven again, "Blanche barely listened to the ramblings of her senile husband. She lay in the silk covers shrinking and in horror. She thought, He is decrepit and weak and easily distressed, and so easily destroyed. When the servants and the priests were gone, she kneeled up on the bridal couch and taunted her old husband and railed at him. Her tongue was sharp with ambition and loathing. She broke his heart. He died at the foot of the bed."

"I called at once for help," said Blanche. "I thought they would judge me blameless. But it seems someone had stayed to listen and had overheard. For a certain kind of murder, the murder of a king by his queen without the brewing of a draught, the striking of a blow, this is the punishment. Confined alive until death in a tower in a cemetery garden. A white queen, a murderess. I am punished. Why," said the old white queen, "is fate so malicious, and are you fate? If I had met him as he was that night, young and strong, handsome and wise, how could I not have loved him? Yet I was sent back eighty years to harm him, as I would harm him eighty years in the future. And as he has harmed me."

"You were his punishment," said the raven. "His pride and his own malign tongue had broken hearts, as his would break. He would brook only perfection, a single sort of perfection, and was intolerant of all others. So this perfection came to him and was lost to him. He might have relinquished the dream still, and would not. He waited until he was a hundred and two years of age to claim a girl of twenty, such, even then, was his overbearing blind pride. It cost him dear."

"While I was punished for my wickedness, willing and casting his life away when I might have been happy elsewhere, and he left in peace."

"Each the other's sentence and downfall," said the raven. "As perhaps each knew it must be."

"And you," she said, "are an angel of chastising God. Or the Devil."

"Neither," said the raven. "Should we not chastise ourselves, that we learn?" He flew to the embrasure of the window. Beyond the tower, the trees were dark as always, the tops of the other dreary towers pushed up. But the sky was blushed with blue. Over the wall it would be spring.

"Despite all sins and stupidities," said the raven, "I love you yet and yet have waited for you, gentle, fair Blanche. And you, whether you wished it or no, waited for me in your bone tower, and at the last as at the first, you were kind."

The white queen wept. Her tears were like pearls.

"Let us," said the raven, "be together a little while, in freedom and innocence."

"Oh, how can you speak?" she cried.

"Oh, how can you understand what I say?"

Then the white queen left her chair. She left her body and bones and old pale blood, for she was white now inside and out. She flew up into the window embrasure. From the prison towers only the souls of dreamers or the wings of birds could get out. Up like arrows flew two ravens, one black as pitch, one white as snow, and away together over the trees, the wall, the road, the city, the world, into the sky of spring.